MW00668527

SURFACE
TENSION

JOHN-MICHAEL LANDER

Can
thank you
for listening and
hearing me.
John-Michael
Lander

Copyright © 2017 John-Michael Lander
All rights reserved
First Edition

PAGE PUBLISHING, INC.
New York, NY

First originally published by Page Publishing, Inc. 2017

ISBN 978-1-63568-591-6 (Paperback)
ISBN 978-1-63568-592-3 (Digital)

Printed in the United States of America

1 CHAPTER

The pack of kids waved their cell phones in the air, each one trying to record the scene that would blast across their social media and go viral. At the center of their attention, two girls circled one another.

"You bitch," I heard one of them shriek.

"Mr. Matthew, can you tell me my grade?"

"Just a minute, Shaun," I mumbled at him and pushed around the desk. It's a teacher's job to break up fights.

"I warned you, whore bag," another shouted.

I pushed past the students. "That's enough," I called out. The cell phones turned in my direction.

Jasmine flung both her arms, slapping Tamara across the head.

"No, you didn't," Tamara shouted. She flipped a desk to get it out of the way and took a fighting stance.

The crowd responded.

"Stop it!" I tried to quickly devise a strategy to end the confrontation.

"I'm tired of your shit." Tamara ignored me, ducked her head, and tackled Jasmine.

The crowd roared with approval.

"That's enough. Stop it." The two girls fell to the floor, slapping, scratching, and pulling hair. I managed to get Jasmine, restraining her with my arms.

Tamara took advantage, grabbed a handful of Jasmine's hair and yanked.

As I reached to free hair from fist, Tamara swung her other hand and sucker punched Jasmine in the stomach, forcing her to bend forward, flipping me over her shoulder.

I landed hard on the floor, feeling pain shoot through my shoulder, knee, and head before blacking out.

Dr. Althea Warner's Office—Dayton, Ohio, July 2016

Althea tapped her lower lip with the end of the pen and furrowed her brows. "What was the cause of the fight?"

"A boy," I replied.

Althea's right brow arched high on her forehead. "How long ago was the fight?"

"About three months ago."

She nodded her head. "And you sustained injuries?"

"I sprained my neck and tore my meniscus, which will be operated on next month."

"All over some boy who probably doesn't even talk to either girl now." Althea Warner's speech was hurried and clipped as she wrote something on the clipboard resting on her lap.

"What?"

"I'm sorry, I tend to speak rather fast. Please let me know if you can't understand me. It's something I have been working on all my life. 'You talk too fast, Alfi,' my mother always told me." Althea nodded her head as if she was convincing me that I was able to understand.

This was a mistake. I've worked with therapists before, and they always end up in a game of cat and mouse or a battle of wits. Why would this be any different?

Althea suddenly stood up. "Would you like some water or tea?" She opened the door that led to the tiny waiting room.

"No, thank you."

"I have some chamomile, ginger spice, or Earl Grey." Althea didn't wait for a response and darted into the other room.

The small, cramped office on the second floor overlooked the parking lot, stuffed with a blue-and-white striped couch and a matching love seat placed at right angles to each other in front of a large window. The desk, occupied by files and an oversized computer monitor, was only a few steps away. Bookshelves aligned the wall behind the desk and housed many psychology, self-help, and life-coaching texts.

"Tell me where you grew up," she called.

"Aulden," I replied.

Althea's head appeared in the doorway. "They have some terrific antique shops there."

"Also the Butter Festival," I added.

Her head disappeared again. "Mostly a farming community, correct?"

"Don't forget football." I laughed at my inside joke. "I was a freak. Unless you were a footballer, farmer, or the Butter Festival Queen, the locals just couldn't understand you. If a sport had nothing to do with the Friday night lights on the Spartan football field, it wasn't considered a real sport." I was proud of my rehearsed response about the town where I grew up.

She returned with a cup and rested back down in the overstuffed chair. "I just have to have my tea at three fifteen." She took a sip, placed the cup and saucer on the table next to the chair, and looked at her clipboard again. "Where do you teach?"

I looked at her with bewilderment. Were we finished talking about Aulden? "Webber Academy."

"The art school in downtown Dayton."

"That's the one."

"What do you teach?" She picked up the tea cup and sipped.

"Sophomore English." My hands shook. I fought the urge to shove my hands under my thighs to stop their shaking. I felt clammy as sweat gathered at my temples. My breath became erratic and shallow.

"And you're pursuing a PhD." Through the reflection in her glasses, I wasn't sure if she was looking at me. "In what?"

"Education."

Althea looked over the bridge of her nose at me. "What do you want to do with a PhD in education?"

"I always wanted to be called Dr. Matthew." I laughed, but she didn't. "No, since I'm teaching at an urban school district, I qualify for the Government Forgiveness Program. When I applied, the representative asked me if I was planning on achieving any other degrees other than my master's. I joked about getting my PhD, and the rep suggested that I go for it and the student loans would be put into the program as well. So I decided to go for it. It's deferring my repayment until 2020."

Althea took a long inhalation and placed the cup back on the saucer. "What did you do before teaching?"

"What does that have to do with what brought me here?" I asked.

"We'll get to that, but I have a way to get to the bottom of things. I like to have a full picture of everything before trying to make a diagnosis. So what did you do before teaching?"

"I was an actor." I rubbed my face and wiped sweat from my forehead and temples.

She smiled. "What type of acting?"

"Theater, television, films." I glanced at the side table and saw a box of Kleenex. I grabbed a couple and dabbed my brows.

"Were you successful?"

"I like to believe I did all right."

"You either were able to make a living, or you weren't." She nodded in agreement with herself. "Tell me some of the things you did as an actor."

"I did a couple of feature films and soap operas."

She put her pen down and leaned in. "Which soap operas?"

"*General Hospital* and *All My Children.*" I loosened my tie, pinched my dress, and T-shirt and peeled them away from my chest.

"Two of my favorites. I have to ask, did you work with Susan Lucci?"

I forced a smile. "Yes."

"What is she like?"

"She is a gracious and kind person."

"Why'd you quit?"

"I didn't quit. Is it warm in here, or is it just me?" I unbuttoned my shirt's top button.

"The air is off. They are working on the circuits. Are you sure you don't want any water?"

"I'm okay. I don't know why, but I feel like I'm in a sauna."

"Relax, and take some deep breaths," Althea stated, comfortable. "So why did you quit?" She sipped her tea again.

"I didn't quit. I choose to come back to help my parents. They were both very ill."

Althea stopped writing and glanced up at me. "You gave up your career to come back and help your parents? How's that going for you?"

"I'm glad I did it." I glanced at the exit.

"Do you miss the acting?"

Without thinking, I responded, "Every day."

She scribbled something in her notes. "How are your parents doing?"

"My father passed away, and my mom is still struggling."

"I'm sorry for your loss." She took a moment as if in respect for the dead.

I noticed a sticker of a hummingbird on the window.

"That's to help keep birds from crashing into the glass. I can't tell you how many birds have kamikazed into that window."

"It works?"

"I'm proud to announce we haven't had a single casualty since the sticker was put there. Are you close to your mother?"

"When it's convenient," I felt another onset of hot flashes.

She cocked her head and looked at me. Was she judging me?

"I mean, it's always been about her. It'd be nice to have her call me and ask how I'm doing. It seems that she only calls when she needs something."

"What do you mean?" asked Althea.

I paused a moment. "She's always been needy. She grew up in a comfortable environment, the big house on Main Street, many gentlemen callers. She was extremely popular and dated all the right boys. She had the latest fashion and hairstyle. She got everything she ever asked for. During high school, the doctors diagnosed her with a heart murmur, and she had to stop cheerleading and quit the dance team. Her parents ushered her to and from school, and her sisters had to carry her books and do her chores so she wouldn't add any stress to her heart."

"Privileged then."

"Yes, but she always seemed out of touch."

"How?"

"She's done strange things. This one time, we were driving home from the grocery store, and all of a sudden, she screamed and sharply veered to the right, almost sending us into the ditch. She started shaking, crying, and shouting, 'Pig! Pig...huge pig in the road!' There was no pig in sight."

"Brothers or sisters?"

I was confused. My antidotes about my mother would usually get more attention. I can't seem to follow this woman. "One each, Caine, an older brother, and a younger sister, Magdalyn."

"I see." Althea wrote down more notes. "What got you into acting?"

"Diving. I was on the USA diving team when I was sixteen years old."

"The Olympics?" she asked.

"No, I never made the Olympic team, but I did go to the World Games."

"What's making you smile?" She asked while studying me.

I touched my face with my right hand. "I'm smiling?"

Althea nodded. "What were you thinking about?"

Matthews' Home—Aulden, Ohio, November 1973

"Go ahead. Put the skates on. Let's try out your Olympic arena," Dad encouraged with a big grin.

He helped me take off my boots so I could put on the brand-new skates. The fresh smell of leather filled my nose as he held open the tongue for my foot to slip in. He tied the laces for me, swiftly pulled me to my wobbly feet, and held me as he guided me around the old barn's foundation he transformed into a skating rink. His big arms held me, trapping me against his chest.

He leaned down and whispered in my ten-year-old ear, "Ready?"

I didn't want to reply too quickly because this was my time alone with Dad. Caine, my older brother, would never partake in such a "girly" sport, and Magdalyn was not due to arrive for a couple of months. Today I had Dad to myself. I didn't want it to end.

"Sure," I responded because the need for his approval outweighed the need to be coddled.

"All right, impress me, Dick Button!" He gently shoved me away, sending me gliding across the icy surface.

My style wasn't Olympic worthy: ankles turned out, knocked knees, hips pushed back, chest too far forward, and arms stretched out to the side for balance. I skimmed across the rink and didn't know how to stop. I continued toward the lip of the foundation until my toe pick met the cement edge, ripped the plastic liner, and forced me facedown onto the hard frozen ground.

"Are you all right?" His strong hands lifted and brushed away dried leaves from my forehead.

I nodded my head.

"Thank God." He ran his hands over my shoulders and down my arms. "Nothing's injured?"

"Let's do it again," I said with excitement.

"Are you sure?"

"I'm sure."

A huge smile crawled across his face, crinkling his eyebrows. He turned me toward the ice arena and placed me on the slick surface. Without a word, he sent me sailing against the cold wind.

"That's it," he encouraged. "Keep your head up. Keep your heels underneath you, and don't let your knees turn in. Make sure your back is straight. Yes. Yes."

My natural abilities took over, and I gathered my skating legs under me. I was able to shift my weight and tilt the skates on an edge that enabled me to curve away from the sides of the foundation. I stopped by, turning both ankles in the same direction, as I squeezed my feet together.

"That's my boy!" Dad yelled.

"Caleb!"

I looked over and saw Mother standing on the front porch, swollen stomach, rubbing her hands with a dish towel.

"I need you to get the turkey out of the oven before it burns," she barked. Mom didn't like being pregnant. She complained she was losing her waist and was always tired. Always grumpy. "Caleb!"

"Be right there." Dad's smile covered his face. "You like it?"

"I love it." I glided over to him, threw my arms around his massive shoulders, and buried my face into his neck, inhaling his aroma of cigarettes and musk.

"I'm glad you like it."

"Caleb!" Mom's voice cracked through the crisp, cold air.

"Coming!" Dad held me at arm's length and whispered. "Keep practicing, and make me proud. I better get inside before all hell breaks loose, or there'll be no Thanksgiving dinner."

"Thank you, Dad."

He kissed my forehead. I felt the warmth of his soft lips. And with that, he was gone, sprinting up to the house. Mom waddled back inside.

It took me a moment to regain my focus. I rotated on the blades and looked at the empty ice rink. I closed my eyes and envisioned Robin Cousins, Great Britain's Olympic champion. I pictured him spinning and spiraling, gliding on one leg, and jumping in the air.

I felt the cold air against my face as I skimmed across the ice. I lifted one of my legs backward and found myself performing a spiral with ease, with my arms stretched out for balance. I safely recovered and pulled my feet together and sent my arms across my chest to initiate a double-footed spin. As the rotations slowed, I flung out both arms and one leg and ceased the spin. I was amazed at how easy skating came to me. Was I a natural? Had I found my sport? I decided right then I was going to be the next Olympic figure skating champion for the United States.

Althea Warner's Office—Dayton, Ohio, July 2016

"What made that experience so important?" Althea asked as she repositioned herself in the overstuffed armchair.

"I'm not quite sure." I looked out the window at the old church tower with a clock on top, thirty-seven more minutes.

"There must be some reason you keep the memory alive." She picked up her clipboard and jotted down more notes.

"I haven't thought about that in a long time. It's one of the fondest memories I have of my father. You know, happy memories. My sister was born soon after, and everything changed. Magdalyn was the 'miracle child' since Mom was not supposed to be able to have another child. Mom miscarried several times after I was born. I nearly killed her because I didn't want to be born, she told me. I was a month late."

"We're you jealous of Magdalyn?" Althea sipped her tea.

"I don't think so." Was I jealous of my beautiful sister? "No, I was proud of her. I wanted to take care of her. I loved her."

"But she took your father away from you," Althea said.

I looked at the therapist. Why does she want me to be jealous of Magdalyn? Was she trying to create something that was simply not there, or was she insightful enough to know that I was in denial about my true feelings toward my sister? Have I always been jealous inside?

"I'm not aware of being jealous of her. I don't want to think I was jealous. I didn't get as much time with my father. Something was always taking him away, yet it wasn't necessarily Magdalyn. No one was spending much time with Dad. He worked and was away from the house all the time. Mom was the one that changed. She was edgy and angry that she couldn't fit back into her dresses. She couldn't wait to get back to work. So I became Magdalyn's surrogate mother by feeding, changing, and rocking her to sleep. Sometimes I pretended that Magdalyn was my very own child."

"Where was your brother?" Althea asked.

I thought for a moment. "Caine was off with his best friend, Zachary Spence. They were inseparable."

"Why does that make you smile?"

"What?" I felt slapped out of a great dream.

Althea glanced over the rim of her bifocals and shook the end of the pen toward me. "Your face genuinely lit up when you started talking about your brother and…" she quickly glanced down at her notes, "Zachary."

I shook my head. "Caine and Zachary teased me a lot for taking care of Magdalyn so much. They called me a momma's boy."

"If you pretended that Magdalyn was your child, who were you married to?"

"You don't have to be married to have a child," I replied.

"So you were a single parent in your fantasy at ten years old?" she asked.

I became filled with warmth from the fantasy. At ten, I knew I was different. I wasn't like Caine. I knew from the moment I was caught running out of the house in one of Dad's T-shirts—which I cinched at the waist with a belt—I was definitely different. I remembered Mom and Dad calling me into the kitchen and asking me if I wished to be a boy or a girl.

Without hesitation, I responded, "I want to be myself," and turned and skipped into the other room. I've always had an active imagination, and sometimes the realities and fantasies blended and were hard to distinguish. I remember holding Magdalyn one rainy day when Mom was working, Dad nowhere in sight, and Caine came rushing into the house followed by Zachary.

Caine had just turned thirteen years old, and Zachary was fourteen. They were completely drenched. I didn't understand, but there was something different about Zachary. His dark hair was glued to his forehead and accentuating his large eyes; his crooked smile was dazzling; and his shirt was pasted to his lean frame. He came over and gently placed his palm on Magdalyn's pink cheek and looked straight into my eyes. Time froze, and I could only hear and feel my heart pumping hard and fast in my chest.

"That's a lot of responsibility for a ten-year-old." Althea broke my reverie.

"I didn't see it like that." I paused for a moment. "I wanted to help. When diving started, I wasn't around a lot. So it was important to do whatever I could to help out."

"You said your father started working longer hours and was away from the house a lot. What line of work did he do?"

"He was an architect slash detailed designer," I said.

"He must have made good money," stated Althea.

"At first, he did, when he was working for a private architecture firm that designed commercial buildings. I don't know why, but Dad left because of some disagreement and went to work for Armco Steel Company. There was an accident, and he broke his back. No one ever really talked about it. I just remember being told by the secretary at school and having to stay with some strange family for months until he was able to come home. When we all returned home, we pretended it never happened. That's when he got religious. He didn't work for a while, except little drawing jobs here and there as a freelance contractor. Then he worked at Hospice of Dayton as a security guard."

"Do you have any other memories of your father?" asked Althea. I nodded.

Matthews' Home—Aulden, Ohio, September 1978

I was balancing on the old tractor tire that was on the ground.

"Davy, why are you just standing there, bouncing on that tire?" Magdalyn asked.

"Just thinking."

"About what?"

"Things."

"What kind of things?"

"Nothing in particular." I sprung off the tire and landed on the green grass. I was amazed at the height that I got from the rubber's recoil. I climbed back up on the tire's rim.

"Come on, it's my turn to hide. You didn't hide very well last time," Magdalyn said. "I found you way too easy."

"Wait, just a minute, I want to try something." I balanced myself with my arms above my head. I compressed down with all my might and swung my arms through, springing into the air. I pulled my knees up and completed a full reverse somersault before landing my feet on the ground.

"That was cool. Do it again," encouraged Magdalyn.

I remounted the tire, positioned myself, and repeated the trick with more finesse. I controlled the liftoff and rotation so that the landing was flawless.

"Daddy, Daddy, my daddy," squealed Maggie. She took off across the yard, waving both hands, as Dad drove up the long driveway.

Dad waved back and called out the opened passenger window, "How's my Maggie?"

Since her arrival, Dad never installed the ice rink again. I attempted it, but it was never the same. I couldn't figure out how he made the water stay within the foundation so it could set and freeze enough to skate. I remember him coming out to me as I was trying to flood the area with the water hose. He was carrying the newborn Maggie in his arms.

"What're you doing?"

I smiled. "I wanted to skate for you again."

He chuckled, and Maggie cooed. He looked at the little girl cocooned in the blanket. "I see you, my beautiful little Maggie. I see you." He wiggled his forefinger around so her eyes would follow, and then he tapped her button nose.

He looked at me. "I don't think that's such a good idea."

"It's still cold." I watched the water splash on the remains of the plastic liner that had become worn and torn. "I fixed the rips with the tape."

"I can see that."

"I want to skate," I whined.

"Maybe next year." Maggie cooed again, and Dad looked down at her rosy face. "Is that right? I agree." He looked up at the sky and then back down to the baby. "Yep, it does look like it's going to snow."

"I just have to make sure the plastic is sealed."

"The plastic is too old."

"I'll get some new plastic from the garage."

"We don't have any more." He pinned his eyes on me and said, "Why don't you play war with Caine."

With that, my dreams of Olympic glory melted away.

I mounted the tire again, turned my back on them, and sent my thoughts to the 1980 Olympics in Moscow. I envisioned the Olympic diving pool, during the men's ten-meter platform finals. Mark Bradley was leading the competition as expected, but Falk Hoffleman from East Germany and Vladimir Alleynov from the Soviet Union were close behind. I was comfortably in sixth. There were two rounds left, and Mark looked destined for the gold medal.

I heard my name over the loudspeaker, heavy with a Russian accent, and I took my position. I was to perform a back two-and-a-half somersaults in the pike position, degree of difficulty, 3.0. I didn't hesitate. I jumped into the air, started spinning, watching colors blur by, and kicked hard. I knifed through the water, pushed off the bottom, streamlined back to the surface, and emerged to thunderous applause. I glanced at the scoreboard. Fourth place.

I climbed the staircase that led up to the ten-meter. Mark patted me on the back and said, "The final round. Nail this dive, kid, and we will both be standing on the victory platform. Make me proud."

My final dive was a front three-and-a-half somersault in the pike position. I felt unusually calm and alert. I scanned the audience and saw Dad and Mom holding little American flags. Dad pumped his arm into the air as he yelled something encouraging, while Mom sank onto the bleacher with her hands covering her eyes, afraid to watch.

I found my starting mark. I took a quick breath and skipped down the cement platform. I launched into the air, spinning while falling, and sliced through the water's surface. I knew it was good.

I became deaf to a silent stadium. I could only use my eyes to witness the results flash on the scoreboard. There on the top line, in first place, was David Matthew, USA, 565.40.

"I won!" I raised my arms and looked into the stands. Dad was hooting and hugging everyone around him, and Mom just stood there crying.

"Who won?" I heard a familiar voice.

My fantasy Olympic victory faded away.

"I did," I said without thinking. I turned and found Dad sitting on the steps of the porch, lighting a cigarette. "Where's Maggie?" I asked.

"She ran inside." He pointed to the front door as he inhaled on the burning stick. "What'd you win?"

I shook my head, "Nothing."

"What're you doing with the old tractor tire?"

"Practicing my takeoffs," I admitted.

His face lit up, and he inhaled on the cigarette again. "You may have something there..." He got up and walked toward me; his gaze was on the tire. He put a foot on the edge and checked the recoil. "Show me what you were doing."

I climbed on the tire and positioned myself. I lifted my arms, compressed, swung through, and performed a somersault.

"Good," he said, nodding his head.

He stepped in the middle of the tire and checked the rubber. "Were you thinking to practice your springboard or platform takeoffs?"

"Both."

"I think there's too much play in the rubber, here. That'll give you a false feeling for the cement platform." He stepped up on the side of the tire and bounced. "This would be good for springboard takeoffs. This could work." He stepped off the tire and went toward the barn.

I wasn't sure what he was up to, but I didn't care. I felt the same rush of warmth that had filled my chest when he created the skating rink so many years ago. I hopped back on the tire and bounced on it like a trampoline, going higher and higher. I bounced from one side of the tire to the opposite side, working on balance and control. I stopped when I saw Dad coming toward me with a large plank of wood.

Without saying a word, he jerked his head for me to get off the tire.

I sprang to the ground like a cat.

He positioned the plank on the tire and stood back, thinking. His eyes were focused and narrow. He rubbed his chin once and then went to work. He slid the end of the plank under the inside lip of the tire, so the plank rested on the opposite side as a fulcrum. I immediately understood what he was creating, a springboard—similar to the real thing. However, the plank wasn't level; it angled up. He propped the back end of the tire, where the plank was supported by the inside lip, with a cement block. This leveled the plank.

He stepped onto the end of the plank that extended out from the tire's edge about two feet over the ground. He used his weight to push the plank down, bounced, and the back of the tire rose off the cement block. He hopped off, and the tire slammed down with a loud thud.

"You weigh less than I do. Stand on the end and bounce. Gently."

I jumped up on the plank's end and lightly bounced. The opposite side of the tire rose ever so slightly.

"Wait a minute. I have an idea." He rushed off to the barn again.

I felt the fall breeze brush through my hair, carrying the scent of drying leaves.

He rushed back. "Step down," he ordered. He motioned with his hand, holding a drill, while the other clutched a two-by-four piece of wood.

I jumped to the ground.

He placed the board on top of the cement block and took the drill with these two long screws and connected the tire to the wood and the cement. The weight of the combination made the dryland board sturdy and stable.

"Try it again," he said.

The plank felt secure. I began to bounce, and the simulation of a real diving board was complete.

"Try your forward approach."

I stepped down the plank, hurdled, and sprung off the end high into the air. I landed hard.

"That's not good for your knees. I know just the thing." He disappeared into the garage and reappeared with an old twin bed mattress. He put the mattress on the ground under the plank. "This should absorb some of the impact. Try it."

I positioned myself on the plank, stepped, and hurdled. I lifted into the air and landed softly on the mattress. "That's terrific!"

"We should move the mattress out just a bit so you land in the middle instead of the end." He immediately repositioned the mattress further away. "Try a back somersault."

I positioned myself on the end of the plank. I forced the plank down and lifted into the air, pulling my knees to my chest. I completed the somersault with ease and landed perfectly on the mattress.

Dad flashed a huge smile.

"Thanks, Dad." I ran to him and wrapped my arms around his shoulders. I felt like a child, not a fifteen-year-old.

He allowed this contact for a moment. "That's enough." He gently pushed me away. He walked to the porch and sat on the steps, pulled out a cigarette and lit it.

I walked over and sat next to him. "Do you think...well, do you think I could make the US diving team?" I rushed out with it. "Maybe?"

"If you put your mind to it." He took a long drag on the cigarette, held his breath, and slowly released a stream of white smoke into the graying sky. "God has a plan for everyone, and you can do anything you set your mind to, David. You have to want it more than anything else in life and work harder than everyone else because we don't have the money."

He stood up and walked inside without saying another word.

I knew then and there that I was going to make the USA team, somehow, someway, because my dad said I could.

Althea Warner's Office—Dayton, Ohio, July 2016

Althea pinched between her brows and forced a smile. "Our time is almost up."

I glanced at the clock on the church tower and realized that time had quickly flown.

Althea looked at her notes. "I have some theories of what maybe causing you anxiety and panic. I'll need more time to confirm them. However, I'd like to try a new approach with you, David. Are you up for it?" Althea folded her hands as if she were praying.

"I guess so." For some reason, I felt this need to make her proud of me. "What is it?"

"I'm not just a therapist. I'm also a life coach. I feel we can make some great strides by combining them both."

"What will I have to do?" I reached into my satchel to get my checkbook to pay for the session.

Althea stood and walked to the bookshelf and pulled out a book. She handed it to me. "Julia Cameron wrote this based on her work with creative people. I think it'd be a great place to start with you."

I read the title of the book, *The Artist's Way*, and flipped through it.

Althea sat next to me. "There's a contract before the section of 'Week One.' If you are interested in trying this approach, I'd need you do three things."

"Are you assigning homework?" I asked jokingly.

Althea chuckled. "Exactly. One, you need to create a contract. Two, you must read the chapters several times before coming back here. And three, you'll need to write three pages every morning, no matter what—three pages filled with streams of consciousness. Don't worry about it making any sense or reason; it's just words you are putting down on paper."

I found the contract and skimmed it. "What's an artist date? It says I have to have a weekly artist date."

Althea waved her hand. "We'll go over that when you come back." She walked to her desk, glanced at the calendar, and wrote on the back of a business card. She handed me the card, and I gave her the check. "I want you to write in the journal all the memories you can. Don't worry about the details, we can go over that here, but make sure you're writing three pages every day."

"I will." I decided that I was going to do everything I could to get through this anxiety and depression. I didn't know what I would write about, but I was going to write. And I felt different. I had an assignment. This approach may be what I needed.

As I positioned myself in the driver's seat, I pulled out my phone and texted Jake, my partner for the past fifteen years. "I think I'm going to work with this therapist." Before Jake could interject a word, I said, "She's a life coach and wants to try this new approach with me. I'm stopping at Kroger's to get a notebook, need anything?"

"No, hurry, dinner is ready," Jake texted back.

I shifted the car into drive, pulled out of the parking space, and thought about the time I was fifteen and preparing for the World Games. *I'm going to write this all out*, I thought to myself. I turned right on to Rahn Road and headed to Kroger's to purchase my journal, a bouquet of flowers, and a bottle of chardonnay.

2 CHAPTER

Leaving for the World Games—
Dayton International Airport, July 1979

Dad's imposing six-feet-four-inch and 195-pound frame of solid muscle was crammed behind the steering wheel of "Old Blue," our Plymouth. His pensive gaze and impatient quality always made riding with him tense. As he pulled in front of Dayton International Airport, he kept looking out the windshield.

"Don't get your hopes up too high."

I wasn't quite sure if I was supposed to respond or not.

Dad always started his declarations by furrowing his brows and tapping his fingers as if to motivate enough willpower to speak.

"Diving's a subjective sport and politically driven." He never looked at me. "They judge divers on their reputation, not the way they're truly diving. Since you've never been in any international meets, the judges won't have any idea who you are, and they'll judge you harder. Mark Bradley most likely will win." His tapping fingers increased on the steering wheel. "What are you waiting for?"

I grabbed my duffel bag from the back and got out of the car. I started to wave, but he was already pulling away. I watched his car curve out of sight.

SSA Flight No. 1425 from Newark, New Jersey, to Oslo, Norway—July 1979

"*Morgen. Kan jeg få din oppmerksomhet*," a Norwegian voice cracked over the loud speaker and switched to English. "'Morning. May I have your attention. This is your captain, Sven Karlsson, and we are traveling thirty-five thousand feet at the speed of 550 miles per hour. We are beginning our descent to Oslo International Airport and should be on the ground at approximately 9:30 a.m. The sky is clear, and if you are on the east side of the aircraft, you will be able to see the sun rising over the North Sea as we arch over Norway."

I lifted my heavy lids and wiped the sleep from my eyes. I rolled my neck, my shoulders, and stretched my stiff spine.

Is this happening?

"Hey, David, look over there," said Patti Lakes, another diver sitting next to me. She pointed out the window that was ablaze with an orange glow.

I unfastened my seatbelt and lifted myself up and over her. Through the small oval portal, I saw the sun peering above the horizon where the ocean met the sky. The white-capped waves, kissed with red, lazily rolled and disappeared under the dark-blue blanket.

"It's beautiful, isn't it?" She leaned in, pressing her cheek against mine to look out.

Patti was a few months younger than me, yet this was her third international team tour as a platform expert. She was on the 1977 Junior World Games in Bonn, Germany, and 1978 Pan Am Games held at Indianapolis, Indiana. She won the gold medal at the Junior Olympics last year, where we met, and recently took the silver behind defending world champion Megan Gunnels, at last month's US Nationals.

As the aircraft descended, my ears popped, and my stomach churned. I flopped back onto my seat, refastened the belt, and inhaled deeply.

Patti took hold of my hand; her dimples dug deep on both sides of her face. I returned the smile before closing my eyes.

Oslo International Airport, July 1979

The USA team gathered around at the luggage claim under the sign for SSA flight no. 1425.

"Let's get up closer." Patti grabbed my arm.

We stepped up next to Mark and Megan, the defending world champions and America's hope to win gold medals at this year's World Games and next year's Moscow Olympics.

Megan Gunnels, a statuesque and lean blond, had a permanent stern crease between her brows from her serious concentration. She had been the darling of US diving since 1977, when at sixteen she won her first national title and a gold medal at the Good Will Games on the platform. She had been the leader of the women's team and was competing in the springboard and platform events at these World Games.

"I hope we can rest before practice this afternoon," complained Megan. "I had the worst sleep on the plane."

Mark Bradley was on the verge of becoming one of the best divers ever. His résumé indicated that he'd medaled at every international meet he entered. He was vying for two gold medals.

"Right. The seats were so cramped that my neck is stiff," chimed in Mark. He stretched his neck from shoulder to shoulder.

"Enough complaining," a deep voice rang from behind us. "We still have a two-hour bus ride."

We all turned to find Dr. Don O'Toole, the USA International and Olympic Coach, standing behind us. His silver hair was immaculately trimmed. His face was kind, but there was a sense of seriousness behind his blue eyes. He wore a jacket and tie all the time, no matter where he was, even on the pool deck.

"We'll make sure we stretch and do lineups before we start any serious practice," said Coach Don. "Jack!" he called as he made his way across the area to the team's assistant coach, Jack Randall.

"All work and no play," piped in Andy Kirkland. He was from Austin, Texas, and was the final member of the men's three-meter springboard team. He had a stout gymnast's built, with broad shoulders that seemed too big for his five-feet-four-inch frame. His red hair and lamb chop sideburns were symbolic of his fiery personality. He was also one of the older statesmen of the team at the ripe old age of twenty-four. Tønsberg was his third world championships, but he never medaled as he had a tendency to choke during the finals. His moment of glory was when he won the gold medal in the USA versus URS dual meet held in Kiev, Russia, last summer.

"We're at the World Games, Andy. It wouldn't hurt if you took it a little more seriously," said Megan.

"And not enjoy life like you? There are other things to living than eating, drinking, and farting diving 24-7," Andy replied.

"Do you always have to be so disgusting?" asked Megan.

"Not always, but always around you." Andy stuck out his tongue and wiggled it back and forth.

I wanted to laugh, but Megan's disgusted look stopped me as she stepped closer to the conveyor belt.

"More room for us," announced Andy. He sidled up next to Patti.

A *beep-beep* sounded, and a red light flashed above the cargo hole where our baggage was carried out on the conveyor belt. Luggage of different sizes and shapes slid down the small embankment and began its journey on the horseshoe-shaped belt.

"Everyone," yelled Jack Randall, "grab your luggage, and get on the bus that's waiting for us outside the sliding glass doors." He pointed to the exit. "Make sure you sign in with Sheryl before claiming a seat."

Jack had been with USA diving for what seemed forever. At first sight, he appeared like a crotchety old man, with a curved spine that made him walk hunched over. He had a tendency to wear his pants too high and cinched tightly at his thin waist, causing his legs to look longer than they were. His salt-and-pepper hair went in every direction. Altogether, he resembled a friendly Ichabod Crane.

"There's mine," announced Patti.

"Which one?" I asked.

"The blue one with the big 'USA' on the side." She pointed to the bag heading toward us.

"Let's go, everyone. Get on the bus," bellowed Jack. "We don't have all morning. We still have a two-hour bus ride." He was shuffling around the room, escorting people toward the exit. "Let's go, people." He looked around nervously, as if waiting for the Headless Horseman.

"Where's your bag?" asked Patti.

"I don't know." I kept looking at the moving conveyor belt. "You go ahead."

"I can wait with you," she offered.

"We don't have all day, people." Jack's voice became harsh. He sauntered up next to Patti.

"David's still waiting for his bag," she explained.

"All right, Patti, you get on the bus," Jack instructed. "I'll see what's taking so long." Jack walked toward the information center.

Patti nodded and headed for the exit, pulling her suitcase behind her.

I turned to look at the cargo hole, as a single box tumbled down and started its journey. The single box reminded me of flying home after the Junior Olympics last year.

Dayton International Airport, August 1978

A dented box wrapped in tape with the word "Fragile" in red ink on the slides, pushed through the strips of plastic as it took its fourth ride on the conveyer belt. This single item, repeating the same rotation, must have been forgotten or lost in the shuffle of the red-eye flight that I came in on from Chicago. The battered box traveled the slow ride, slightly banking off the curved metal edging and rotating into a new position until it exited through the plastic straps at the opposite end of the luggage claim area. The belt came to a halt with a loud hiss.

I glanced down at my worn green duffel bag and a large tag identifying, "David Matthew, Ohio." My eyes burned, and my hands shook from the lack of sleep. I boarded flight number 673 in Lincoln, Nebraska, at 11:45 p.m., and flew down to Dallas, Texas. I switched planes and flew north to arrive in Chicago, Illinois, at 3:30 a.m. Finally, I boarded flight number 712 to fly southeast to arrive at Dayton International Airport at 5:30 a.m. That was forty-five minutes ago.

I remained standing in the same spot—afraid that if I moved, Dad wouldn't be able to locate me and think that Coach Trevor gave me a ride home. My teammates and their parents weren't scheduled to leave Lincoln until later in the afternoon. I took the red-eye because it was the cheapest flight my mother could find. I told her I wanted to travel with the team, and she said that it was impossible. At fifteen years old, I was becoming a seasoned traveler.

The main artery of the airport awakened with life as pilots, flight attendants, kiosk managers, and ground crews streamlined through the metal detectors, flashing their badges and carrying Styrofoam cups of coffee while pulling their luggage behind them on wheels. Passengers started gathering around counters beneath banners for each airline to purchase, upgrade, or change their itinerary. The PA system came alive with announcements of arrivals and departures.

I grabbed my duffel bag and made my way out the revolving door. A heavy gust of stale air pushed against me as I stepped out onto the covered patio area. I wandered over to an empty bench and sat, hoping that I was visible for my father to find me. It seemed that I was always waiting for him.

The rising sun was streaking the eastern sky with strands of rose and amber. The August morning's heat mixed with the exhaust fumes from the arriving, idling, and departing vehicles. I found myself watching people hugging and saying a teary "good-bye," "see you soon," and "have a great trip."

I waited.

I unzipped my duffel bag and retrieved a plastic bag. I pulled out a pink Beanie Baby with a Nebraska flag sewn over its heart. This gift was for Magdalyn, who loved everything "girly." For Caine, my older brother, I had found a model red car with a white stripe over the doors, which looked like his Torino. For Mom, I always found tiny bells with flags of the state I visited. And for Dad, I couldn't find anything, so I figured that I would present him the medal that I won. I pulled the medal out from the bottom of the bag; it sparkled in the morning sun as it hung from a red ribbon with the Junior Olympic emblem, five rings representing the five regions of the United States. The face of the medal was copper; a woman with an olive wreath was reaching both hands into the sky; "1978 Jr. Olympic Championships Lincoln, Nebraska," was engraved around the outer rim, and on the back was etched, "8th Place."

There was something else in the bag, a Polaroid that I forgot that I stored there on the last connecting flight. It was a candid shot of Patti Lakes, a new friend from Pasadena, California, and me. We were wearing our medals—hers, of course, was gold from winning the women's ten-meter platform. Patti and I hit it off the moment we met during the warm-ups and became inseparable throughout the duration of the competition. Everyone thought we were brother and sister, with our blond hair, dimples, and bright smiles.

"David," a voice called.

I looked up and saw the red Renault with Mom in the driver's seat. She was leaning over the passenger's seat, with the window down, trying to get my attention.

"Come on." She waved her hand for me to hurry as she glanced at the rearview and the side mirrors.

Relieved it was Mom, I quickly gathered my things and rushed to the idling car. I threw my duffel bag into the back, sat down, and fastened the seat belt.

"Didn't you hear me?"

"What?" My head was pounding from the lack of sleep, the lack of oxygen, and the heat of the rising sun.

"I was honking and calling for you." She shifted into drive, and the little vehicle surged forward.

"Sorry. I guess I wasn't paying any attention. I was expecting Dad."

I noticed her fingernails manicured with fire-engine red nail polish. She was wearing a black cocktail dress, dark-tanned hose, and black pumps with gold stitching. It was not even 7:30 a.m. I was curious as to why she was so dressed up, but there was a part of me that didn't want to know the reason. My eyes were drawing close as I leaned my head against the door, allowing the wind to brush my bangs from my forehead.

"I thought Dad was picking me up," I mumbled.

She pulled the car among the congested curving driveway without looking, causing another driver to lay on his horn. "Something came up."

"He forgot, you mean," I said with disappointment.

"Now, he has had a lot on his mind lately. I volunteered," she replied.

"Wow, thanks for being so considerate. Wait a minute, what about work?" I asked.

"I'll go in later and make up the time," she said as she grabbed my chin.

"Super!" I pulled from her grasp, leaned back, and closed my eyes.

"What's that supposed to mean?"

"Nothing. Do you have any aspirins? I have a major headache."

"Look in my purse. If I don't, we can buy some as soon as we get into town."

I opened her purse that was resting between us and found several boxes of diet pills. One box was empty, and the other contained the last two large, green, and oblong tablets sealed in cellophane. I glanced back at Mom. She had a faint grin on her painted red lips, and her mascaraed eyes rapidly darted from side to side as she scanned the Airport Access ramp that led to I-70. I recognized these symptoms; she was in her numb, euphoric state from the pills. This would explain her "bubbly" personality, because she was speeding and feeling no pain.

She must have felt me gazing at her because she looked over and saw me holding the box. Her cheeks reddened, and her dilated eyes widened as if she had been caught smoking behind the barn. She quickly ran a shaky hand over her high forehead and along her coiffed hair.

"The sun is murder this morning." She pulled her sunglasses from the visor and used her teeth to extend the shade's arms. She slid them over her ears and adjusted them to rest comfortably on the bridge of her nose.

I remained in the same position, holding the box of diuretics.

"What?" Then she added with a jovial and phony pretense, "Not there. I keep the aspirins in the outside pocket." She took the boxes of diet pills and laid them in her lap, and keeping her eyes on the road, she blindly reached for the front pocket of the purse, fumbling for the zipper as if reading Braille.

"I can find them," I said.

She withdrew her hand, as if she were a scolded child, and clutched the steering wheel. She glanced up into the rearview mirror before merging onto I-70 East. "I need to get more of my girls." That was what she called her diet pills. "They've been doing wonders."

I found the small bottle of aspirin and unscrewed the lid. It was empty. "Nada," I stated as I held the bottle upside down.

"I thought for sure I had some. We can get some more, I have to stop anyway."

I placed my head back on the headrest and watched the landscape whiz by.

"I swear I've some aspirins in there somewhere. Are you sure you looked near the bottom? We can get some more, I have to stop anyway." She always repeated herself when she was under the influence of her "girls."

She flipped on the turning signal to merge onto I-75 south toward Downtown Dayton.

My forehead rested against the vibrating window frame of the Renault, as the morning sun shed its rosy hue onto my shut eyes. I felt myself sink into the softness of the seat.

* * * * *

"Come on, David. Look alive. We're almost there," Mom said. She shook my shoulder. "It's a beautiful day."

I stirred and sat upright in the seat. "What time is it?" I asked as I stretched my spine like a cat.

"A little after nine," she said.

She veered the car north on State Route 73 and turned right onto Main Street. The town of Aulden was waking up, and people were opening the many shops that aligned the main strip. Mom pulled the car into a parking space outside the Humbler Inn.

"Mom, what's going on?" I asked as I stared at the entrance. I could see people peeking out. The door swung open, and a woman with a microphone and a cameraman exited and made their way toward our car.

"Mom?"

"The town's proud of you," she said.

"Mom, what'd you do?"

"Nothing." She patted me on the cheek.

"I just want to go home and sleep," I begged.

"Pull it together. I went to a lot of trouble to set this up. You be nice," she directed me.

"But, Mom!" I said.

"No 'but, Mom.' You'll go in there, and you'll be pleasant. There are people that want to help you with your diving. I told them that you'd be honored to meet with them. So you be a good boy and make me proud." She flashed a crooked smile, patted her hair, and checked her lipstick in the rearview mirror before opening the door to get out.

"Mrs. Matthew?" the woman reporter asked.

"Why, Laura Summers, what a pleasant surprise," Mom said with such sweetness you would have thought she was competing for Miss America; all she needed was to swear that she wanted world peace. Mom waved for me to get out.

The cameraman rushed to my side and pointed the camera at the window. I tried to hide.

"Wait, Darren," Laura Summers bellowed. "Focus on me, and we'll do the lead-in. Shoot David as he is coming out of the car and joining his mother and me. Then follow us into the restaurant."

"Whatever you want," the cameraman said. He adjusted his baseball cap backward on his longish brown hair and then aimed the camera toward Laura. "In five, four, three, two..." He pointed his finger at Laura.

"Hello. This is Laura Summers. Welcome to *Summers' Beat* where we catch up with local events and happenings in the Miami Valley and surrounding neighborhoods. Today we find ourselves in front of Humbler Inn in Aulden with Lydia Matthew."

Mom smiled adoringly toward the camera.

"And I believe we have a celebration in store for today. Can you explain?" Laura pointed the microphone toward Mom.

Mom took the microphone out of Laura's hand. "My son, David Matthew, has just returned from the Junior Olympics in Lincoln, Nebraska, where he won the bronze medal."

I cringed. I heard a tap on the car's hood. I looked up and saw Mom motioning for me to get out. I opened the door to have a camera shoved in my face. My cheeks felt like they were on fire as I made my way to Laura and Mom.

"How does it feel to have done so well at the Junior Olympics?" Laura asked.

"Um, good," I said into the microphone.

"Are you planning on representing the USA at the Moscow Olympics in two years?"

"That's a big—" I started to qualify.

"That's his big dream," interrupted Mom, "if all things work out and if we can get enough funds to send him there."

"Well, let's go in and see what's happening," Laura instructed. She motioned for the cameraman to follow.

We walked into the lobby of the restaurant, where a huge banner read, "Welcome Home, Junior Olympian!" People stood in small groups around the restaurant and clapped as we entered. I wanted to disappear.

An elfish man in a pinstriped suit walked up to Mom and wrapped his arm around her waist. She giggled as they walked to the back of the room.

I was escorted to a seat. Laura sat next to me, and the cameraman positioned himself behind her.

"What do you want to say to everyone, David?" coaxed Laura.

I wasn't sure what to say. My head hurt, and my eyes burned. "I want to thank everyone for coming and supporting me. It means the world to me to know that so many people are cheering me on here at home," I said with a plastic smile.

"The Spartans are winning state this year. Yeahhhhhh!" Dwayne, the football captain, appeared over my right shoulder, stuck out his tongue, and flashed a victory sign for the camera. Someone led him away. "Go, Spartans!"

I laughed.

"Yes, Dwayne, we're aware that Aulden has a great football team." Laura looked into the camera. "This is live, and anything can happen. David, what are your next steps to getting to the Olympics?"

"First, go home and sleep," I honestly admitted.

The people laughed at my joke.

"Yes, yes, I'm sure that will happen soon. But seriously, what does it take to become a nationally ranked diver like yourself?" Laura asked as she put the microphone to my mouth.

I thought a moment, and it dawned on me that this could happen, like one-in-a-million chances—but what if it did?

"Well, having this experience at the Junior Olympics has opened my eyes to what I'm going to have to do to get to the next level. Trevor Foxx, my coach, and I are going to get together to make a plan over the next couple of days. I'm going to have to increase practice time and travel to more competitions to get my name known. And then, with the help of God, I'll be able to go to the Olympic trials. I'll have to dive extremely well and place in the top 3 to get a ticket to Moscow."

"Sounds to me that there is very little time to rest and recuperate before you start all over again. How many hours do you practice?"

"Right now Trevor has me working out twice a day, two hours in the morning and then four hours at night. It takes about forty-five minutes one-way to get to the practice location, so my day is filled," I stated simply.

"You travel forty-five minutes to practice?" asked Laura.

"Yes. But my best chance is on the ten-meter platform. The closest platform to practice on is at Ohio State University," I explained.

"The odds seem to be stacked against you, and yet you have qualified for the Woodlands Texas International Cup later this month."

"Yes. But I'm not sure I'll be competing. Diving is very expensive, and since I went to the Junior Olympics, I may have to wait until next year for Woodlands."

"You're a junior in high school this year, correct?" she asked.

"I'll be a sophomore this fall at Aulden High School," I corrected her.

"This is truly an amazing accomplishment, and we wish you all the best." Laura turned to the cameraman, "This is Laura Summers with another segment of *Summers' Beat*. Thank you for watching." Laura winked her left eye. "That should be good enough." She rose.

I automatically stood as well.

"Good luck with everything, David," murmured Laura. She headed toward the exit with the cameraman in tow. Mom rushed after them.

"David."

I turned to find the elfish man who talked to Mom. The man's Brook's Brother pinstriped suit was immaculately pressed, and a pocket square matched his tie.

"David, I'm Harold Hall." He held out his hand.

I shook it.

"I've been following your successes, and your mother was telling me about your adventures," Mr. Hall said. He reached inside his jacket and pulled out an envelope. "I'd like to help you out."

He handed me the envelope.

"Inside you'll find a letter that explains what I'm willing to offer. Read through it, and then give me a call. We can have dinner and talk about it."

I took the envelope. "Yes, sir, Mr. Hall."

"Please call me Harold, or Hal." His smile seemed too friendly, like a used-car salesman.

"Yes, Hal," I stated with some reservations. It felt awkward using the first name of an adult I didn't know.

"I must be getting back to my office. It's a pleasure meeting you, and I look forward to talking with you soon. Congratulations on winning the medal." He patted my shoulder and disappeared amid the small crowd of people.

I was alone. There were people around Mom, listening to her give her Academy Award performance. No one was sitting or talking with me; they'd simply glanced at me while they were laughing with Mom. I opened the letter.

"Dear David, I am very interested in your Olympic endeavors and would like to provide some assistance…"

"David," a familiar voice called over the noise.

Mom was waving for me to join her. She enjoyed being the center of attention.

I folded the letter and obediently walked to her side, with a huge smile on my face.

Dr. Althea Warner's Office—Dayton, Ohio, July 2016

Althea laid her clipboard on her lap and clapped. "This is a good start. Tell me more about this…" she looked at the last page of my homework she assigned, "Harold Hall."

I felt resistant to talk about him. Why was it important to talk about him? I just sat there.

"You said he wanted to help you with your diving. How did he find out about you?" she asked.

"I don't know."

"He just showed up out of thin air?" She chuckled.

I shifted on the couch and took a deep breath. "He was like an uncle."

"But he wasn't a real uncle, was he?"

"No."

"So how do you think he found out about your diving?"

"Maybe through the newspaper," I offhandedly responded.

"Maybe. Maybe the uniqueness of diving caught his attention while reading the *Aulden Starr Newspaper*." Althea nodded and scratched her forehead. "Did you know J. K. Rowling's new book is written under a pseudonym?" She got up and went into the other room. "May I get you some water or tea?"

"No, thank you," I called to her.

I heard her preparing her tea as she hummed *Moonlight Sonata*. She returned with a purple cup and saucer, placed it on the side table, and repositioned herself in the chair. She saw me looking at the cup.

"I have a different color for each day of the week. Crimson for Monday, pink is Tuesday, purple for Wednesday, alabaster for Thursday, and fuchsia is for Friday. At home, I have paisley for Saturday and a rose print for Sunday." A storm was moving in, and the room dimmed. "Do you like that scent? It is natural oils I'm trying out." Althea inhaled. "I believe that is lavender. It helps soothe you."

"It's nice, not too overpowering," I responded by looking at the machine on the side table sending out puffs of the flowery scent.

Althea picked up the clipboard and jotted down some more notes. "So Mr. Harold Hall found out about your diving through the newspaper, but how did he know you were going to be at the Humble Inn that morning?"

"I'm not sure."

"Okay. How did anyone know about the gathering, like Laura Summers?" She tapped her pen on her lips.

"Mom invited them?" I guessed.

"Did your mom do this often?" she asked.

"Sometimes. She was always trying to help."

Althea looked back at her notes. "So what did Harold Hall do for a living?"

"He was a lawyer and wanted to help me with going to meets and things." I crossed my arms to my chest.

"You seem very defensive."

"I'm not." I looked out at the church steeple to see how much more time I had.

Althea remained silent and sipped her tea.

After an awkward pause, I felt that I had to defend Harold. "He was like a father figure. He understood me. He talked with me. He took me places and introduced me to people that helped with the diving costs. It's a rather expensive sport. He helped me get my driver's license and my scholarship to college. He helped me with my student loans. He introduced me to influential people in Aulden, Linden, Dayton, Columbus, and even Cincinnati."

Althea nodded her head. "Who were these influential people?"

"Other lawyers, doctors, and wealthy individuals who wanted to help someone like me." My head started pounding, and my palms sweated.

"And did they help you?" she asked.

"Yes, and the family."

"I see." She wrote down more notes.

The church tower's bell rang, indicating the end of the session. Althea stood, handed me back my journal, and went to her desk. I gathered my satchel and pulled out a check to give to her.

She took the check without looking at it. "You should check out J. K. Rowling's book, it is nothing like *Harry Potter*. And keep up the good work. Continue the morning pages, and bring in more for our next meeting."

3 CHAPTER

Bus to Tønsberg, Norway, July 1979

As I boarded the bus, everyone became quiet and stared at me. I looked at Sheryl, the team's assistant manager, as she stood next to the front row of seats.

She glanced down at her clipboard and then back up at me. "David Matthew?"

"Yes," I meekly replied.

Sheryl placed a checkmark next to my name and motioned for me to find a seat.

I hesitated as I looked toward the back of the bus for any available seat. I recalled when I was five years old, lost during my first day at a new school. The assistant principal dragged me to every bus and held me up in the air by my armpits and said, "Does anyone know this kid?" It must have been the fifth bus before my older brother, Caine, claimed me. I ran to him and hid my face in his shoulder.

"David, sit with me," Patti called.

I nodded and made my way, relieved to see a friendly face.

"Ain't that sweet, a budding romance," mocked Andy, "a World Game crush."

"All right, pipe down, Kirkland," demanded our coach, Dr. Don. He was towering in the front of the bus next to the driver.

Jack came rushing up the steps. "Is everyone here?"

Sheryl glanced down at her list. "Everyone's here and accounted for."

"Good. Everyone needs to get settled," Coach Don announced. I slid next to Patti.

"Where's your luggage?" she asked.

"Lost, it seems," I responded. "They're going to send it when they find it."

"All right, everyone, listen up," Dr. Don said. "We've got a two-hour ride to Tønsberg. The first thing we need to do when we arrive is register. Make sure you have your passports, AAU, and FINA cards. They'll give you identification badges that you must have on you at all times. Security will be tight, and they'll not let you on the pool deck without them. Don't lose them!" He took the clipboard from Sheryl and flipped several pages. "Remember, you are repre-senting the USA, every minute of the day. There'll be camera crews and reporters from all over the world following your every move. You'll be on constant display. Be careful of what you say, how you say it, and to whom you say it. If you're nervous about speaking to a reporter, make sure that one of us or a chaperone is with you. And let me remind you how important these World Games are, because of next year's Olympics. Any questions?"

Andy raised his hand, and everyone on the bus moaned.

"Yes, Andy?" called Dr. Don.

"So we'll get registered, and then I'm assigned to room with Megan?" His face flushed red.

"Real cute," said Megan without looking at him.

"What I meant to say was that, after we register, we'll practice," said Andy.

"That's what Dr. Don said," piped in Jack.

"So let's get this bus rolling," Dr. Don proclaimed. He patted the driver on the shoulder and made his way to the front seat. Jack settled in next to Dr. Don, and Sheryl sat across the aisle from them. The three huddled in some impromptu meeting.

The driver shifted the bus's gear and pulled away from the front of the airport.

"Can I sit by the window, Patti?" I asked politely.

"Sure." She shifted herself so that I could shimmy under her. She flopped down next to me and put her head on my shoulder. I reached over and interlaced our fingers.

The landscape reminded me of a quilted blanket—with different colors of green, yellows, blues, and browns sewn together. In the distance, I saw a farmer plowing a field and sending a plume of brown dust into the air behind him. The sun was hiding behind the long stretch of clouds, with the threat of showers. Three hawks circled lazily in the sky, looking for prey.

The bus slowed as it entered a small town adorned with clapboard buildings with sharp-angled thatched roofs hugging tightly to the narrow road. The people of the town were typical Nordic descent with blond hair and prominent cheekbones.

"They could be our relatives," noted Patti.

"What do you mean?"

"Look at the both of us, and then at them." She pointed to the locals shopping, working, or walking. "The blond hair—maybe we should've been born here?"

The idea of knowing where you come from was entertaining. Since I was the only blond in my family, Caine thought it was important to tease me by telling me that my real father was the milkman, the semi driver, or the carnie at the carnival. When I was younger, he had me convinced that I was adopted and not a real Matthew. I believed him so much that I was always trying to figure why I was different. I knew I was different in appearance, but there was something else that didn't seem quite right.

Matthews' Home—Aulden, Ohio, September 1978

The stale air mixed with exhaust made my stomach churn as the bus descended into Mount Holly, a section of Aulden situated at the base of a steep hill. The harsh afternoon sun weighed on the houses, barns, and fields that lined the curving two-lane road. The wind blew through the half-opened window, adding to the mugginess that smothered like a wool blanket.

I had started riding the bus again since Caine had decided it wasn't cool to have his little brother in his "hot rod"—a red Torino with white checkmarks detailed on both sides. The car was his tribute to the television show *Starsky and Hutch*. I tried to tell him that we both could be in the car—since his dark hair resembled Starsky's and with my blond hair, I could be Hutch. But he wasn't thrilled with that casting because he wanted to be Hutch, the one that got all the girls. And besides, his best friend, Anthony Spence, was already cast as the sidekick even though they both had dark hair.

As the bus jostled past the Hawkins' farm, my heart started to pound with the anticipation of two possibilities: Dad being home early and the construction worker on the job of the new neighbor's house across the street. The last half mile stretched like an eternity. As we approached my stop, I quickly glanced to see if Dad's car was in the driveway. It wasn't. Then I glanced over to see the skeleton of the new two-story house. The back side seemed to be enclosed, but the front side facing our house was still open, like a huge dollhouse. I watched from my window and prayed to God, *Let him be here today.*

He rounded the far corner of the structure, carrying several two-by-fours on his tanned bare shoulder, his shaggy blond hair stuffed under the yellow hard hat.

The bus rolled to stop, and the doors flung open.

"Matthew. Are we going to get off the bus here today or what?" announced Sue, the bus driver. One of her fat hands was gripping the steering wheel, while the other rested on the lever that swung the double doors open. Her stern eyes glared at me in the huge rearview mirror. "Let's go!" she ordered. "We don't got all day now."

I rose and stumbled down the narrow aisle.

"Have a nice trip? See you next fall," said Josh, a skinny kid with bad acne.

"Shut up," I said under my breath.

"Matthew!" Sue yelled.

I staggered to the exit, bumping into seats.

"Matthew, tell your mom that Sonnie has her order in at Quackenburger's," Sue said as I reached the front of the bus. Sonnie was her husband and ran the only grocery store in town.

"I sure will."

I flung my book bag over my shoulder and descended the three steps to the graveled driveway. The double doors slammed closed. The bus hissed as the breaks released and groaned as it crept forward like an old man with arthritic joints. A cloud of exhaust and heat bathed me in the bus's wake. When the cloud dissipated, there was nothing between me and the construction site, except the road. I saw the blond guy stretching to hand the boards to a man on the second level. The blond's broad shoulders and his muscular back tapered down to a small waist. The tool belt hung loosely around his hips and accented the roundness of his butt in his snug Levis.

I stood there as he handed off the last board and turned. I dropped my head because I didn't want him to know I was watching. When I glanced back up, he was gone.

I decided to cross the road to get the mail, which would position me even closer to the construction site. I pulled open the mailbox, retrieved the parcels, and automatically flipped through the envelopes.

The blond came around the corner of the house, again carrying more boards. His chest was gleaming with sweat, and I noticed the light patch of hair that streamlined down his abdomen to his belly button and then thickened and darkened as it ducked behind his waistband. *What was it about him?*

I turned and marched back across the road and up the driveway. I heard the pounding of nails into wood, the shrillness of electric drills, and the high-pitched burring of the saws. As I went through the back porch, I was overwhelmed with the odorous decay of rotting garbage heaped in the corner. A host of flies swarmed in circles above. I held my breath as I made my way to the kitchen door.

Bear, our black German shepherd and Labrador mix, jumped against the door, wanting to get out.

"Down, boy," I shouted. I opened the unlocked door.

Bear stood on his hind legs, placed his huge mitts on my shoulders, and licked my face.

"Ugh! Down, boy!" I lifted his massive paws off my shoulders and dropped them to the ground.

He skirted around me and ran out the door. He paused to sniff at the garbage bags.

"No! Bad dog!"

He glanced at me over his broad shoulder before bounding out the back porch door that was jarred open and then to the backyard.

"Oh, man!" I saw the present the dog had left on the dining room floor. "I hate this!"

I dropped my book bag on the chair by the door and grabbed the paper towels by the oven. I gagged as I scooped up the large load and placed sheets of paper towels on the floor to soak up the yellow liquid.

I grabbed my book bag and made my way up the stairs to my room on the landing and opened my window. The blond across the way was handing more boards to the man on the second level, and the sun was bathing him in gold. I sat on the edge of my bed, watching. Suddenly, I remembered the binoculars in Caine's room. I retrieved them and adjusted the focus. His chiseled face streaked with dirt and sweat; eyes were shrouded beneath bushy brows; lips were surrounded by a growth of golden day-old beard; chin dimpled; and strands of hair sprouting out from under the protection of the yellow hard hat.

I removed my shirt and stood in front of my mirror. I wondered if I was ever going to have a similar physique. My flesh was smooth and devoid of any hair. I rubbed my chin and wondered when, if ever, I would have to shave. As I examined my reflection, I realized I wanted to look like him, stubble and all.

I looked through the binoculars and saw him remove his hat and run his hand through his lionlike mane. *I have to get closer.* I thought about the front porch, where there were the bushes. *I could hide and watch.*

Without thinking about the ramifications of being caught spying, I sailed down the stairs and opened the front door. He was nowhere in sight.

I crept onto the porch as if I were searching for something. I took my time to migrate to the porch's edge, where the evergreen bushes were aligned in a row. I glanced over to the construction site, and when I was certain no one was watching me, I jumped down into the flower bed and positioned myself behind a bush. I pulled the glasses to my eyes as the blond came into view. He lifted the boards to the awaiting man again. Once the boards were taken from him, he turned, facing me. I shrunk behind the bush. *Did he see me? No way, there is no way that he saw me.* I braved it, leaned out, and watched again. He was still standing there, closer than ever. He wiped the back of his gloved hand across his forehead, exposing the swatch of damp brown hair under his arm. I touched my armpit and only found sprouts of hair like goose down. I watched as his brown gloved hand pressed against his round pectorals and wiped sweat and dirt down to his waist. As the glove slid down his abdomen, he flattened the hairs in his wake. I mimicked him and felt only smooth skin. *I have to get closer! How?*

Lemonade!

I'll make lemonade and take it over to him. Wait a minute. I'm going to have to make enough for all of the men so that it won't be obvious. I waited until the blond disappeared to get more boards then hopped up from behind the bushes and rushed into the house. Bolting upstairs, I threw on a shirt and hurried to the kitchen. I opened the cabinets to find the lemonade mix and the plastic Tupperware pitcher, which I filled with ice. I scooped in some flavored powder and shoved the pitcher under the faucet. My hands were shaking so bad that I almost spilled the mixture. *Shit!* Once I regained control, I finished filling the pitcher with water and stirred it with a wooden spoon. I grabbed a stack of blue plastic cups and made my way to the front door.

Before I knew it, I was standing at the construction site, holding a pitcher in one hand and a stack of glasses in the other. The blond was nowhere in sight, only the older man that was shoveling gravel into a wheelbarrow.

"Excuse me," I spoke with a dry mouth.

The man turned with a start, "Yeah?"

"I thought…I'm from…across the road, and since it was so hot, I thought you guys might be thirsty," I said.

The man's brows arched and met above the bridge of his nose. He glanced over toward our house. "From over there with the big black dog?"

I chucked. "Yes, that's Bear. He's a big baby. He'd lick you to death before ever biting." I held out the pitcher and glasses. "Would you like some cold lemonade?"

He shifted his eyes down at the pitcher and then back toward me. He slowly smiled, exposing yellowish teeth behind his spreading and graying mustache. "Damon," he called, "do you want something to drink?"

A voice called back from behind the half-constructed building. "Yeah, a beer would be great."

"You'll have to settle for lemonade."

"What the hell are you talking about?" The blond, Damon, rounded the building with two more boards balanced on his shoulder.

"This kid has some lemonade for us," said the older man.

"Oh, that's nice." Damon stopped next to me, bent down to place the boards on the ground, and exposed a slight crack of his buttocks.

"What are we waiting for?" the older man demanded.

"Right." I gave a nervous laugh and handed the older man a glass and poured him some lemonade. I turned to Damon and froze. Damon took a glass and the pitcher; his fingers grazed mine. He poured his drink and gave the pitcher back to me. I stood there while he drank.

I want to look and act and smell just like him.

Matthews' Home—Aulden, Ohio, October 1978

Two months since I watched Damon drink the lemonade, the neighbor's house was near completion, and Damon was no longer around.

"David, tell your mom that Sonnie has the ground chuck on sale today and tomorrow only—the good ground chuck," said Sue Quackenburger as she waited for me to exit the bus.

I glanced up, blocking the afternoon sun with my hand. "I sure will."

"Watch your step." Sue looked in the large rearview mirror. "All right, you rug rats, settle down and stay seated." She closed the door and shifted the bus into drive.

I froze when I turned and saw Old Blue parked by the back door. I felt like I stood there for a lifetime before I took in a deep breath and walked toward the house. Bear was on the chain in the backyard and barked a hello.

The kitchen was silent. The air was filled with coffee and cigarette smoke. I glanced in the living room, and no one was there. Maybe Dad was praying in the woods. I climbed the stairs to my room and found Dad sitting on my bed, surrounded by my drawings hidden under my bed.

"Your figures' hands, feet, and cocks aren't proportional. They are too big. This pulls the viewers' attention away from the rest of the composition." He gathered some sketches and made room for me next to him on the bed.

As I sat, he was demonstrating and speaking.

"Always base your proportion with the size of the head. There'll always be exceptions if you're painting pornography, but always make your figures' extremities in proportion."

He lit a cigarette and let it hang between his lips. He placed the pencil's lead on the figure's cock and etched a new line. "You'll want to make sure that the lines aren't completely straight. The human body is never a straight line. This will give your figure life and movement."

He shaded the tubular shape with the side of the pencil's lead in arching movements. "Always shadow circular shapes in this way, it'll give the illusion of depth and circumference."

The shape became lifelike, and the shading added dimension to the drawing. "Remember, whenever drawing a human figure, there's an essence or light coming off the skin. This light is energy or heat. So when you shade, make sure to include this band of light."

I watched how the band of light added even more dimension and a photographic quality to the image. He continued to reshape the hands and feet.

"Hands are the hardest part to make realistic. Many people don't take the time to explore the fingers' shapes and how they bend. They assume they know and then proceed to draw mechanically. Look at your hand. See how everything comes together to give the illusion of a whole hand?"

I looked at how my hand's natural lines curved and flowed with the shape of the bones under my skin.

"Turn your hand over."

I looked at my palm, and he ran his forefinger over the flesh. "See how the lines dictate the life of the hand?"

Dad went back to the sketch. "Let the viewers' eyes fill in most of the hand's lines for you. Give just the hint of the line connecting, but leave blank spaces as well." The hands came alive, looking natural and not stiff.

"You might want to use less body hair in your drawings too, it distorts the physique's line. If you're going to include hair, make sure you're aware how the hair grows. Hair doesn't just appear. It's in alignment with the body. Look at my forearm. The hairs wrap around the arm starting from the underside and span out over the top of the forearm until you get to the opposite side. Now this is where the hairs start growing in the opposite direction, and then you can see a line where the hairs meet, like this." He showed how the hairs create a line on the inside of his arm along the natural line of the little finger.

He turned the sketch and pointed to the figure's thigh. "You need to be aware that the hairs on the legs extend out from the patch of pubic hairs surrounding the cock. As the hairs extend over the thighs, just like the forearm, they grow in a wrapping formation." He exemplified this by placing his hand on his thigh and motioning how the growth patterns move across the upper and under the thigh until they meet. "You did a good job with the hair patterns here. You see how you allowed the hairs to help keep the circular evolution of the human body. Nice work."

He stopped, laid several sketches out, and examined them. Without looking at me, he asked, "Why are you drawing Zach naked? Why are all these of Zach?" He looked at me. "Did he pose for you?"

I shook my head.

He slowly stood up, letting the drawings fall to the floor.

"They aren't Zach," I managed to say.

He looked at me with stern eyes. "They all look like Zach."

"But they aren't. I was just practicing the figures from your art book." I picked up the drawings from the floor.

Dad's head cocked as he took a step closer. "Why do they all have the same hairstyle, lips, eyes, and hairy legs?"

"I don't know. I just drew them without thinking." I looked down at the sketches in my hands. All the figures were similar in the fact that they had Zach's dark gothic appearance. "I had no idea."

"Is that how you see him, naked and all out of proportion?" He gently took the sketches from my hands. "It's unnatural to draw images of the flesh in such provocative ways."

"But what about the woman you drew, the one I tried to copy?" I asked.

"That's different. That was an assignment." His neck started to turn red, as the veins on each side began to pulse.

"But…"

"No buts." He held up the sketches. "These types of drawings will cause you to burn in hell and are against the Bible, which states, 'He who sins sexually sins against his own body.'" He looked at the sketches, then back to me, and calmly asked, "Do you think Zach is attractive?"

I quickly shook my head.

"Then why do you draw him?"

"I just drew those pictures. I'm not sure why they look like Zach." My face flushed from lying. I have often fantasized about Zach, and by drawing him, I felt that I was near him.

Dad slowly nodded his head and sucked air through his lower teeth. "Leviticus 20 says, 'If a man lies with a male as with a woman, both of them have committed an abomination, they shall surely be put to death, their blood is upon them.' An abomination," he stressed. He took a moment to look out the window. "Maybe we should refrain from drawing any more nudes of Zach, or any man. You don't want to bring disappointment and shame to the family, do you?"

I didn't say anything.

He calmly stood there and said, "I asked you a question. Don't you see the temptation that these drawings have?"

I flinched. "They're just drawings."

"Smut. You're drawing smut. I can't have such smut in my house. You will obey my request, or I'll forbid you from drawing anything. Do you understand?"

"But it wasn't…"

"Do you understand?"

"Yes." I hung my head in shame.

"Yes, what?"

"Yes, sir."

He gathered up all the sketches remaining on the bed. "Why don't you pray for forgiveness?"

I wasn't sure if he was suggesting or demanding me to pray. I didn't want to take a chance. I prepared for the wrath of anger to spew from him, not this calm and controlled demeanor. I felt my muscles start to tremble with the anticipation of physical abuse. None came.

I knelt on the floor and rested my folded hands on the bed. "Dear God, forgive me for my misguided ways. Please accept my apologies if I offended you with my drawings, I was in no way wanting to offend anyone. Please help me to see the temptations of the flesh and help protect me from its sinful ways in the future."

Dad placed his large hand on my head. "You are not alone, my son." He leaned down and kissed me before removing his hand.

I remained on my knees next to the bed, afraid that he could still be there watching me. I imagined tearing up the sketches and gathering all the pieces of evidence and rushing to the silo. I could see clearly: I struck the match against the side of the box, and the paper accepted the red and orange flames. I watched the torn paper crinkle with the heat. I witnessed my illustrations char to ash. When I felt it was safe to stand, I found that all the sketches were gone. Dad had taken them with him.

Dr. Althea Warner's Office—Dayton, Ohio, July 2016

Althea set her pink teacup on the side table, picked up my pile of papers, and settled back in the armchair.

"Were you attracted to the blond construction worker?" she asked.

"How do you mean?" my voice came timid.

"Were you sexually attracted to him?" She gazed at me with her gray eyes.

"I'm not sure if I was sexually attracted to him. I was drawn to how he looked and acted. He was different. He was blond. No one else in my family was blond. I wanted to grow up and look like him. He was sexy and beautiful," I replied as honest as I could.

"How did it make you feel inside when you were around or thought of the construction worker?"

"I felt nervous, scared, and afraid all at the same time."

"Have you ever felt this way with anyone else before the blond construction worker?" She wrote notes on my papers.

"The only other time I felt similar to this was when I was around my brother's friend, Zachary Spence," I responded. "But Zach wasn't blond, he was more of a dark gothic figure."

"Describe him to me," instructed Althea.

"Well…he was tall and thin. He had messy dark hair, his bangs always fell across his bushy eyebrows. Zach's brown eyes always seemed to sparkle and dance. He had pronounced cheekbones, angular jaw, and a cleft in his chin. He always had a five o'clock shadow of stubble surrounding his plump red lips. He wore dark clothes, long coat, and torn straight-leg jeans that revealed his hairy thighs."

"Do you think you had a sexual attraction to Zach?" Althea asked.

"I'm not sure I understood what that meant at the time. I knew I wanted to be next to both Zachary and the construction worker, but for different reasons. It was like the construction worker was pure and Zachary was the dark version of attraction. Zachary was what I was used to since my father and brother were dark haired, and the construction worker was more of what I wanted to be. Does that make sense?"

Althea looked confused. "Oh, I'm sorry, I was thinking of something else, but I do believe it makes sense. Did you think your father and brother were attractive?"

"Yes." This question caught me off guard and made me uncomfortable. I quickly added, "They're both dark haired and blue eyed. They looked alike. Does this make me sick?"

"Why?"

"Isn't it wrong to be attracted to your father and brother?" I ran my hands through my hair.

"I didn't ask if you were attracted to your father and brother. I asked if you thought they were attractive. There's a big difference. Thinking your father and brother are attractive doesn't mean you are attracted to them sexually. It is how one bases his attraction on when he begins looking for a partner. You've heard the ideology that a daughter looks for a husband that resembles her father, and a son will find a mother-figure type for his wife?"

"I thought that was just a gross generalization," I said.

"It is, but there's still some truth to it. Were you aware that you were gay?"

"No. I had no idea what that meant. All I knew was that I was different. I knew that Caine talked about girls the way I felt about Zach. Caine had a Farrah Fawcett poster on his wall, while I had Bruce Jenner and Mark Bradley. Yet it didn't make any sense why I'd be any different. I grew up in the same house as Caine, and I wasn't influenced by anyone who was gay. Dad and Caine were the only males I was around growing up—it wasn't like we were allowed to have people over. Dad was extremely private. He didn't want the outside world to know our business. We even stopped going to church because according to Mom, Dad had a disagreement with the priest. That's when he built a sanctuary in the woods' clearing near the house with three full-size crosses to represent Calvary. He explained to us that God told him to do this to be closer to the Holy Father and to bring a daughter into this world. No one questioned his validity or actions. We accepted it as truth. I remember being a bit jealous that God personally contacted him. I wanted to know what God looked like. He would never go into detail.

"Dad started reading the Bible more and creating religious drawings and paintings. He had always dreamed about being an artist but was constantly told there was no money in such nonsense. His paintings were extremely detailed and looked like actual photographs. He spent more and more time working on his illustrations, and everything else became secondary. Dad's painting of Jesus on the cross was very sensuous. I'm not sure if it was Dad's interpretation, but his Jesus was beautiful and very human. Jesus's expressive blue eyes were looking up toward heaven, the crown of thorns caused droplets of blood to caress his forehead like fingers, and one drop gently traveled down his cheek. His lips parted and his long brown hair cascaded over his shoulders. I remember thinking that if I could look like Jesus, I would be beautiful and 'normal.' But I wasn't. I was always reminded when I looked in the mirror that I was different. I was a disappointment, because I was blond.

"I started copying Dad's paintings and added my personal interpretations to them. At first Dad seemed proud that I acknowledged his desire to paint and shared his expertise. I learned that Dad had once been accepted into a prestigious art school but had to drop out because of the tuition. He showed me his art books, assignments, and sketches. I practiced and practiced, and I started to improve. I wasn't talented like him, but I was able to express emotion through my art. My version of Jesus won a blue ribbon in a local art show because Mom entered it without my or Dad's awareness. Dad said that my Jesus was too 'girly' and looked too much like Zachary. He stopped sharing his work with me after that. I never knew what he meant by 'too girly,' so I stopped painting Jesus and focused on horses."

"Why horses?" asked Althea.

I felt myself grin. "I'm not quite sure. But in my teenage mind, I thought horses represented the strength and power of an athletic man. I was free to draw the animal's legs without the ramification of drawing a man's leg." I suddenly stopped and buried my face in my hands. "This is so embarrassing."

"Why?"

"The lengths I took to hide and pretend that I was okay or 'normal.' How naive I was to think that I could hide my passion for masculine, hairy legs by drawing and painting horses." I took a deep breath and chuckled. "I have never admitted that to anyone."

"Was Zachary gay?" Althea asked as she wrote on the clipboard.

"I don't know. I don't think so. All I knew was that I felt pulled to him. So I drew and painted his image. Not all at once. At first I was not even aware that I was sketching Zach. I remember having this dream during a nap on the couch. I woke breathless and felt excited. It was something I had never felt before. I grabbed my sketch pad and etched a faint outline of a person sitting. I recall that as I started shading in shadows, the image began to develop. I remembered this slight moment, when I was shading edges of the ripped jeans, if I dared to illustrate the hairs on the image's thighs. This was a huge decision. I really wanted to, but I was not sure if I could correctly illustrate the effect. My heart started to race, sweat started to appear, and my hands shook. I was worried that I would ruin the drawing, but I had to try. So I sharpened the pencil to a fine point and lightly drew some fine lines on the image's exposed thigh. The effect was exactly what I wanted, and the thrill was overwhelming. Feverishness came over me as I darkened the lines, and the hair on the thighs looked real to me."

Althea picked up her cup and took a long sip, studying me over the rim as steam circled her head. "Why was body hair so important to you?"

I scratched the base of my neck and said, "Because I didn't have any. Mom used say that it was because of the Cherokee Indian on Dad's side of the family and it must have skipped to me."

"What do you mean?" she asked as she placed her cup on the table.

I glanced up at the ceiling and took a deep breath. "As I hit puberty, only one area seemed to develop. I was completely embarrassed by it. It was as if God had forgotten the body hair and focused everything on one area." I gave a nervous laugh and looked at Althea.

"You'd think I would have been proud about it. But I wasn't. I was made fun of at school, especially during gym showers. I was called 'Monster,' 'Nellie the Loch Ness,' and was constantly asked if I ever tripped over it. I remember trying to hide it. I wanted to make it disappear. I used to tell myself that it just looks like that because I had very little hair, and the hair I had was blond and seemed to disappear when wet. I got so paranoid that I felt that when someone spoke to me, they were only looking and talking to my crotch."

"But then you went into a sport that the uniform is nothing but a Speedo," said Althea.

"Ironic!" I said. "But I was constantly trying to find ways to hide it. I used to wear Mike Peppe swimsuits that were made from this really thick material of acetate, cotton, and rubber. I had this idea that the material would compress everything, so no one would be able to see anything."

"How did that work for you?"

"I thought it did its job. It allowed me to think more about diving. But I have always been ashamed and am constantly still trying to hide myself." I squirmed and shifted to a new position, crossing my legs and hunching over.

"You can't even say it, can you?" Althea asked.

"I don't understand your question."

"You have skirted around calling it a penis, cock, or dick," she stated.

"Oh my," I replied without knowing I did.

"See, you are uncomfortable."

"No, it's just…I don't know. I feel that it's just something that I've been embarrassed about all my life. So what? I used to sleep in sweats no matter what the temperature, because I didn't want it to show."

Althea didn't respond. She picked up her clipboard, nodded her head, and wrote down some notes.

"So you have a huge cock."

"Oh my god."

"Yet you were also concerned about not having body hair. Why?"

I looked up at the church tower's clock and was disappointed that I still had fifteen more minutes. I looked back at Althea and felt her anticipation for the question.

"I felt different, not normal. Everyone else had body hair. I had none." I pulled up my sleeve to expose my forearm. I ran my palm across it. "Nothing. Everyone said I had girl's skin, smooth as a baby's bottom, and my skin glowed better than a woman's. I wanted to have hair because it proved that I was a man. Everyone would peacock around the locker room, strutting and exposing the hair on their bodies. I wanted to hide because I looked like I was ten."

"Except for the size of your dick."

4 CHAPTER

Tønsberg, Norway—Bus and World Games Registration, July 1979

The bus's brakes hissed and came to a complete stop.

"Wake up, sleepyhead," Patti said.

I rubbed the sleep from my eyes, as the bus's interior came into focus.

Dr. Don stood and announced, "We're finally here."

The bus erupted with cheers.

Holding up his hands, Dr. Don continued, "We'll first go to registration. So get your AAU and FINA cards and passports out and ready. This shouldn't take long. We'll go in as a group and look for the USA marker, most likely it'll be the last table. When finished, gather at the souvenir area. Remember that you're representing the USA every minute of the day."

"Wait just a moment before y'all leave," shrieked Sheryl in her high-pitched voice. "Listen up to who your roommate is. For the girls, Megan Gunnels will room with…"

"Andy Kirkland," Andy's muffled voice rang out.

Everyone cracked up.

"Yeah, right, like in your wet dreams," shot back Megan.

"Oooh, she got you, bro," Mark encouraged.

Andy stood and feigned he was stabbed. He fell dead in the aisle.

"Megan," Dr. Don piped in.

Defensively Megan retorted, "He started it."

"Enough," placated Dr. Don.

"May I finish?" asked Sheryl. No one responded. "For the girls—Megan Gunnels and Patti Lakes, Amy McGill and Mary Kimball, and Cindy Vanberger and Jennifer Connors. The boys—Andy Kirkland and Matt Davis, Bruce Bryans and Tim Morse, and Mark Bradley and David Matthew."

Can this be happening? Am I going to be housing with the defending world champion and my idol?

The stifling afternoon sun greeted us as we climbed off the air-conditioned bus. The USA team gathered outside the Nordic building with two Viking statues guarding the entrance.

A lady wearing a white polo shirt with the 1979 World Game insignia stitched on the front left panel intercepted Dr. Don, Jack, and Sheryl before they could enter through the glass doors. The Norwegian smiled and talked to them. We watched as Dr. Don nodded his head in agreement and turned to Jack before he entered the building with the guide.

Jack and Sheryl approached us.

Jack said, "Please only bring in your AAU and FINA cards, passport, and wallets. Leave everything else on the bus. Security is extremely tight."

"I'm available for a strip search," joked Andy.

Megan retorted, "You're such a nimrod."

"Very funny, but this must be done as seriously as possible," reminded Jack.

Some athletes climbed back on the bus. Patti and I remained on the curb.

"What's with all the security?" I asked.

"Ever since the Munich Olympics, security's tight. And now that Russia's threatening Afghanistan, everyone's edgy. They want to keep the athletes safe," she explained. She looked through her purse for her ID cards.

We lined up and entered the building. The first thing we encountered was the metal detector, which looked like a portable white door frame. A red light flashed and a high beep sounded if it detected anything.

Patti placed her purse on a table for the guards to search and walked through the archway. Nothing happened, and she smiled back at me.

My palms felt sweaty as I stepped up to the metallic configuration. *What would I do if the machine indicated metal on me?* I took a deep breath and stepped through. Nothing beeped or flashed.

Andy followed me. The moment he stepped in, it started beeping and flashing red lights. The guards stiffened and surrounded him.

"What? No way," demanded Andy. "I've nothing on me." He started emptying his pockets, removing coins, a Saint Francis medallion, and a wrinkled magazine photo of Brooke Shields. A tall, husky guard held his hand up for Andy to stop. The guard pulled out what looked like a black paddle with metal tubing running up one side, curving, and running down the other side. The guard indicated for Andy to hold his arms out to his sides and then waved the wand inches over Andy's body. It started beeping when it passed over his waist. The guard lifted Andy's shirt to reveal a large silver belt buckle.

"What can I say? That's my Texan longhorn," Andy said with a smile.

The guard allowed Andy to pass through.

I leaned in close to Patti's ear and asked, "Will that suffice as a strip search for him?"

Patti playfully hit my shoulder and whispered, "Stop!"

"I survived," Andrew announced loudly. He squealed and fell into Patti's arms as if he had fainted.

The crowds in the lobby laughed and proceeded with their business.

We passed into a rotunda with a high-domed ceiling painted with murals depicting battles between Vikings and farmers. Hanging down from the center of the ceiling was a banner welcoming the athletes of the world in their native languages. The atmosphere was electric.

Patti grabbed my hand and started leading me to a table in the far corner where Sweden, United States, and USSR flags were draped above.

"Patti!" someone called.

Patti stopped suddenly, and I bumped into her.

Megan was waving. "We're supposed to get our pictures taken first."

Without a word, Patti led me to queue up behind Megan and Mark. Andrew followed us.

The area was crowded with athletes, coaches, chaperones, reporters, and volunteers. The noise was bouncing, ricocheting, creating an orchestra of multilingual cacophony.

"I thought we had to sign in first," said Patti.

"That's what I thought," replied Megan, "but Jack told us to go here first since the line was shorter."

"Mr. Matthew," a squeaky voice called.

I turned to find Sheryl sternly looking at me.

"You need to go to the sign-in area before getting your badge." She tilted her head and pointed toward the long tables on the opposite side of the room.

"Oh, okay," I quickly said. I released Patti's hand and started toward the registration tables.

Patti grabbed me and said, "Sheryl, we've been told to get our badges first."

"Yes, that's correct." Sheryl's Minnie Mouse voice raised in pitch. "You four are to get your badges first, since you're established in international meets. David has never competed internationally, he'll need to be processed through the regular registration format." She remained standing with her arm extended in the direction that I needed to go.

"Finally, I'm a part of the A-list," said Andrew.

Megan turned her back on him.

"What? Was it something I said?" Andy mocked shock.

Megan didn't respond or even look at him; she shook her head.

"Sheryl, I've no problem going to register first." I sounded like Mom, in her sweet and pretend way. I started walking toward the far end of the room.

"Thank you," Sheryl said as I passed.

I walked through the milling athletes, coaches, and chaperones from all over the world. Each country seemed to be in small clusters, speaking languages I've never heard before. There was so much going on that I was having some trouble figuring out which group belonged to which country. I was able to recognize the maple leaf on the Canadian warm-ups; the King's red, white, and blue of Great Britain (which always made me think of the mathematical Xs and plus signs); and the white sweat suits with the large red circle on the back of the Japanese athletes.

A team with "Italia" in blocked letters on the back of their jackets stood in a huddle toward the center of the room. One of the athletes looked over his shoulder and caught me staring at his group. His golden curls hung loosely above a face that seemed to have been designed by Michelangelo. His emerald eyes locked on to mine, and I froze. His face brightened with a grin.

I immediately glanced away. When I glanced back, he was nowhere to be seen.

I paused for a moment before making my way to the table surrounded by red uniforms with the white hammer crossing a sickle. I recalled my father warning me about the Russians: "They make their athletes into coldhearted, ruthless machines from the time they're born until they die. The commies are nearly impossible to beat. They are sent to Siberia if they finish second."

As I waited for the Russian comrades to complete checking in, and hoping that they didn't see me standing there alone in my patriotic uniform, I noticed the huge mural on the wall behind the table. It depicted an image of Vikings battling to get back to their ship. Two warriors in the foreground looked familiar with their heavy and prominent brows, and the eyelids were at half-mast and shadowing the pupils. *Where have I seen this before?*

Matthews' Home—Aulden, Ohio, October 1978

I climbed off the school bus and noticed that the neighbors had moved into the new house across the street. As I walked up the gravel driveway, I was disappointed when Bear didn't come galloping down to greet me, which meant that he must be in the house or chained up in the backyard. My stomach dropped when I saw the Old Blue Plymouth parked by the back door entrance.

As I passed the dining room window, I saw Dad at the kitchen counter, pondering over several piles of paper. One hand clutched his favorite coffee mug, and the other propped his head up with a short cigarette smoldering between two fingers. I wondered what he was so intensely focused on, but also hoped that I could slide past him and go to my room. Just then, a black face leaped up against the window's screen, causing me to yelp and earn Dad's attention.

Bear panted with glee as his big red tongue hung out to the side of his mouth and his black nose pressed against the screen.

"Down, Bear!" Dad ordered.

The massive dog's head swung around and glanced toward Dad and then quickly returned to me before clumping down from the window's ledge.

"Davy, come here, I've got something to show you," called Dad.

This sent a sheet of ice through my veins.

As soon as I opened the door, Bear greeted by lapping my face with his wet tongue.

"Down, boy," I instructed. I pushed against his large chest, forcing him back onto all fours. He quickly spun around, chasing his tail with excitement.

"He's glad to see you," said Dad.

I remained at attention by the door, not sure what to do or where to go next.

"Come here, I want to show you something," he encouraged. He lifted the burning stub of his cigarette to his lips and inhaled.

I put my bag down on an empty dining room chair next to the door and made my way around the kitchen counter.

"Mom working?" I asked.

"As usual. She said she was going to be late tonight." He scratched his temple. "I was going to tell her that she should have a room there and not worry about coming home, but I think she might like that idea."

"She sure does like to work," I dryly admitted.

"Maybe she's got a secret man hidden somewhere."

"No," I tried not to allow myself to even entertain such a notion.

Dad waved to me to hurry. "I can't believe I didn't see this sooner," he triumphantly proclaimed. He twisted the butt of the cigarette in the already-overflowing ashtray.

"You're home early," I said.

"I took the afternoon off. I wanted to tinker around with The Luper."

Dad was always developing ideas and contraptions. His latest was what he called "The Luper," a car engine that ran completely on water. He knew this would revolutionize the automotive industry and help the US from being dependent on the Middle East for gasoline. Most importantly, it would make him a millionaire.

"When I was in the basement working out the configurations of the model's specs, I had this image. This idea rushed into my head like a bullet. So I came up here and started putting what I saw down on paper."

Before him sat three piles of papers; some were lined with notes scrawled in blocks and running at different angles across the front. Some were tracing paper, onionskin, with sketched portraits. And a final pile that was scribbled with numbers that looked like they had been printed from a machine, but on a closer look, I recognized the detailed script of tight circles and lines that belonged to Dad's penmanship.

"Sit," he ordered. He gathered the papers for his presentation.

I reluctantly lowered myself onto Magdalyn's stool next to him.

"Now look at this first." He pulled out a sheet of paper with notes and used his thick index finger to point to the upper right-hand corner. "According my calculations, there's been a major disruption in the way the stars have been lining up. Look at this."

He directed my focus to the center where a jumble of numbers had been added and divided and multiplied, resulting in what looked like a date: 56 BC.

"Do you know what that means?"

I shook my head.

"Come on, use your noodle." He reached for a dented Pall Mall package and flipped up the lid, took out a fresh stick, and placed it between his lips. The whole time his blue eyes were encouraging me to provide the correct answer.

I hesitated because if I couldn't come up with the correct answer, he might go into a rant. I concentrated on the numbers and notes to try and come up with a guess. I was able to decipher the names of Caesar, Hitler, and Carter. *What do these three names have in common?* I also located what looked like the following dates: 56 BC, 1935, 1945, 1976, and 1979. On the lower section of the first page, I saw words, such as, *the Holocaust, Ides of March, Hindenburg, Vietnam, Pearl Harbor, Black Plague, Noah's Ark, WWII,* and *WWI.*

None of this makes any sense.

He must've read my mind, because he added, "Don't be too literal."

Leaning back, he lit the cigarette with his lighter. He took a deep drag and blew the smoke high into the air then waved his hands over the sheets of paper.

"Think of these as messages, as codes to help you come to a central idea. What would all these things point to?" He folded his massive arms across his chest. "What do you see?"

"I'm not sure," I replied.

"Try," he said with an edge of impatience.

"I am." Nerves caused beads of sweat to gather along my forehead.

"What do you see?" He took another long drag on the cigarette before he placed it carefully on the lip of the ashtray. He held his breath for what seemed an eternity before exhaling; the gray smoke lingered above the paperwork.

I inhaled the burnt cloud and coughed.

"I see names and dates," I said with as much enthusiasm as I could muster. I tried not to breathe in any more tar.

"Okay, yeah. What do these names have in common? Let's start with them."

"Well, there's Hitler," I said. I pointed to his name on the list.

"Good."

I continued and said, "Caesar and Carter."

"You're correct. What do these three names have in common?" He asked, looking like a child receiving a gold star for a job well done.

"I'm not sure," I slowly said.

"Don't give up so easily. Think," he gently demanded.

"Is this Jimmy Carter?" I guessed.

"Of course," he said with glee.

"They're all leaders," I supplied another guess.

"Exactly! Leaders of what?" His excitement forced him to lean onto the counter and hoist himself up to arm's length. His face was inches from mine. I felt his heat radiating from his high forehead and smelled the burnt remnants from the inhaled cigarette.

"Well, Caesar was leader of the Romans. Hitler led the Nazis. Carter is the current president of the United States," I stated.

"Correct. So you see the literal meaning of what these men led or are leading—since Carter is still president. But think outside of the box, and tell me, what were they leading their people to?" His blue eyes encouraged me to continue.

I started to play the game for reasons I wasn't completely aware of. "What's confusing me is Carter's name."

"Why?"

"I can think of other presidents that seem to be more in line with Hitler and Caesar," I qualified.

"That's what I thought at first as well. Now think."

"Eisenhower, Kennedy, Johnson, Nixon, and Ford were presidents during Vietnam," I said.

He quickly added, "But Kennedy was assassinated. So he's eliminated."

"Roosevelt was in office during the Holocaust," I added.

"But that wasn't his doing." He leaned back on the stool to give me room to organize my thoughts.

"He declared war after the bombing of Pearl Harbor," I quickly added.

"He was forced due to the monsters all around him. He had no choice," Dad explained.

"What does Carter have to do with the other two?" I asked helplessly. "He was a peanut farmer before politics."

"That's all a veneer. Look here." He pulled out the portrait sketches he'd made on the onionskin paper. He held one up and asked, "Who's this?"

The image's masculine features were thick and dominant. The brows were heavy and prominent, causing the eyelids to appear at half-mast and shadowed the pupils. The jaw line was strong and sharp, culminating in a deep cleft in the chin. The hairline receded above a high forehead. I noticed an olive wreath encompassing his head.

"Is this Caesar?" I guessed.

"That's correct." He shuffled some papers around and pulled out another portrait and laid it beside the Caesar sketch. "Who's this?"

At first I was thrown by the similarity of the figure's head shape to that of Caesar. The mouths were identical, with thin tight lips that seemed to curl up at both ends. Instead of the olive wreath that Caesar wore, it had a shaded area under the nose that resembled a little mustache. This gave this sketch away immediately, "Hitler."

"Correct again." He looked around the table in frenzy. "Now, where'd I put the other one? I just had it a minute ago."

I noticed a pile of papers on the stool next to me. "Is it in this pile?"

"Don't touch them," he demanded. "They're in a certain order, and I don't want them messed up."

I pulled my hands away as if they'd been burned. He reached across my chest and grabbed the pile. He leafed through the papers and, with a sigh of relief, said, "Here it is." He put the final sketch out for display next to the other two.

I looked at this one with more curiosity. Again the shape of the head was similar to the other two, as if this were a template he'd used for his sketches. The shallow cheekbones indicated a thinner face, but the chin and the eyes were identical. There were no added features like the olive branch or the little mustache, just a clean shaven face—except that this image was smiling with a huge grin, filled with large teeth and pulling the skin taut around the mouth's edges. There was only one name left, yet I wasn't convinced that it resembled the current president.

"Is this Carter?"

He smiled with a pride that I hadn't seen in a long time, which released a flood of warmth within me. He nodded his head, "Exactly."

He arranged the portraits next to each other with Caesar on the left, Hitler in the middle, and Carter on the right. He floated his hands over the pictures as if he were magically placing a spell on them.

"What's similar about all three?" he asked.

My stomach tightened as I realized I wasn't interested in playing this game any further. But I felt trapped since I had allowed it to go this far. My only option was to continue to pretend that I was interested. I took my time and examined the three sketches, mulling over them to find the similarities and differences.

"I'm not quite sure," I said.

"That's what I thought." He quickly gathered the pictures into a pile and picked them up. He placed the Caesar sketch on the countertop. "Take a good look."

Then he placed the Hitler portrait on top of the Caesar sketch. The thin onionskin allowed the image from below to bleed through the image on top. The head shapes fit perfectly on top of each other. The eye sockets, the arch of the brow, the length and width of the nose, the shape of the mouth, and the curve of the chin were in synchronicity. The only contrasts were the shading and the shadowing of the interior face structures like the cheekbones, the temples, the jawline, the hair, and Hitler's little moustache.

"Interesting, huh?"

He placed the Carter sketch on top of the Hitler portrait, and again the head shapes aligned. The shadows and shading of all three sketches merged into an image of a skull composed of deep eye sockets, two oval holes for the nose, sharp cheekbones, strong jawbone, and rows of teeth. I was entranced by the mechanics it took to devise the exactness of each portrait to be able to have an end result of the skull.

"That's neat. How'd you do that?" I asked.

"I just drew the faces and then laid them on top of each other, and this was the result. It was meant for me to find this." He grabbed his coffee cup and turned to the sink. "I was amazed myself," he said while rinsing out the cup and filling it with fresh water. He walked to the cabinet and opened it. "I'm sure you could imagine my surprise when I placed all three sketches on top of each other."

He took down a jar of Maxwell House instant coffee and scooped out two teaspoons of dark granules. The air filled with the aroma of the coffee. He used the spoon to stir the concoction, placed the cup inside the microwave, and turned the dial. He turned to me and smiled.

"What do you think that all means?"

"I'm not sure. What do you think?" I instantly regretted asking.

"Are you sure you want to hear it?" he asked with a tone of caution.

"Of course, I want to hear it."

The microwave beeped. He removed the steaming coffee cup out of the metal box and placed it on the counter before his papers, scooped six spoons of sugar, sat himself on the stool, and prepared for this dissertation.

He started out slow and monotone, "It all has to do with the Rapture and the Antichrist."

He tasted his coffee, eyeing me over the lip of the cup. He placed the cup on the counter and shuffled through some more papers.

"Choose you this day whom ye shall serve, Joshua 24:15." He twisted a sheet of paper in front of me. "It is your choice." He leaned back into his stool and crossed his arms. I felt his challenge.

Remain cool.

He slowly began, "For the Lord himself shall descend from heaven with a shout, with the voice of the archangel, and with the triumph of God, and the dead in Christ shall rise first." His eyes burned with anticipation. "Then we which are alive and remain shall be caught up together with them in the clouds, to meet the Lord in the air." His voice paused and quivered. "And so shall we be with the Lord. Wherefore comfort one another with these words, Thessalonians 4:16–18."

What the shit?

I didn't know how to respond. I knew never to disagree with him on anything dealing with religion. I started trembling.

"God says that signs will provide the evidence needed to prepare for the Rapture, and these signs are showing themselves again." He pulled the picture of Caesar clear from the bottom of the pile of sketches. "Caesar was thought to be a tyrant to many, causing suffering. He called himself god. It took his best friend to end his life, which resulted in a major civil war."

He pulled out Hitler's portrait and tapped his fingertips on it. "Hitler thought he was god and the savior of Germany. He persecuted and murdered hundreds of thousands of Jews, political rejects, and fags. He thought he was ridding the world of degenerates to make the world a better place. He was a powerful speaker and was able to get anyone to follow him and do his bidding. What he failed to realize was that there's no perfect race and that taking on the role of god was going to end disastrously. He ended his life in a bunker along with his wife. The result of his egotism was a major world war."

He took a deep breath. His face turned red. "Now this monster…" He lifted up the picture of Carter. "This snake in the grass has everyone fooled. Everyone thinks he's a naive peanut farmer. He's the most poisonous kind of snake—even more vicious than any viper along the Nile. Look at his beady little eyes. How can anyone trust him? He sits in the oval office and thinks his shit don't stink. But what's he doing?" He slammed the paper back on the countertop, stood, and leaned over the sink, looking out at the backyard.

Silence filled the room.

He turned, and his eyes were dark black. "I asked you, what's he doing?"

I flinched and automatically brought my hands up to protect my face. "I don't know."

"Think, damn it!" He slammed his hands on the countertop, causing me jump. "Tell me what Carter's doing."

"I-I don't know," I stuttered.

"Think! It's not nuclear science!" he shouted.

"I really don't know." I felt my eyes flood.

"You need to know. Your future world depends on you knowing what he's doing." He leaned in close, forced my hands away from my face, and grasped my chin with a vise grip between his forefinger and thumb. He forced my head from side to side. "There's no need to cry about it. That's your problem, you're too sensitive. You're just like your mother." He shoved my head back.

I almost fell off the stool.

He stood with his hands on his hips, glaring at me.

I repositioned myself and hid my fear.

"You and your type aren't strong enough to fight against what he's planning to do. You'll see. Just like the Jews in the concentration camps and Sodom and Gomorrah, you'll see firsthand."

He reached for his cigarette, causing me to flinch again. He took a deep drag and exhaled the smoke through his nose like a dragon.

"I'll tell you what he's doing in the big office. He's preparing for the end of world. It says in the scriptures that the meek shall inherit the earth, but what people don't realize is that the meek will cause this world its demise. Carter is the epitome of the meek that will end the world as we know it. He's not even aware he is." He snubbed the cigarette into the ashtray. He grabbed his coffee cup and started pacing. "He sits there, doing nothing to prevent the threats of war. He sits there, forcing the little man to work to support the rich, when he was once a little man. He's allowing the commie Russians to build nuclear weapons and attack surrounding countries." His anger crawled up his neck, forcing his veins to thicken and pulse. "Carter's the Antichrist. Mark my words, his actions are going to cause the country we know as Russia to no longer exist. It'll fall apart like Caesar and Hitler. It'll no longer be called Russia. This'll set off a nuclear war, and we'll all be obliterated." He smashed his coffee cup into the sink.

I covered my head as coffee and shards of ceramic rained down on me, the countertop, his papers, and the floor.

He stomped out of the room and yelled over his shoulder, "Clean this mess up."

World Games Registration—Norway, July 1979

Someone grabbed my elbow and ushered me forward.

"Let's go, we don't have all day, newbie," Sheryl voice squeaked. She positioned me in front of the registration table. "This is David Matthew, USA."

The person at the table never glanced up as she scanned down a list of athlete names. "Last name?" she asked as if she never heard Sheryl.

"Matthew," replied Sheryl.

"FINA card and passport." The woman held out her hand to receive the requested articles, without looking.

As I dug into my pocket, I noticed the blond Italian leaning against the wall beyond the table, looking at me. He smirked and slightly nodded his head.

I found myself grinning back.

"David?" I heard a voice pull me back to the registration table. "Your IDs?" Sheryl was impatient.

"Sorry." I pulled the AAU and FINA cards and passport out of my pocket and handed them to her.

"Don't give them to me. I don't want them. Hand them to the registration personnel." Sheryl pointed toward woman at the table, who was still holding her hand out.

I quickly slipped the cards and passport into the waiting hand. She glanced at them and handed the AAU card back. "I only need the FINA card and passport."

I glanced over to Sheryl, who shrugged and shook her head.

"Sign here," the registration woman pointed to a line.

I grabbed a pen and signed my name.

"Welcome to the Games. You are officially registered," she said with a thick Norwegian accent. "Here are your FINA card, passport, and your welcome bag. Please go to have your picture taken for your badge." She finally looked.

"Thank you," I replied.

Sheryl grabbed my elbow and twirled me around, causing me to smack right into the blond Italian.

"Excuse us," Sheryl demanded. She pulled me, and I left the Italian behind without saying hello.

Sheryl guided me through the maze of athletes, coaches, and chaperones. She forced me on to a stool.

"Smile," said a voice behind a camera.

I had just enough time to lift my head and force a smile before the camera flashed a blinding white light.

Dr. Althea Warner's Office—Dayton, Ohio, July 2015

Althea scanned my writings and nodded, "Good, very good. I feel you are beginning to trust the process." She placed the papers on the floor next to her feet. "Did you lose power?" she asked as she rubbed her eyes.

"Excuse me?"

"You know, from that storm last night."

"Yes, we did for about twenty minutes," I replied.

"It must have been bad here, because when I came in this morning, everything was off." She picked up the clipboard and tapped the end of the pen against it. "You have not mentioned anything about your partner."

"What do you mean?" I asked.

Althea shrugged. "You do have a partner, don't you?"

"Yes." I wasn't sure what she was trying to say.

"You haven't told me anything about him, and you haven't written about him in your morning pages. I was just curious, why?"

"Oh," I let out a breath. "I have been focusing on that certain time period of my life, and he wasn't a part of it."

"What is his name?"

"Jake," I replied.

"How did you meet Jake?"

I shook my head.

"You don't have to tell me," she said.

"No, no. It's just…" I stopped and decided to give the edited version. "We met when I was dancing at a bar. He was playing pool.

Hardly anyone was in the place due to the snow, and I walked up to him and joked, 'If you lose this game, you'll win me.'"

"And did he? Lose the game?"

"We've been together for fifteen years," I said proudly.

Althea smiled and clapped her hands. "That's incredible. And is he supportive about all this?"

"Extremely. He encouraged it. Jake is the grounded one, nothing seems to bother him."

"Is he older?"

"No." I smiled.

"So he is younger. How much younger?" she asked.

"Oh, jeez. I stole the cradle, so to speak. He is fourteen years younger."

"That would make him…"

"Okay, that's enough."

"I see. Have you shared much about your past with him?"

"Not really. I'm not sure what to share."

Althea nodded and wrote on the clipboard.

"What does he look like?"

"Jake Gyllenhaal."

"Nice. Tell me about you two."

"We have a ranch-style house and two Boston Terriers, named Bella and Barkley."

"I love dogs, they are God's gift to us. They keep us sane and loved. And by the smile on your face, you know what I'm saying."

"Bella and Barkley are my best friends," I admitted.

"And how is the sex life?" she asked nonchalantly.

"Excuse me?"

"Fifteen years is a long time."

"I'm really uncomfortable with this."

"Why?" Althea asked.

I squirmed in the couch and glanced at the church tower clock. "It's something I don't feel comfortable talking about."

"But it's part of relationships," she qualified.

I felt myself shut down, defensive, and my mind went blank.

"Are there problems?"

"No, not really," I rubbed my forehead, "I don't know."

"Can you explain it?"

"Recently, I feel that I'm not attractive enough. I hide myself and not really been pursuing it." I felt my face heat up.

"Is Jake all right with it?"

"He seems so. He's the type that doesn't pressure sex. He seems to just go along."

"Is he asexual?" she asked.

"I don't think so. It's me. I have issues when it comes to intimacy."

5 CHAPTER

Sandefjord Natatorium, Tønsberg, Norway, July 1979

The Sandefjord natatorium made me feel small. The seating areas wrapped around the Olympic-size swimming pool and were decorated with every nation's flag. The ten-meter was the focal point of the diving well, and the massive cement structure towered high above the water with a huge white banner stating, "1979 FINA World Springboard and Platform Diving Championships, Tønsberg, Norway," in red letters. Divers were practicing on the three-meter springboards and the various platform levels in a manner of controlled chaos while the coaches shouted instructions and corrections in different languages.

"Let's go, divers, we only have a forty-five-minute practice slot," shouted Jack. "It starts in ten minutes."

Patti, Megan, and the other girls threw their bags into a pile on the deck and started stretching out.

I can't believe I'm actually here, I thought. It was like a circus, where acrobats were performing difficult tricks from different levels. The familiar smell of chlorine filled my nostrils, and my heart pounded in my chest.

While I watched the other countries' divers practicing, I realized how much I loved the sport. I loved the feeling of flying through the air, twisting, turning, and spinning. I loved the feeling that I had a sense of control over something in my life, that if I practiced hard enough and was determined enough, I could be good enough at something and get to go places. I realized that training never felt like hard work; it was a way to clear my head. I loved the feeling of winning at a sport that took more finesse than a jock throwing, catching, and tackling a football. I felt at home here.

"What are you waiting for, blondie?" asked Mark. He playfully punched my shoulder. "Will you partner me for stretching?"

"Sure."

Mark removed his sweats and sat in front of me. A charge of electricity sprang through my being when we placed our feet together, grabbed hands, and spread our legs. We both automatically leaned toward the other with our faces only inches apart. I saw his eyelashes accentuating his blue eyes and his lips looking ever so inviting. For a moment, I thought he was going to kiss me right then and there as he nudged closer to me. I lost my breath, closed my eyes, and prepared for the experience.

"Are you all right?" Mark asked.

I opened my eyes to see him grinning. "Yes, I guess."

Mark chuckled and said, "You're cute."

I thought I was literally going to die. Mark Bradley said I was cute.

"Are we going to stretch or stare at each other's eyes?" he asked.

I have no problem staring at his eyes, but I said, "Stretch. We need to stretch, I guess."

Mark pulled me toward him while he leaned back. As I lengthened my lower spine and hip flexors, I was presented with a view of his crotch, only inches away and hidden by a thin layer of spandex. We held this position, and then I leaned back and pulled him forward toward me and a view of my crotch hidden behind my sweatpants. I noticed his long neck, wide shoulders, and how his back tapered into a V-shape and snuck under his Speedo, which housed his round and firm gluts. I was amazed at how flexible he was, as his chest rested on the floor. I felt the effects of the excitement of being this close to him. As he sat up, he noticed the effects and grinned.

"Is everyone here?" asked Jack.

"Andy hasn't checked in," Sheryl said. She rechecked her clipboard.

"What do you mean?" Jack's voice was urgent.

"He didn't check in with me," explained Sheryl.

"Great. This is just great." Jack stomped toward the locker room.

The locker room's door swung open, and Andy rushed out with a towel tied around his neck like a cape. He darted past Jack and ran around the Olympic-size pool as if he were flying. He screamed at the top of his lungs, "I am Captain America. I am Captain America. I represent the U S of A, the red, white, and blue of freedom."

He stopped and struck a Captain America pose for a brief moment before repeating his performance of flying and shouting around the length of the pool with Jack fumbling after him. Andy managed to get to where we were, tore off his cape, and started stretching.

We all tried not to laugh and pretended to concentrate on our stretches.

Megan said in a hushed whisper, "Stop it, guys. Remember the shit we had to go through the last time Jack got so angry?"

Andy asked, "Meggie, did you say 'shit'? I'm so shocked. You've got such a potty mouth. What's the world coming to?"

"Just stop it!" Mark demanded.

Jack marched toward us, out of breath, looking like a mad ostrich. Sweat beaded on Jack's forehead and stained his underarms. He tried to catch his breath. "Andy, I…I…what the…" he stuttered as his neck flamed red. "I'll talk with you later…Dr. Don wants you to only focus on the required dives for this practice. That's what the preliminaries will consist of. You'll practice your optional dives later."

"Thank you, Jack," said Megan.

Andy pretended to cough as he said, "Shit."

Everyone tried hard not to laugh.

"Who said that?" demanded Jack.

No one responded, but we all either buried our faces or looked down at the tiled deck to keep from losing control.

"That'll be enough of that." Jack shook his finger at us.

A whistle blew, and the divers in the pool started to clear.

"This isn't over, but we've to get on the boards and practice. Let's get to it," Jack said. He clapped his hands and limped toward the diving well.

We all busted up laughing as we made our way to the pool. Mark wrapped his arm around my shoulders and led me. I was a part of the team.

Trip to Ohio State University, Columbus, Ohio, April 1978

When I heard the car pull up the graveled driveway, I grabbed my jacket and duffel bag, stuffed with towels, swimsuit, and sweats. I had the front door open and ran to the car before it came to a complete stop. I was anticipating Trevor's arrival. He had asked Mom yesterday during practice if he could take me to Ohio State University to practice platform with the college team. He informed her that it would be an overnight adventure. Mom eagerly consented.

I climbed into the passenger side of the red Mustang convertible. The top was down, and the leather seat was warm from the afternoon's sun.

Trevor guided my duffel back to the space behind the two seats. "What's all this? You moving in?"

I laughed as I situated myself in the copilot's seat and strapped myself in.

"Are you ready?" he said. He clasped his large mitt of a hand on my leg above my kneecap and squeezed it firmly. His smile caused his eyes to appear like slits as they conveyed the onset of our adventure.

"Let's blow this popcorn stand," I said.

He took his hand away from my leg and reached behind my seat. He majestically presented two long-necked bottles of Miller beer. He handed one to me and placed the other between his thighs. "We need something for this road trip," he said. He cocked his head, smiled, and reached for the gear shift.

The car jerked. "Sorry, it sometimes sticks. I haven't gotten it looked at yet." He lifted his right arm over my head, rested it on the back of my seat, and twisted to look behind the car and guided it back down the driveway.

I took one last look at the front porch, hoping that my two days away would be easy and void of any drama. As my red horse–drawn carriage began to back away from my prison, I saw my mother dart out the door. I hoped that Trevor was unaware of the oncoming flight of what appeared to be the Wicked Witch of the West.

"David!" she shrieked over the engine's humming.

She hustled down the lawn along the driveway, flailing her arms over her head, as her teased hairdo bounced in all directions. I prayed that Trevor remained focused on our escape, but to no avail; he was distracted by the echoing of the high-pitched calling and halted the vehicle.

As I watched her approach, I automatically slipped the beer between the door and my calf, shivering as the coldness kissed my leg. Trevor, with the style of an expert, simply placed his arm over the beer bottle as if it were an armrest.

Mother finally reached the car. Exasperated, she grabbed hold of the driver's door. As soon as she caught her breath and patted down strands of flyaway hair, she transposed herself into a coquettish girl for Trevor's benefit.

"Trevor, will David need some money?"

"No, I don't think so. Everything's taken care of. We'll be staying with some friends of mine, eat pizza, and he'll be home by tomorrow afternoon," said Trevor.

"No rush," she giggled. She pointed a finger toward me. "Do everything Trevor tells you to do. I don't want to hear that you chickened out of anything. This is a great opportunity."

She paused as she lifted a trembling hand to her lips; her eyes welled; and her cheeks reddened. Her performance was enhanced with the quivering of her lower lip as she looked toward Trevor.

"I don't know how to thank you. This means so much to David, and I'm so grateful for you. Thank you." She managed to push a tear over her right lower eyelid and directed it to dramatically roll down her cheek as she clutched her hands to her breasts.

I pressed the cold bottle harder against my leg. "We know this, Mom. You tell him this every time you talk to him."

"I appreciate it, Mrs. Matthew," Trevor said gallantly.

"Lydia, please."

"Okay, Lydia." He flashed me a smile.

"You be good, Davy." She kept her eyes on Trevor.

"Bye, Mom."

She reached over Trevor, resting her chest on his shoulder, to hand me something that was wadded up in her clenched fist.

"Just in case."

I accepted the crumpled-up bills, and she stepped back from the car.

Trevor repositioned himself with his arm resting on the back of my seat, released the break, pulled out of the driveway, and shifted into drive.

Mother waved, "Have fun. Be safe. Thank you so much, Trevor. You're an angel."

I saw Dad looking out of the kitchen window with a cigarette in his mouth.

Trevor guided the Mustang onto the main road and said, "Your mother's loony." He flashed that incredible grin and pulled up the beer bottle. "To our road trip." He waited until I pulled up my bottle and clinked the brown necks together. "Let's open these suckers."

* * *

The wind whipped through my hair, stinging my face. The car's speakers pumped out Donna Summer's version of "On the Radio" as Trevor and I finished our second bottle.

"There should be another round of beer," Trevor announced. He pointed toward the space behind the seats.

I unfastened my seatbelt, pivoted, propped myself on my knees, and reached over the back. The last two bottles were jammed down against the frame and the floorboard. I had to lean farther to retrieve the prized possessions.

"Woo, tiger, be careful!" Trevor grabbed my waistband. "We're going seventy-five miles on the freeway.

"Got 'em," I triumphantly proclaimed. I flopped back onto the leather seat and held a bottle in each hand over my head. "Yahoooo!"

"Don't lose them," he ordered. He passed an eighteen-wheeler, cutting lanes with the agility of a cat.

I secured one bottle between my thighs and twisted the top off the other. "For you, Kemosabe," I handed him the sweating brown bottle.

"Thanks, Tonto," he replied.

I smiled.

The freedom I was feeling was beyond anything I had ever experienced. It was as if I'd left all cares behind with the exhaust fumes from the tailpipe. The humming of the engine, the wailing of Donna Summers, and the buzzing from the previous two beers had propelled me into a state that was like flying. I felt that nothing could bring me down. I twisted the top off the bottle between my thighs and released the cap into the oncoming gust of air, sending it sailing behind us. I quickly gulped a mouthful of sudsy liquid as I watched the farm lands whiz by.

"Cow!" I hollered with all my might.

"What?"

I dropped my chin and repeated, "Cow."

"That's what I thought you said, but why?" he asked.

"It's a game we play." I repositioned myself in the seat so that I could focus on Trevor.

The wind manipulated his dark-brown curls, causing them to dance upon his head. His Foster Grants were reflecting the lanes that were ahead of us. His smile was ever so contagious.

"Whenever we go on a trip, we look for things along the side of the road," I explained. "It really could be anything, but the first one to see it has the right to call it. The more bizarre the sighting, the more points you get for originality."

"You keep score?" he asked.

"Not really, it's just fun to call things out when nobody else is expecting it." I looked out the window. "Buzzard!"

"Where?" He looked in the review mirror.

Donna Summers ceded to Gloria Gaynor's "I Will Survive." As the intro started pounding, I let out a screech that any teenage girl would have been proud of.

"I love this song." I cranked up the volume and started gyrating to the beat. "Don't you just love her?"

I didn't wait for his response as I broke out in my best voice, using the bottle as my microphone.

"First I was afraid, I was petrified. Kept thinking I could never live without you by my side. But I spent so many nights, thinking how you did me wrong. I grew strong. I learned how to carry on..."

"Pig!" Trevor shouted.

"What?"

"Pig...I won." He pointed behind with his thumb.

I shook my head, more interested in continuing my performance, "I should have changed my stupid lock, I should have made you leave your key, if I had known for just one second you'd be back to bother me."

Trevor chimed in, and we started rocking out as loud as we could. We didn't care if we were out of tune or what the truck drivers thought of us as we passed them. We were having a great time, and I was free from ties at home.

We sang, "Oh, no, not I. I will survive, as long as I know how to love, I know I will stay alive."

* * *

"David, this is Deb Willis," Trevor made introductions.

"It's a pleasure to meet you," the thin woman quickly shook my hand, while shouting across the pool, "Mark, make sure that you reach through the takeoff, and don't rush it. Jennifer, that's better on the entry."

Trevor pulled me aside, "Deb won the bronze medal at the '76 Olympics in Montreal. She's amazing. Why don't you go ahead and get ready."

The atmosphere was a circus. Divers—in a calculating and precise precision—were jumping, spinning, and plunging from all the different levels of springboards and platforms. The platforms looked like hands extending from the back wall, supporting two to four athletes on each level. The divers alternated takeoffs from the three-, five-, seven-and-a-half-, and ten-meter levels by quickly taking position and shouting out their level. A spotter on the pool deck confirmed the announced location by parroting it back. The only areas that did not seem to need constant identification were the three-meter springboards positioned as bookends to the massive cemented platform structure. The pounding sound from the springboard's recoil against the metal stands echoed continuously throughout the cavernous building.

I watched in awe as a diver perched high on the edge of the ten-meter platform. The young woman looked elfish as she positioned herself for takeoff, toes wrapping the edge of the cement flooring and arms extending over her head.

"Ten-meter!" she shouted.

"Okay, ten," the spotter replied.

The diver demonstrated the perfect arm swing and takeoff. She lifted into the dense air, elegantly touched her toes, reached back, and stretched for the water. She knifed the surface and disappeared with little splash.

"Leslie, that was on the money," Deb called when the diver came to the surface. "Could you come here for a moment?" she motioned her over. "Mike, let's make this one count," her attention went to the diver on the three-meter springboard.

He approached the end of the metal board, hurdled, and propelled himself into three-and-a-half somersaults in the tuck position. He snapped out of the rotation to dive into the water.

That is awesome, I thought to myself.

When the diver's head broke the surface of the water, Deb was quick with her correction. "Mike, you're still ducking your head and dropping your shoulders when you reach the end of the board. That's cutting off the height of the dive. Do it again."

He acknowledged the critique with a simple nod and swam back to the pool's edge to climb out.

"Seven and a half," shouted a deep voice.

"Okay, seven and a half."

The diver appeared from way back on the platform as he skipped, hopped, and whipped himself off from the end and started immediately to spin and twist. After completing the revolutions, he flung open his arms, piked at the waist, and reached for the water. He misjudged the entry and overrotated, sending a tsunami of a splash in my direction.

"Tim," hollered Deb, "what's the rush? That's the takeoff you needed, more control on the finish, and that'll be fine. Remember, you have another two-and-a-half meters when you take that to ten. The way you're going, you'll be flat on your back."

"Five."

"Okay, five."

Leslie pulled herself from the pool and walked dripping wet to Deb's side.

"Leslie, this is David," Deb made the introduction without looking at either of us as the hollow splash sounded of someone hitting the water. "Jennifer, that's nice, take that up, you're ready." She leaned in to Leslie, "David is going to practice with us today, can you show him where to put his stuff and take him to the tower?"

"Sure," Leslie nodded at me. "Come this way."

I felt a case of nerves sprout in my stomach as I obediently followed her.

"Three."

"Go ahead, three."

"Put your things here. All you have to do is go through that door over there." She indicated the open arch at the base of the wall where a huge crimson letter *O* with a buckeye and green leaves wreathed around the lower-right curve. "That's where the stairs are to the platforms. I'll see you when you get up there." Leslie hurried back to practice.

"Thanks," was all that I could muster before she was gone.

I quickly undressed, grabbed my chamois, and followed her instructions. Once I entered the archway under the huge *O*, I felt a strangeness that I hadn't felt in a long time. I wasn't sure if it was nerves, anticipation, or the result of the three bottles of beer Trevor and I each consumed on the way here. Whatever the reason, it was creating a knot in my intestines. I hadn't had a real tower practice in three months. I took a deep breath and mounted the steps. I hesitated at the five-meter level, but the daredevil inside talked me out of playing safe. Since I was among such elite divers, I would have to appear elite as well. I climbed on and went to the top.

When I reached the ten-meter platform, I was greeted by a group of girls in the corner talking. One of them I recognized as Leslie.

"Girls, this is Dave." Leslie quickly looked at me. "It's Dave, right?" she clarified. She dried her shins with a pink chamois.

"Dave…David," I stammered.

Leslie introduced the girls, "This is Jennifer, Wendy, Mary, and Nancy."

"Hi," I said, giving a quick, little wave.

"Like he's really going to remember all our names," said Mary.

"He's so cute," said Nancy. "How old are you?"

"Ah, fifteen," I blushed.

"Fifteen!" the girls repeated condescendingly.

"I'll be sixteen in January," I quickly added.

"So you're a sophomore," Nancy asked.

"Yes," I replied.

"In high school?" she asked again.

I nodded.

"I'm Wendy." Another girl reached for my hand. I automatically shook it. "Look at his green eyes," she commented as she peered closer. "Is that your real eye color? I mean, you're not wearing colored contacts or anything?"

I looked around uncomfortably before stating, "These...I mean, this is my color, I mean, I wear contacts, but they're not colored. They're clear."

"He's blushing, that's so cute," Jennifer piped in.

Wendy added, "Look how long his eyelashes are. They're longer than any girl's I've ever seen." All the girls leaned in and inspected closer. "Do you know how much I'd save on mascara if I had those lashes? I'd never buy another tube. You've prettier eyelashes than any girl! Have you ever put mascara on to see how long they would be?"

"No," I shook my head. I was at a loss for words and could only stare at my palms.

"Girls, leave him alone." It was Mark Bradley!

I would've recognized him anywhere since I have a poster of him next to Bruce Jenner on my bedroom wall. He'd won the World Games last year in Berlin, East Germany. He appeared hurried, as if he had some other place to be.

"Are you hens ready? We're up."

"Go ahead," instructed Leslie.

"Okay." He slapped me on the shoulder, "Don't let them bother you. They'd rather gossip than practice." He quickly took to the edge of the platform. He lifted his arms and yelled, "Ten."

"Go ahead, ten," the spotter's voice bounced off the ceiling.

Mark bent over, cupping his fingertips on the lip of the platform. He pushed off his toes and straddled his legs up into a perfect handstand. He held the position as his diaphragm pulsed in and out. He lowered his legs slightly to get the snap he needed and whipped himself off the platform. There was a slight delay before I heard the water break from his entry.

"That was really Mark Bradley?" I asked dumbfounded.

"The one and only," answered Leslie.

"What's he wearing?" one of the girls questioned, followed by a sarcastic giggle.

I turned to find the gaggle of girls looking at my swimsuit.

"That's a Mike Peppe suit, isn't it?" Leslie tried to lessen the obvious bashing.

I glanced down at my dark-green swimsuit. The drawstring was untied and dangled over the waistband. I felt exposed, naked, as if they could see everything that I had been trying to hide.

"I didn't know that they still made those," Wendy proclaimed.

"What's that material?" Mary asked.

"Burlap?" Nancy snickered.

"No, it's more like canvas," Wendy validated as she reached over and felt the material. "It hides everything. It compresses everything."

"What's he hiding?" Nancy giggled.

"I wonder if it gets heavy when it's wet." Wendy said. "Imagine trying to swim with that on. Does it weigh you down?"

I just shrugged.

Leslie interjected, "Come on, girls, and leave him alone. Dave, why don't you go ahead?" She shot Wendy and the others a stern look.

"We're just curious," defended Wendy.

I walked to the edge of the platform, and I sat on the lip. I held up my arms and lifted my legs into a pike position.

"Wait," I felt a hand on my shoulder. I dropped my legs to dangle over the platform's edge, looked back, and found Leslie preventing my takeoff.

"Three," a faint voice wafted up from below.

"Go, three," affirmed the spotter.

I waited to hear the echo of the splash.

"Carrie, I like that lead-up, take it up," Deb's voice carried across the water.

"Ten," announced Leslie.

"You're up, ten," the spotter shouted.

"Now go," Leslie let go of my shoulder.

I pulled my legs back up into a pike position, rolled off, wrapped my arms around my legs, stretched for the water, and cut through the surface. I torpedoed toward the bottom and raced back to the surface. I glanced over to Trevor and Deb, who looked at each other. Trevor indicated for Deb to give her criticism.

Deb smiled, "That's pretty nice, David. Make sure you flatten your back and pull in your core so you don't scoop."

I had started to swim to the pool's side when I heard Trevor call, "David, come here."

I nodded. I got out and scampered to the area where I left my duffel bag. I rummaged through it and pulled out two towels. I wrapped one around my waist and the other around my shoulders. I then made my way to Trevor and Deb.

"Seven and a half."

"Go, seven and a half."

As I approached Trevor, he was pulling something out of his briefcase.

"Listen, I'm not trying to sound weird or anything, but Deb agrees with me. That suit you have on isn't doing you any good."

Deb piped in with an aggression that at first seemed offensive. "It's ugly. It's an old man's suit, and the square cut is making your legs look stubby. I hate it." Her attention went back to the pool. "Mike, let's go on. I want to see reverses and inwards today."

"I don't have any other suits," I whispered to Trevor.

"Here, go put this on." He handed me a balled-up crimson Speedo that looked like a Band-Aid. I start to object but, he ordered, "Just do it."

* * *

The locker room was empty, without any evidence of life, except for the trickling echoes from the showerheads and the denseness of mold and musk that filled air.

95

I found a corner and unwadded the Speedo. It was similar to the one that Mark was wearing, crimson with a gray stenciled *O* in the right corner of the front panel. The Lycra material seemed flimsy and unsupportive.

How could I wear this? It'd reveal everything that I had been trying to hide, trying to ignore, trying to pretend wasn't part of me. By wearing this, I'd be advertising and putting all my junk on display.

I stood there in that spot for what seemed to be an eternity, not moving. Then it dawned on me that this was Trevor's Speedo, that he actually wore this when he was diving. I pulled my canvas old-man suit off and stepped into the Speedo. The material hugged my body in a way that sent a pleasure through me. I was not sure if it was the softness of the material, the way the suit was cut, allowing my legs more movement, or the way the pouch was roomier—whatever the reason, the result was a momentary embarrassment as I stretched the material's front panel to its limits.

Once I was able to get myself under control, I went to the full-length mirror just outside of the showers. The reflection wasn't what I anticipated. The crimson suit didn't just change the image in the glass. It brought out a confidence that I had never recognized. The way the material draped my midsection was aesthetically pleasing to the eye, pronouncing my solid build and accentuating my Adonis belt.

As I stood there, frozen in this space and time, I knew something was immediately different. I tried to label the change, but I was at a loss and decided that it wasn't important at that moment. All that I knew was that I wanted to dive.

* * *

I entered the pool area. I walked with an air, chest out and head high. As I approached the diving well, the divers all ceased and looked at me. Then they started clapping, hooting, and whistling. My cheeks burned with heat as I approached Trevor and Deb.

Deb looked me up and down and smiled, "Now we're talking. Get up there, and show me what you can do."

Trevor gave me his thumbs-up sign. He playfully slapped my buttock as I walked away.

I climbed the stairs to the ten-meter and came upon the gaggle of girls. This time they just looked and smiled.

Wendy broke the silence, "Hope you can dive as good as you look!"

"Wendy, he's only fifteen," Leslie piped in.

"God forgive me," Wendy confessed.

"Take a cold shower, you overheated bitches," Mark flatly stated. "Who's up?"

"I'm going," said Leslie. She walked the cement plank.

Mark stood near me, drying off with his chamois. "Nice suit."

"Thanks," was all I could say.

"Ten," shouted Leslie.

"Go, ten," the voice echoed from below.

As I was standing there, I noticed that the human body was beautiful and perfect in its simplicity and artistry. I glanced over to the huddle of girls and was overcome with the lines and curves of the female physique. It was like I was seeing females for the first time, how their bodies curved slightly in certain areas, especially from the chest to the waist and then to the hips. I became aware of the swollenness of their beasts and how their swimsuits displayed the round areolas and semihard nipples behind the Lycra material. I was entranced by the smoothness of their legs as the thighs converged to the slightly bent knees, continued down and expanding to present calves, and then tapered to the thin ankles. I couldn't help but look.

Curiosity peeked her head out for my attention again as I glanced over at Mark standing next to me. He was leaning his back against the railing, presenting an uninhibited display of masculinity. His lines appeared harder and curves seemed more streamlined, connecting every part of the body to the next. It could have been attributed to the lesser material covering the body, but his chest was firmly developed with round pectorals; rib cage enclosed a hard sheet of rippled abs; and a path of fuzz drew my attention south from his tight naval to his narrow hips. This region was masked by the wet crimson Lycra material that accentuated the curved head of his penis and the heaviness of his pouch. His thighs extended out from the hips and were clustered with curly hair that laced the length of his legs.

"Who's up?" Mark chided. "Hey, new boy, you go ahead."

"Sure," I replied. I walked to the edge of the platform and turned around. I measured my approach by skipping and hopping down the cement. I spun around to face the takeoff area. I raised my hand and shouted, "Ten."

"Go, ten," the voice filled my ears.

I took a deep breath and released it. I elevated on my toes, tilting my weight forward, took two skips and hopped to the platform's lip, projected my body into the air, threw my arms forward, grabbed my legs behind the calves, squeezed, rotating three-and-a-half somersaults before plunging into the water with a precision I knew I was capable of—a perfect entry.

"That was some practice," Deb proclaimed as she rubbed her tired eyes. "You did good, kiddo," she added as she drained the rest of her chardonnay from her glass. "Maybe one day you can win an Olympic medal of your own. But make sure it's gold, bronze did nothing for my career."

I felt pride as I held her Olympic bronze medal in my hands. It was heavy and engraved with, "1976 Olympic Games, Montreal, Canada," on the back.

"Thank you," I childishly tried to accept the compliment.

I examined the medal one more time before handing it back to its rightful owner. I couldn't help but imagine myself wearing a medal like this around my neck as the "Star Spangled Banner" played in my honor.

"That's so cool, thanks for letting me hold it."

"And he's polite," she chuckled. She put the medal back on a shelf above the television. Then she looked over to Trevor, "Why's he hanging out with you?"

Trevor just shrugged as he gulped another mouthful of beer.

"Don't let any of your habits rub off on him." She leveraged her hands on the back of the overstuffed chair and extended her spine. "Ya'll can stay up all night for all I care, but this beauty must get her sleep." She started to the door leading to the hallway, stopped, and turned, "Really nice job today, David. Trevor, when are you planning on heading out tomorrow?"

"When we wake." Trevor released a loud belch.

I tried to stifle my laugh; for some reason, I have always found bodily noises humorous.

"Nice, real nice," Deb rolled her eyes and pretended to bang her head on the door's frame. "Just like college—will you ever change?"

"I hope not, because that's why you love me," he boasted. He blew her an air kiss.

Deb pretended to catch the kiss. "Right! You're drunk."

"Not completely, not yet," he corrected her.

"Yes, you are, and stay out of my room. I don't want some drunken fool waking me up. I need my sleep. I've a really early morning tomorrow." Deb started down the hallway again and called over her shoulder, "There's more beer in the fridge, but I'm not contributing to the delinquency of a minor."

Trevor held up his finger to his lips to be quiet, and then we heard the bedroom door shut.

Trevor glanced over to me. "Hurry, get two more brewskies."

"I think I'm done."

"No, no, no, no." He shuffled closer toward me as we sat on the couch. His words began to slur together, "No, I brought you here to loosen you up. You act as if you have a goddamn stick shoved up your ass all the time. You need to learn to let go. Go with the flow." He accentuated his point by waving his hands in the air as if to bat away gnats. He studied me with glassy eyes, then cocked his head, put his arm on the back of the couch behind me, and scooted closer until our thighs were touching.

"You did great today, you really did. I'm proud of you," he stammered. He pointed his free hand against his heart. "You did me proud." He paused a moment as if he'd forgotten what he was about to say. "Oh, yeah, you think too much." His index finger tapped my forehead. "You got to get out of your head and stop analyzing everything all the time."

"You really think I did well today?" I asked.

"Cross my heart." He demonstrated by making a huge X" on his chest and then on mine.

I felt a sense of pride. I did well today; even Mark told me that he was impressed and that I could have a bright future if I kept practicing.

Maybe Trevor is right, maybe I do think too much, I worry too much, I'm afraid too much.

"We had a breakthrough today, so we need to celebrate. Go get us some beer."

"I'll get you one, I've had three and that's enough."

"No, no, no! I can't drink alone. I can't celebrate alone. Bring one for both of us…It'll be the last one. I promise."

"Okay."

I tried to stand, but my legs were wobbly. I wasn't aware of what the effects of the sudsy liquid would have on me. Earlier it was liberating and brought a sense of power or confidence. Now it was causing me to feel odd, unstable, and unsure. I staggered to the makeshift kitchen. It took forever to reach the refrigerator; it seemed that with every step I made, it appeared to slip further away. Somehow, maybe by sheer determination, I reached the handle and swung open the door. The beers were on the bottom ledge, and I almost toppled over as I bent to retrieve them. I pulled myself together and retraced the path I took. I found Trevor facedown on the couch. I set the beers on the coffee table and hoisted him up, resting him against the back of the couch.

"What, what?" He slobbered.

I reached over and wiped the sputum from his chin. He grabbed my wrist and pulled me next to him. He stared deep into my eyes. I could smell the mixture of beer and chewing tobacco. He didn't say a word but just looked at me. His free hand touched the side of my face, roamed over my ear, and wrapped around the nape of my neck. He pulled me closer, as if he was inspecting me for some flaw. I tried to pull away, but he restrained me. His hand on my neck traveled upward and clinched a fistful of hair. He forced my head down against his chest. I stabilized myself by bracing my hand against his shoulder. He relinquished my trapped wrist and forced my head to his stomach, which caused me to fall to my knees. I felt his breath as his diaphragm rose and fell. He managed to unbutton and unzip his pants. A cloud of musk filled my nostrils. He started to guild my face to the dark, thick, and curly bush that escaped from the confines of his pants. I pushed away, and he grabbed the collar of my shirt, keeping me at eye level.

"What? What's wrong?" he questioned me.

I was scared and confused. I didn't know what to do. I was trapped.

"No one'll ever know. It'll be our secret," he encouraged with a crooked smile and guided my eyes down. His member was awake and begging to be freed from behind the unzipped material. I looked back at his eyes. "It's all okay. Trust me." He guided my head down again, but I resisted, sitting back on my heels.

My head was spinning, and I felt like I was going to puke.

"It's no big deal, it doesn't mean anything."

He pushed my head down to his crotch, and I allowed it for a second. A fleeting moment of desire overtook the morality of the situation.

I heard Dad's voice: "You shall not lie with a male as with a female, it is an abomination." I knew that once I took this path, there was no turning back. Was I ready for this?

"No!" I shot up and pleaded with my eyes.

"It's okay, baby. I want you to. I'd love for you to. I'll tell you what to do. It's okay, just go for it." He pulled out his erection, and he wiggled it. "I want you to do this for me."

"I don't know…" I tried to pull farther away.

He grabbed my head. "You'll do this. You'll do it 'cause I asked nicely. Remember what your mom said…" He forcefully guided my head down. "Just open your pretty mouth and wrap your pretty lips around it, like a lollipop or a cream sickle. That's it, yeah, that's right. That feels so good, babe. You are a natural. Oh, I love it…Yes…you are a cocksucker.

My head throbbed as I stumbled toward the Mustang brightly bleeding red from the harsh midmorning sun, causing me to squint. I halted my steps, hesitating as I tried to figure out how to successfully get to the car.

I fumbled with the silver handle, trying to open the door, before I simply gave up and hoisted my duffel bag back into the space behind the seats. The flood of nausea was overpowering and demanding my full attention. I rested, propping myself up along the side of the car, hoping that my head would stop spinning.

How am I going to make it home riding for an hour and a half? Thank God that it's a warm day and the car's top is down. If I get sick, I'll just do it over the side.

"You ready, Tonto?" Trevor came bounding out of the apartment building looking fresh, rested, and donning a bright smile.

Immediately, my hands tried to cover both my ears and eyes at the same time. "Not so loud," I mustered up a measly response.

"Oh, no," I heard him laugh, "are we suffering a bit?"

"I don't believe *we* are," I said with much disdain.

"Here, drink this." He handed me a thermos, slapped me on the butt, and raced to the driver's side. "What's that saying, 'Bite the dog that bit you,' or whatever it is. Just drink it."

I unscrewed the plastic lid that acted also as a cup and placed it on the car's trunk. I twisted off the corkscrew protector and was greeted by a strong smell of tomato and pepper.

"What is it?"

"An old family recipe. I don't want to tell you until you drink it. Believe me, this'll make you feel better in no time."

"I don't know. My stomach and head…" I couldn't finish.

"Have I ever led you astray?" He flashed that perfect devilish smile.

I thought of a couple of questionable topics that could fall into the category of him leading me astray, but I didn't have the courage to voice them at that time. Maybe I would later. I glanced into the concoction inhabiting the inside of the thermos. Small, dark specks were floating amid a sea of thick red juice and a ribbon of yellowish mucus spiraling like the Loch Ness, and disappearing in the thick substance as I moved the canister.

"What's in this stuff?"

"Just drink," he said. He pulled open the driver's door and positioned himself behind the steering wheel. "And hurry up so we can get on the road. I'm starving."

"You can eat?"

"Let's go. Drink up." He placed his arm on the passenger seat and slapped his opened palm against the leather.

Without any further delay, I closed my eyes and lifted the odorous mixture to my lips, tilted it back, and drank. I felt particles of substances that I couldn't identify slide over my tongue and down my throat. I thought I was going to gag. I pulled the thermos quickly away, turned my head in case I was going to puke, and quickly guided my hand to my mouth to prevent it.

Whatever you do, don't puke. Not in front of Trevor.

I forced the upsurge back down with sheer willpower. I stood with my eyes watering and turned to face him.

"Mmmm, good," I said with a smile.

"I knew you'd like it." He patted the leather again, "Get in."

I handed over the thermos to him, along with the corkscrew lip and plastic cup.

"You could've used the cup."

"I didn't want to see what was mixed up inside. I saw something yellowish…"

"The raw egg."

I felt my stomach retch.

"Not in the car."

I quickly spun around and fell to my hands and knees, dry heaving without any success. I felt like a cat trying to rid itself of a massive hair ball. The only thing that emerged was a strand of saliva drool.

"Better now?" I heard the glee in his voice.

"I'm fine." I pulled myself to my feet.

"If you think the color green's fine, then great. Your face is green."

"No, no, I'm fine." I pulled open the passenger door and flopped heavily into the seat. I had to wait a moment for my head to stop spinning before I could pull my legs in. Once I was recovered, I slammed the door.

"Not so hard," he said.

"Sorry," I replied.

We sat there without Trevor starting the engine. His hands were positioned on the steering wheel, and he stared at his knuckles. He had this dumb look on his face, as if he were trying to conjure up the words he needed to say. Stubble accentuated his lips, and his thick lashes shadowed his eyes. The image of him on the couch filled my mind again and brought on shame and confusion.

"Hey," he started with a quirky smile, "I'm proud of you."

This confused me even more.

"I'm proud of you. You did everything I asked. Deb thinks you could really go places with your diving."

There was a moment of relief, and yet more confusion. I wasn't sure how to respond.

"This may seem strange, but I got you something." He reached behind his seat and pulled out a blue glossy bag. "I hope you like it." He handed it to me.

"Thanks." I wasn't sure why he was giving me something. I opened the bag and looked in. I reached in and pulled out a black Speedo swimsuit.

"Look on the front," he smiled.

I unfolded the Lycra material, and on the right front-side panel was a scarlet *A*.

"For Aulden, your school."

"Oh!" I was speechless.

"I didn't know how to tell you that the other suit wasn't any good. And when you were wearing mine, I could see that you felt better. You dove completely different."

"I love it. When'd you get it?" I asked.

"I've had it for about a week." He started the convertible's engine.

"What'd you have done if I refused to try your suit on or if I dove poorly?"

"First of all, I knew you wouldn't dive poorly, even if you had your 'old-man suit' on. I knew you'd rise to the occasion, especially when you saw that you were diving alongside Mark Bradley. As for the Speedo, I was hoping you'd see the light. When you came out of the locker room, I was amazed by how well you looked. I knew you were a changed man. And if you didn't put it on, I'd have had another suit for myself."

"Thanks." I wasn't sure to feel good or not. I couldn't help wondering if this was a gift for being his little "cocksucker" or for diving well or both. And somewhere in my mind, I didn't care what the reason was; either way, I've a new suit.

"What's for lunch?" he asked as he put the car in reverse.

Dr. Althea Warner's Office—Dayton, Ohio, July 2015

The tinkering of Althea preparing tea and humming something classical made me realize how small the office space was. Today, for some reason, I felt like the room had shrunk and the walls were closing in.

"Do you know what I'm humming?" Althea's voice carried from the anteroom.

"No, I'm sorry," I called back.

"It's *Un bel dì vedremo* from Puccini's *Madam Butterfly*. Do you ever go see *Live from the Met*?

"No, what is it?" I asked.

"It's this arrangement with the Metropolitan Opera, and they stream the performances live into movie theaters across the country. The idea is genius, because it is presenting opera to larger and newer crowds."

Althea came through the doorway, carrying her tea, humming the aria, and conducting an imaginary orchestra with her free hand.

She paused in the middle of the room and performed the final notes as her hand lifted high above her head. Her face glowed as if she were accepting the crowd's appreciation.

"Oh, I always wanted to be an opera singer, but I was a violinist instead." She placed her teacup on the table. "*Madam Butterfly's* Cio-Cio-san was played beautifully by Kristine Opolais, and the tenor…" Althea placed her hand over her heart, "the tenor was played by Roberto Alagna." Althea slowly sank into the chair. "You know the story?" Althea didn't wait for my response before excitedly and quickly sharing her version. "It is about this fifteen-year-old girl who is going to marry an American Naval officer, but the officer is only marrying her out of conveyance until he finds a proper American woman. Cio-Cio-san is so excited that she secretly converts to Christianity, but her uncle finds out and comes to the house to denounce her and throws everyone out. Then the two, Cio-Cio-san and the Naval officer meet up, sing a beautiful duet, and spend the night together."

"It sounds like *Miss Saigon*," I said.

"Exactly. It was unbelievable. There's an encore performance in two weeks. You must see it," Althea said.

"I'll put it on my to-do list," I responded.

"You won't regret it." Althea picked up her clipboard and nestled into the chair. "You were talking earlier about your frustrations in the classroom."

I felt the gears shift in my head to try and catch up with change of topics. "I was talking about *The Scarlet Letter* and how difficult it is to get the students to read it. They want the story told to them or to watch the film, but they're reluctant to read the book."

"I see," said Althea. She shook her pen toward me. "I have another teacher that says that there is so little motivation on the students' part. She felt that *No Child Left Behind* has been detrimental and, in fact, is leaving many children behind."

"I think the ideology on paper looked like a solution, but unless you are in this classroom, it is difficult to imagine what would work and what is a theory," I said.

"This teacher said she is frustrated because the school is more interested in the scores on the tests, so the teachers have to stop their lesson plans to teach to the tests," Althea added.

I nodded my head and wondered how any of this was important in figuring out my depression and anxiety issues.

"Well, teachers are being evaluated by the scores their students receive on high-stake tests. And if the class doesn't reach certain expectations, the teacher is rated accordingly and could lose their position."

"How are you motivating students with *The Scarlet Letter*?" she asked.

My minded shifted again to try and keep up. "I'm not sure I am. I had the students complete a journal of how they interpreted each chapter. They had to create a summary and illustration to transfer Hester Prynne to a relevant situation happening today. And the final project was to create a short film depicting their modern version and present it to the class.

"We had a film festival, and after every student had a viewing, we cast ballots for our Academy Awards. One student depicted Hester Prynne as a pit bull, and how she was discriminated and misunderstood, based on generalizations by the other pure-bred dogs in this isolated community. The dog, Daisy, ended up winning best actress."

"That sounds so creative," said Althea.

"They had a great time. But it wasn't in alignment with teaching to the test," I said. All of a sudden, I felt uncomfortable.

"I'm sure the students are going to remember *The Scarlet Letter* for the rest of their lives, and by connecting to a situation that is relevant to them helped with the comprehension. What's wrong?"

I glanced up.

"David? Are you all right?"

"Yes, I think so."

"What happened?" Althea asked with a compassionate voice.

I took a deep breath. "It just dawned on me that I'm teaching students who are the same age as I was when I won the World Games and everything that went with it. I realize that every day, I'm faced with triggers being subconsciously tripped."

Silence filled the air.

"Just the other week, a young man came into my room and asked to talk. He shared with me that he was gay. I had suspected, but I have the worst 'gaydar' in the world. He sat across from my desk and started speaking, in a rush of emotion. He said that he had a boyfriend who was older, much older, in his thirties. The student shared that they have been sexually active and that his mother and grandmother were supportive of this. When I asked why, he responded with, 'He helps pay the bills and groceries.' I didn't know what to say or how to react. I explained that I was going to have to report it. He was fine with that, almost relieved. When I shared it with the assistant principal, I was informed that they were aware of the situation and that nothing could be done since the parents and guardians were aware. The boy has a history of this."

"You did what you were supposed to do," said Althea.

"But I feel like I let him down. It was like he was asking me for help. He sat there with his eyes welling up and shaking, sharing with me. I did nothing."

"No, you did the right thing. You reported it to your superiors. Now, if they do nothing about it, it is no longer your responsibility," Althea informed.

"But I know that feeling of being alone, abandoned, or having no one to turn to."

"Do you draw anymore?" Althea asked.

The question seemed too random, and I threw my arms up.

"No. I haven't drawn since college."

Althea stood and walked to the bookshelf to pull out a copy of *The Artist's Way.* She flipped through the book while instructing, "I want you to go on an artist date this week." She flipped through the pages. "Here it is. An artist date on page 18. You need to set aside a block of time. You do this alone. Go to a museum, the theater, or walk through the woods. You could go to an art supply store and walk around and look at the paints, brushes, canvases—whatever, anything, something so you can nurture the artist child in you," explained Althea.

"When will I have time for that?" I said, only half joking.

"Make the time." She placed the book back on the shelf. "Continue the morning pages, and take yourself on an artist date. Go and watch *Live from the Met.*" She sat down at her desk and pulled out the calendar. "Same time next week?" she asked.

I felt as if I was being dismissed. I grabbed my satchel and headed to the exit, which was a separate door from the one I entered.

"Turn the lock to the left."

"What?"

"The lock, turn it to the left to unlock the door." Althea never looked up from filling out her client report.

I did as instructed, freed the door, and exited.

6 CHAPTER

Youth Hostel, Tønsberg, Norway, July 1979

I couldn't sleep. It could've been the fact that I was excited about the next day's preliminaries. It could've been that the sky was still light at 10:00 p.m. It could've been that I was rooming with the defending world champion and Olympian, Mark Bradley.

I heard him softly purring in the bed across the room. One arm was lazily lounging across his forehead, protecting his eyes from the brightness. His lips barely met before a puff of air separated them. His chest was visibly rising and lowering in a gentle rhythm.

I sat there, wondering if the other divers were asleep and if any of them snored or softly purred like Mark. I watched the dust particles dancing along the stream of light from the window before coming to rest on the cotton sheet that reached to just below his chest.

He shifted his hips and freed a leg from under the sheet, exposing a naked thigh, knee, calf, ankle, and a foot stretching and then relaxing on the mattress.

My eyes danced, hands shook, and my heart raced. I felt beads of sweat on my forehead and neck. I was unable to control myself. Something took over my being, and I crept closer to the sleeping champion. I froze as the wooden floor squeaked under my foot.

What will I say if he wakes?

He didn't stir.

I approached more cautiously, slower, testing my weight with every step.

If I can just make it to the chair next to his bed.

I was filled with relief as I reached the back of the chair, lowered myself to the seat, and pulled my legs up against my chest. My body heat was confined beneath the sweatshirt, sweatpants, and socks that I had on despite the warm night air.

I watched him sleep. I watched the hypnotic movement of his breathing.

He shifted ever so slightly, disengaged his right arm from under the sheet, and subconsciously rubbed his fingertips across his chest and pushed the hem of the sheet down, exposing a dark path of hair running down his flat stomach.

I forced a hand over my own mouth to keep from making any noise.

He flopped his hand to the edge of the mattress and exposed his palm to the ceiling. There was vulnerability in the position he had taken, and yet I couldn't take my eyes away. His diaphragm expanded and collapsed, emphasizing his stomach, which was divided into sixths under his rib cage. Devil's horns guided my eyes, like a well-planned painting, from the top of his hips and ducked under the sheet, pointing to what was hidden. I wanted to remember every detail so I could draw him.

I want to see.

Without thinking and without reason, I reached for the sheet.

A noise outside caused me to pull my hand back. I remained still. I watched. I waited.

I forced myself to look away.

What are you doing? Nothing! I just want to see.

I tried to pull myself away, but I didn't move. Something had regained control of my mind. I looked back at the sleeping champion. Calmness came over me. I reached and slightly tugged the sheet down a little, testing the state of Mark's sleep. He didn't move. The sheet slipped over his hip bones and revealed the beginning line of dark, curly hair—like a tree line of a forest.

My heart pounded, sending loud pulses to bang in my ears. My eyes widened, wondering what to expect.

I waited to see if he was still sleeping soundly. I listened to his purring for a while.

He didn't move.

I reached and carefully tugged the sheet. The fabric scaled down, exposing his nakedness.

I stared at the perfect construction of his form, from the protecting arm covering his face, the roundness of his shoulders, the firmness of his chest, and the flatness of his stomach.

A sadness filled me as I watched Mark sleep, unaware of my intrusion. I felt my throat tighten up. It was becoming hard to breathe, and I felt like I was going to suffocate. I felt my eyes bulge as my shoulders started to shake. The room was going dark.

Aulden, Ohio, Motel 6, January 1979

"Someone's here," called Caine from the living room.

A black car's headlights fought through the falling rain as it pulled into the driveway.

I sat at the dining room table, watching the beams, as the car came to a stop. My head ached, and my palms sweated. I looked over to where Dad was sitting at the kitchen counter with a cigarette pinched between his fingers, its embers dangerously close to his skin.

A coffee cup, a box of Pall Malls, and an overflowing ashtray were positioned before him.

"It's not the red Corvette or the blue Mustang or the gray Lincoln Town Car. It's definitely a black Cadillac. Nice ride," reported Caine.

I looked out and watched the wipers momentarily clearing the windshield so that a shadow of a man could be seen, before the image was distorted by the rain pellets.

I glanced back at Dad.

He slowly lifted his hand and inhaled deeply on the cigarette stub. He held the inhale and crushed what was left into the pile of already-discarded cancer sticks. Slowly and methodically, he released a thin and even stream of gray smoke, which dispersed into the room. He drained the remains of the coffee and set the cup down on the counter without a sound. Picking up the box of cigarettes, he lifted the lid, jerked the box, and removed a new stick with his lips.

Say something. I wanted to scream at him. *Don't just sit there and pretend this isn't happening.*

He calmly lit the cigarette, inhaled, released a plume of smoke, rested his chin in his palm, and stared ahead into nothingness.

"David," called Mom from the front hall. "He's here."

I wasn't going to move.

The front door opened and Mam called out, "He'll be out in a minute."

I saw the driver wave, climb back into the seat, and close the car door.

Dad just sat there.

"David, let's go," her voice barked.

I got up and walked toward the front hallway. I stopped and looked at Dad with pleading eyes.

Don't make me do this. Tell her I don't have to go.

He stared straight ahead.

I walked past him.

Mom was at the end of the hall, dressed in her best blue dress, white heels, and her hair sprayed up like a football helmet. She stood there with her plastic smile while holding up my jacket. I was amazed that she didn't have to work, always home when one of the cars came to pick me up, and always dressed nice as if she was meeting with them.

"Come on, it's not nice to keep people waiting, especially when they've come all this way to pick you up."

My pace slowed as I passed the living room, where Magdalyn and Caine were watching *Star Trek*. I would have given anything to sit in there and watch it with them, even though I hated science fiction.

"Stop dawdling." She pulled my attention back to her. She shook the jacket as if that would hurry me.

I felt the heat of the radiator as I passed it. I ran my fingers on the pipes, hoping that they would burn. I felt nothing. I was numb. I stopped and looked back down the hall. I saw Dad still sitting there, still staring straight ahead.

Help! I yell as loud as I could in my mind.

"David!"

I turned to Mom and slowly shook my head. "I don't want to go," I mumbled.

"What?"

"I don't want to go."

"Speak up, I can't hear you," she emphasized her authority by raising her volume.

"I don't want to go," I restated.

"Why? What's this nonsense? The man's already here." Mom was beginning to lose patience with me.

"I'll tell him I can't go tonight, something's come up." I dropped my head and started to fiddle with my hands, clasping and unclasping them.

"There's no way that you're not going. Come on, put this coat on." Her tone dropped two octaves.

"No, I can't." I felt my armpits sweat.

"Why not? What's all this?" Her face started to turn red.

My mouth went dry, my tongue felt like it swelled up, and I felt clammy. "He tou—" I tried to speak, but the words got stuck in my throat.

"What? David, this isn't the time to play." She grabbed my wrist and attempted to guide my hand into the jacket's armhole.

I pulled it away and started clutching my hands into fists and nervously rubbing my knuckles.

"David, enough of this nonsense," she demanded.

I glared at her, and a strange calmness came over me. My voice growled, "He touches me."

Mom was stunned, her mouth flew open, and her eyes widened. She cocked her head as if she didn't quite hear me correctly. "What?"

I stepped closer to her so that Magdalyn, Caine, and Dad couldn't hear—although I wanted Dad to know. I wanted him to rescue me, to keep me from having to go.

"He touches me," I stressed each word so that I knew she could hear them.

"Where?" she seemed concerned.

I indicated downward with my eyes to where my hands were clasped. I looked back up at her.

"I don't understand." Her lips tightened in a thin line.

"He touches me down here." My lips quivered.

"Down where?"

I grabbed my crotch with such rage and shook it. "Down here!" I glanced over my shoulder to see if Dad got wind of our discussion. I shook it again, harder. "Right down here!"

Dad didn't move. He kept staring at nothing.

"No!" For a moment I thought she understood and finally, something could be done about this.

I have wanted to tell you for months, but I didn't know how.

I looked at her. "Yes." I felt like a scared little boy, my eyes welling with liquid.

Her brows crinkled, and her lips tensed. "No. No. No, you're mistaken." Her voice was soft and sweet.

"No, I'm not," I pleaded with much shock as tears raced down my face.

"Why'd he do that? He's an important person in the community. He wouldn't…" She took a deep breath, causing her chest to rise. "You shouldn't make up lies about people. It's not a very nice thing to do, especially with someone that has helped our family as much as he has." Her voice was even, and she pointed in the direction of the waiting car. "Harold Hall said that this man, this man that drove all the way out here to pick you up, that this man is a very respectable person and wants to help with your diving. If it wasn't for this man, Magdalyn would never have been able to get those treatments for her chin after the accident." She took a pause and stepped toward me. "You've got to do your share to help the family. We're all making sacrifices for you so you're able to travel to all the meets."

"I've never asked you to!" I said with a low, gravelly voice.

With a crack, the palm of her hand made contact with my cheek.

My eyes watered, and my flesh stung. I couldn't move.

"You're going." She guided the jacket to my shoulders. "This man has come all this way and is kind enough to take you out to a nice dinner at a nice restaurant. You'll go, and you'll be pleasant and polite. And don't let me hear of anything different." She forcefully shoved me out onto the porch and down the steps.

The rain felt soothing on my heated face. I walked in a trance to the awaiting car.

Mom stood on the front porch, arms crossed in front of her chest. "Have a good time," she said with such sweetness.

I felt the warmth of the car's headlights through my pants as I passed to get to the passenger side. The door latch popped, and I opened it. I glanced back up at Mom.

She waved. "Thank you." She gave a huge smile. "David, I can't wait to hear all about it when you come home."

I climbed onto the seat and shut the door. I looked through the windshield and saw Dad watching from dining room window.

"Are you ready?" the man asked. He placed a hand on my knee. I just nodded.

* * *

I sat on the edge of the bed, holding my underwear in my hands. A coughing fit echoed from the bathroom, reminding me that I wasn't alone in this Motel 6 room with its twin bed, dresser, broken television, and a closet-size bathroom. The door was open, and I could see him cleaning up, Dr. Malcolm Shultz.

I recalled him grinning. His fat cheeks were spotted as rosy-red corpuscles pushed against the paper-thin surface of his skin—all the result of his taste for Dewar's, Camels, and the hope that the sun would keep him looking young. His body was an overstuffed sausage with a hard, protruding belly and flabby man breasts. His hairless and varicose-veined legs seemed too skinny and too weak to support his torso. His cologne was an attempt to mask the overpowering body odor.

Staleness reeked from my mouth as the taste of his bitter tongue lingered behind. I could still hear his guttural grunts of pleasure and the repeated words, "Oh, yeah. You're so sweet. You're so pretty." I wanted to vomit, as burning liquid rushed up and ambushed the back of my throat.

I noticed a sticky matter at the base of my stomach. I grabbed the moth-eaten sheet and tried to wipe it off. I rubbed harder, unsure if the mess was his, mine, or a mixture. I wanted it off me.

"How you doing, baby?" Dr. Shultz asked as he came back into the room, holding a wet washcloth in his hands. "Let me." He gently pushed my hands aside and laid the warm cloth on my lap. He struggled to bend over, willing his joints to function, and started to wipe the area. "You're such a beautiful boy."

What do I say?

As he cleaned me, he ran his tongue along the length of my neck. He sat back on his heels, leaving his palms on my thighs, and looked at me. He looked at me for a long time.

"I want to remember this moment. How beautiful you look with the light coming in from the window behind you. How sweet you've been to me." He giggled like a girl and used the edge of the bed to aid in standing. "My joints don't work like they used to." He staggered to his jacket, resting on the back of a chair, and pulled something out. He slowly turned to me and stretched his arm out toward me.

I immediately closed my eyes, wondering if I would feel any pain.

"Here," he softly said.

I slowly opened my eyes, expecting to come face-to-face with a gun and hearing Dad's voice reminding me that I was going to hell. To my relief, Dr. Shultz was holding out an envelope.

I didn't reach for it.

He cocked his head and offered it to me again.

I remained still.

He grinned, "You're truly something. Hal said you were special, but I thought he was just trying to sell me. But he was right on all accounts. I want you to have this." He started to hand it to me again and then quickly pulled it away. "But you have to promise me something." He waited for me to respond.

A siren's wail filled the space as an ambulance sped past.

I finally broke my silence, "What?"

"This is for you. This isn't for your mother. Hal informed me that you give everything to your mother. Promise me that you'll not let her know that I gave this to you. I'll make sure everyone in your family has their examinations and whatever medical treatments that are needed. I promise I'll continue working with Magdalyn's chin, but I want to know that you'll keep this as a secret for yourself. Promise?"

"What is it?" I asked.

"You got to promise me first."

"All right, I promise," I said flatly.

"Good." He handed me the envelope.

I looked inside and found four fifty-dollar bills.

"Happy Sweet Sixteen, young man."

Youth Hostel, Tønsberg, Norway, July 1979

"David?"

I heard a voice far away, but I wasn't able to tell where it was coming from. All I could tell was that I was in a cave with colorful stalactites and stalagmites that were impeding me from walking to what I thought was the exit.

"David! Come on, man, open your eyes."

I stepped forward and grabbed hold of a stalactite, and it dissolved.

"David, can you hear me?"

I pushed against the wall of the cave. As beacon of light fell on my face, I knew it was the way out. I reached for the light.

"That's it, David. Wake up," the voice seemed to become clearer and more recognizable.

"What happened?" another voice filled the air.

I opened my eyes and saw Picasso-like images. The colors bled together in a blurry vision and then started quickly swirling, causing dizziness.

"I heard this thud, and I woke to find him lying on the floor. I tried to wake him, but he wouldn't open his eyes."

The swirling slowed down, and I started to see images. There were two faces looking down at me. I recognized Mark and reached for him.

He grabbed my shoulders and pulled me into a tight hug.

I started crying.

"It's all right," Mark whispered in my ear. "Everything's all right."

I felt someone cup the back of my head. "He has a bump here. We'll have to get it checked out."

"I'm so sorry," I said between tears. "I'm so sorry."

"You're fine now." Mark kissed my cheek. "You scared me."

"I didn't mean to." I squeezed him harder.

"I'm going to go let Dr. Don know about the situation."

"Thanks, Jack. I'm not sure what I would've done without your help."

I felt Mark reach and shake Jack's hand.

"No problem, Mark. See if you can get him to rest. There are only a few hours before we have to get up and get ready for the prelims," said Jack.

"I will."

I heard the door close and assumed that Jack went to talk to Dr. Don. Mark maneuvered and guided me down on his bed. He pulled the sheet up and cuddled next to me, cradling my head on his chest.

"Rest, David. I'm here, and I'm not letting go."

I felt safe and secure. I closed my eyes and matched his breathing.

Dr. Althea Warner;s Office—Dayton, Ohio, July 2015

The office room was dark.

"In the dream I'm behind a massive wall and there's this man standing on the other side. There I am, a wall, and there he is." I looked to Althea and waited.

She gestured with both hands and asked, "Why is there a wall?"

"I don't know. But I'm not able to get past the wall. No matter where I move, somehow, this wall maneuvers as well to keep me at a distance from the man."

"Tell me what you see," Althea leaned in and took notes.

"A hand. A child's hand. It's my hand. It's small and reaching around a wall to the man."

"What kind of wall?"

"I think it's brick. It has a rough texture, like brick," I said.

"Why can't you walk around the wall?"

"I don't know. I just know I can't, or I'm not allowed to. All I can do is reach."

"What are you reaching for?" she asked in a hushed tone.

"The man. He is standing on the other side of the wall."

"What does he look like? Describe him for me."

"He is blond and has a defined muscular body. He is not wearing a shirt, and he is reaching for the child."

"Can you see his face?" she asked.

I froze.

"What's wrong?

I slowly shook my head.

"You're safe here, nothing is going to happen," she ensured. "Who is it?"

"It's…it's…it's me."

The image disappeared. I looked around the room and focused back on Dr. Warner.

Althea began writing without saying a word. I watched and heard the pen scribbling against the paper.

"I'm sure Freud would've had a field day with this," I joked.

"Or Jung," she stated and kept notating.

"What do you think it means?"

She stopped writing and looked at me. "What does this dream mean to you?"

"I'm not sure, but it's like I'm splintered. There are two of me— one is a child, and the other is a mature man. It's like, if the two could just touch the other's fingertips, then they would be able to fuse together into a complete, whole person."

"This is not uncommon for a child to create split personalities in order to protect himself from situations that seem too hard to handle at the time. It could be some tragic or emotional issue that forces the child to splinter. What we will need to do is to explore and look back at specific times to see where you felt you needed to deflect the situations in order to survive," Althea said.

I looked at her and was in awe. This was one of the few times she appeared to be a doctor of psychology.

"Maybe there are some clues in your morning pages? Maybe these clues can indicate why you felt the need to protect yourself—if, indeed, you splintered your personality. Dissociative identity disorder seems more complex than what you appear to have. It is when the person develops two or more distinct personalities, or "alters,' which control the person's behavior at different times. But when these alters take over, the person does not usually remember some of the events that occurred while the other alter is in the driver's seat. However, I don't think that you have DID, or MID, because of how you function and relate. Yet I believe that there are degrees of splintering that, like all scientific findings, vary on a scale. A person may have a mild case of DID and may find that he can't remember everything that happened in his childhood or past, like moments of blank spots, in order to deal with the reality of the situation. Sometimes the person feels dizzy or even experiences blackouts when a situation triggers overwhelming unconscious fears."

She took a sip of tea and replaced the cup in the saucer.

"What is important is to understand or look at the 'myth' of yourself, which you developed as a child through the impressions placed on you. This myth is carried into adulthood and effects the decisions, behavior, and one's sense of self. The developed myth determines how one views the world, relationships, and self to his surroundings. Unless we, you and I, can find and become conscious of this distorted myth and correct this myth, change is going to be difficult."

My mind started racing, trying to unearth anything that could have contributed to this distorted myth of me, or my anxiety. Nothing stood out as unusual. My childhood was what I thought was normal—at least, to how I perceived it, since I had no other childhood to compare it to. Although I felt like I was coming up empty-handed, I felt that this session was delving into an area that could be life-changing.

Althea feverishly wrote on the clipboard. She paused and cocked her head.

"It may also be a form of PTSD."

"PTSD?" I asked.

"Post-traumatic stress disorder, PTSD. So tell me about your artist date?" Althea asked.

My mind shifted from finding my myth to PTSD and then to the banality of the homework she had assigned.

"Well, I wasn't going to do it. I'm overwhelmed with teaching and my PhD work," I responded. "Yet I decided that I was going to make time and go. So I went to the Dayton Art Institute. I just walked around until I came on Cristoforo Salari's sculpture entitled, *The Dead Christ*. I was mesmerized. It was beautiful, the white stone was carved in such details, and the beautiful face and body were perfection. I wanted to hold the figure in my arms. I wanted to be Mary and cradle this man. He looked so peaceful." I felt a tear and quickly wiped it away.

"How did you feel inside?" Althea asked.

"It's crazy, really. There was this urge to want to draw again, or paint. I wanted to create."

"Did you?"

"Well, when I left the museum, I found myself stopping off at an art store. I bought a sketch pad and some pencils. But when I got home, I lost the drive to draw. I tried, I did. But it seemed like a waste of time and effort. I couldn't do it," I said.

"Why do think that is?" Althea was leaning and resting her chin in her hands, intensely watching me.

I shook my head and threw my hands up, "I don't know."

"If you did know, what would be the reason?"

I covered my face and threw my head back against the couch. *Here we go,* I thought to myself. *Here comes the psychobabble bullshit.*

"Why do you think you couldn't draw?" she prodded.

I uncovered my eyes and looked directly at her. "If I knew the answers, why would I be here every week and paying you money that I don't have?"

Althea cocked her head, and her face flushed red. She sat back into the chair and dropped her hands into her lap.

"I'm sorry, I don't know where that came from," I said.

"It's all right. Maybe we touched on something that you are not ready to address."

I felt anger rise from deep inside my gut and start climbing, grabbing each rib to hoist itself up toward my throat.

"I'm just tired of trying to please everyone, and then there is no one to help me when I ask for it."

"You don't think I'm helping you?" Althea asked with pain behind her eyes.

"No, not exactly."

"I'm not your mother, and I don't intend to be," she announced.

I felt like she said this as if she had rehearsed it and probably said it to many clients. "I never asked you to be my mother. I wouldn't be here if you were."

"I'm glad that is clear and settled." She got up and walked to her desk. "I will not be available next week. If you are interested to continue, we can schedule a time now or you can call."

"Let's go ahead and schedule now."

My mind was reeling as to what just happened. I collected my check and presented it to her.

"Tuesday in two weeks," she coldly said.

I started to leave but stopped. "I'm not sure what just happened, but I never intended to project you as my mother."

"Good. I'm glad you said that, because I felt that I was being attacked."

"I'm confused. I thought we were talking about why I couldn't draw, and then you're telling me that you're not my mother," I said as I tried to find something to focus on.

"Until you can trust me to help you, we're just wasting my time and your money. I've another client waiting." She forced a smile.

I didn't know what to say. I just walked out.

7 CHAPTER

Sandefjord Natatorium, Tønsberg, Norway, 1979— Competition: Preliminaries

As I treaded through the puddles on the tiled flooring toward the springboards, The Sandefjord natatorium was in a hushed state. Giovanni Pizzini, the eighteen-year-old "golden angel" Italian that I bumped into at registration, prepared to perform his final required dive of the preliminaries. He stood perfectly still and focused as his muscular body glistened with droplets of water. A whistle sounded, and he took four steps to osculate the board and send him flying up into the rafters. At the apex, he touched his pointed toes, looked back, reached for the water, and entered with a small splash.

The capacity audience erupted with claps, whistles, and hollers—which echoed throughout the building.

Giovanni broke the surface of the water and waved to the crowd. He swam to the side of the pool and climbed out.

"Poing?" the Norwegian announcer asked for the scores.

The seven judges from all over the world, sitting in strategic positions on both sides of the diving well, keyed in their desired points into their remotes. The awards flashed up on the large scoreboard at the far end of the pool.

"8.0, 7.5, 8.5, 8.0, 8.0, 7.5, 7.0," read the announcer. The scoreboard calculated the total and flashed that Giovanni Pizzini, ITA, was currently in third place.

Giovanni grabbed his light-blue chamois and headed toward the hot shower at the base of the massive platform.

"Nice dive," I shyly mumbled as he passed by.

He smiled and placed his large hand on my shoulder. "Now your turn," he stated with a thick Italian accent.

All I could do was smile back. He withdrew his hand, leaving a warm spot on my shoulder.

"Hasse Havdevt of Norway," the announcer projected over the loudspeaker, causing the crowd to explode with a deafening roar. The square-built Norwegian scaled the ladder of the far three-meter and immediately adjusted the fulcrum while the announcer continued, "Hasse's final dive in the preliminaries will be a front one-and-a-half somersaults in the pike position."

I walked to the nearest three-meter, grabbed hold of the ladder, and I rested my right foot on the third rung. Extending my arms over my head, I stretched to the right and then to the left and then leaned forward to stretch my hamstring and then switched legs. I didn't want to watch Hasse's dive, so I closed my eyes and rolled my head on its axis, feeling confident since I had not missed any required dives in the first four rounds and had averaged 8s and 8.5s.

"David?" I heard someone whisper.

I opened my eyes and saw a man holding a large camera in front of his smiling face.

He lowered the lens, and his eyes gleamed. "I'm Mike Drake, the corresponding photographer for the Associate Press in London." He held up his Kodak camera. "Do you mind if I take a quick photo?"

I simply grinned and nodded back to him.

I heard the shutter click. "Thank you, mate. Keep up the good work." He disappeared amid the crowd of milling divers, coaches, and volunteers.

My mind returned to the task at hand. I closed my eyes and took a slow deep inhale. *Focus, David. All I need to do is get a good compression, wait for the board, extend through my toes, get my arms over my head, touch my toes, check my arms to the side, and stretch for the water.*

I heard the springboard clap against the metal frame and the echo resonating throughout the stadium. I waited until I heard the splash of Hasse entering into the water, and the natatorium rumbled with thunderous applause for the home country's leading diver.

I opened my eyes, scaled the ten-foot ladder, and stepped onto the springboard.

"Poing," the announcer waited for the judges. The scoreboard illuminated as the announcer read, "8.0, 7.0, 7.5, 7.5, 7.0, 8.0, 8.0."

As I adjusted the fulcrum, I glanced at the scoreboard. What I discovered unnerved me. In third place was Mark Bradley of the USA, second place was Hasse Havdevt of NOR, and leading was David Matthew of the USA.

Me! How can this be? I haven't done my final preliminary dive yet.

My heart started racing, and all the breath escaped my lungs as if someone pummeled me in my stomach. I was trembling as I adjusted the fulcrum forward, and my foot slipped, causing me to almost collapse onto the metal plank, but my arms were supported by the railings. There was an, "Oh," sound from the crowd. I slowly stood, forced myself to take another deep breath, and proceeded to successfully make the proper adjustment. I regained my composure, focused on the end of the board, and wiped my fingertips over my Speedos—feeling the stitched USA label on the right-front panel.

"The leader going into the final round of the preliminaries is David Matthew, USA."

All I heard was my own breath and the unmetered rhythm of my heart thumping in my ears. For the first time, I was nervous.

"David will perform an inward dive in the pike position."

I felt small, mounted on the springboard, as I glanced out toward the fifty-meter swimming pool. A huge red flag was mounted on the far wall with a blue cross outlined with white. I counted at least six television cameras and their crews focusing in on me from different locations around the pool's deck. Looking up, I saw a cameraman perched on the five-meter platform adjacent to the springboards. The crowd had countless handheld cameras perched and ready to record this moment. I even pretended that Mom, Dad, Caine, and Magdalyn were seated in the USA section, cheering and waving little American flags.

Silence.

I walked down the flimsy board, turned, and extended my arms out to the side to maintain balance with my toes on the end. Dad's voice added the rambling within my head:

"You'll never break through the politics of the games. You don't have the right last name. Judges are never fair, they only vote for the one that's expected to win. You'll be competing against guys that have already proven themselves. Don't expect anything."

Stop it! I shouted inside my head. *Just stop it.*

I slowly and systematically lifted my arms to the side, rising up on my toes. A slight moment passed before I swung my arms through, compressed my weight down, extended through my legs, and the recoil propelled me up and over the board. I touched my pointed toes, reached my arms to the side to check my position, pressed my legs to the ceiling, reached for the water, and streamlined to the bottom of the seventeen-foot depth. When I resurfaced, I was welcomed with a deafening noise that rumbled like thunder throughout the stadium.

"Poing," the announcer requested in his monotone voice.

Silence.

I pulled myself out of the pool and sat on the ledge, watching the scoreboard light up.

"9.0, 9.5, 9.5, 9.0, 9.0, 8.5, 9.5."

The thunder erupted once again.

I waited.

There it was for everyone to see. My name was at the top of the leaderboard by almost 100 points:

1. David Matthew, USA, 220.65
2. Hasse Havfvent, NOR, 121.80
3. Mark Bradley, USA, 121.25
4. Giovanni Pizzini, ITA, 118.05
12. Andy Kirkland, USA, 110.00

Is this real?

I wasn't able to feel my body. It was almost as if I'd been stolen away by some body-snatcher and had been robbed of all feelings.

Before I knew it, Mark pulled me into an embrace and kissed my forehead. I was quickly surrounded by the other competitors, hugging and slapping my shoulders and back.

I found myself alone in the locker room after the prelims, trying to comprehend what just happened. I watched the water wring out of my Speedo as I squeezed it between my hands. The droplets fell to the cement floor and raced toward the drain beneath the bench I was sitting on. My muscles tingled with exhaustion and excitement. I had to concentrate to lift my foot up to rest it on the edge of the bench to tie my shoe.

I wrapped the wet swimsuit in a towel and was about to stuff it into the duffel bag when I saw something in the bottom. Reaching down, I pulled out a stuffed frog.

Oh, Magdalyn, you're so sweet and funny.

We had this game where we hid this stuffed frog in the other's book bag, suitcase, under the pillows—anywhere we thought of—so that it could be found by the other later. She kept this frog by her side as she recuperated after getting out of the hospital.

Magdalyn's Accident—Aulden, Ohio, 1978

"Magdalyn, quick!"

She rushed to my side.

"Look, Maggie." I held back the white lace curtain in the dining room to reveal the outside world. "Just look at that. Isn't it beautiful?"

Magdalyn squeezed alongside me to get a better view, "Wow."

"Let's go outside."

We watched Caine packing the side of a snow mound that created a sled course, curving and running down the hill on the far side of the driveway. He paused a moment to wave at us. Dad made his way back to the house from helping Caine.

Magdalyn leaned in to the framed view, placing her tiny hand against the pane. Her breath clouded the glass.

"Magdalyn!" Dad called. He rushed in through the back door. "Ya wanna come out and play?"

She shrieked, "Yeah!"

"Where's your snowsuit?"

"I'll get it," I offered. I rushed to the hallway and returned with a bright-pink snowsuit.

Dad unzipped the suit and held it to the floor for her to step into. "Come on, my Maggie, we're going to go sled riding. We're going to have the Olympic Games today, and you're going to be the champion of the world, the prettiest gold medalist ever. So hurry up," he encouraged.

"Okay, yeah." She giggled and rushed into the snowsuit as if she were popping herself into an envelope. She sealed herself up with the zipper.

Caine threw open the door, and a gust of cold air pushed into the room. "It's almost done," he proudly announced.

"Now wait a minute, sweetie. We've got to get your hood on," Dad instructed. He placed a wool cap over her pigtails and pulled the red snowsuit's hood over the cap. He knelt down and tied the hood in place with a bow under her chin, leaving her rosy cheeks and big eyes exposed. He quickly slid her mittens on each of her hands.

I grabbed my jacket and sat on the floor, slid on my boots, and tied them.

"Close that door, do you want to let out all the heat?" Mom said as she rushed in from the bedroom, hugging her breasts for warmth.

"We're going, we're going!" Dad rushed Magdalyn out the door. Caine chased after and slammed the door closed.

I quickly followed, cramming a hat on my head and buttoning up my jacket.

"Don't stay out too long, lunch's going to be ready soon," Mom said.

"I'll tell them." I gently closed the door behind me.

By the time I reached the hill, Caine was putting the finishing touches of packed snow on the launching area. The course was designed with tubular curves here and there and a straightaway that led to the road.

Magdalyn had to take large, slow steps in the deep snow; occasionally, she fell to her knees. Dad helped her to her feet, lifting her out of the small drifts that entrapped her.

"I'm taking a test-run," Caine shouted.

He shoved off from the starting line and flopped himself belly-first onto the red plastic sled. He sailed through the tubes of snow, curving to the left and then to the right, and headed toward the next series of turns. He flung around the final set of curves and stream-lined through the straightaway with ease.

"Yahoo, that was incredible," he hollered up the hill. He started back with the red plastic sled in tow.

"It's now time for the champ to take to the slopes," Dad boasted. He lifted Magdalyn onto the icy track. As he put her down, she slipped onto her padded bottom. We all laughed as she blushed.

"Come on, Magdalyn, show 'em how it's done," I encouraged.

Caine held the sled in place at Maggie's feet. "What country are you representing?" he asked.

Magdalyn took a moment to think about it and then said, "The USA."

Dad picked her up and placed her carefully inside the sled. "Hold on to the yellow straps on each side."

Caine announced, using his best Howard Cosell voice, "Here we are, ladies and gentlemen, at the Olympic Games, where USA's own Magdalyn Matthew is about to take her trial run in pursuit of an Olympic dream. This will be the first chance for the world to get a glimpse of this remarkable talent."

Magdalyn adjusted herself in the sled, took hold of the yellow straps, and braced her legs against the sides.

"Ready, my Maggie?" asked Dad.

"Ready."

"All right, hold on tight. One...two..." Dad slid the sled back and forth for momentum, "three!" He released the sled with a huge shove.

The sled sailed through the first turn with ease, riding high on the lip of the embanked snow, slid back into the tunnel with a jolt, and whipped down toward the second curve that banked to the right. Magdalyn whirled through the curve, squealed with glee, picking up more speed as she headed to the second set of curves. She whipped through the two curves remaining low in the icy tunnel and flew through the straightaway to the finish line. We screamed with excitement as she came to a rest at the end of the race way, stood, and victoriously lifted her arms over her head.

Dad ran down to congratulate the champ and to bring Magdalyn and the sled back to the starting line.

Caine's Howard Cosell imitation continued, "Ladies and gentlemen, this just in, it's unofficial, but I think USA's Magdalyn may have broken the world record. Let's try and get a word with her coach."

Dad reached the top of the hill, holding Magdalyn and the sled.

"Coach," Caine held an imaginary microphone up to Dad, "how do you feel about Maggie's performance here today in this first trial run?"

Dad, without missing a beat, took on the role of the coach, "I think it went as we had planned, but I'm a bit concerned with the construction of the first turn. I think they need to build up the snowbank there. She almost flew over it the last time."

"So you think they should build up the first curve's embankment?"

"Yes, definitely," Dad said. He held up his hands, indicating that the interview was over, and walked away from the imaginary cameras.

Caine looked into the imaginary cameraman's lens. "And now let's get a word from our...wait a minute." He listened to his imaginary earpiece, "Yes...it's official, a new world record. Ladies and gentlemen, USA's Magdalyn has just set the precedent here on the Olympic Hill, even before the competition has officially begun." He bent down to her. "Congratulations, you've just broken the world record. How do you feel?"

"Good," Magdalyn proudly responded. "Let's do it again."

"What are you going to do if you win the gold medal today?"

"Go to Disneyland," she boasted. She hurried to the starting line.

"There you have it, ladies and gentlemen. Magdalyn is ready for her second run. This has been Howard Cosell, bringing you live updates from Olympic Hill," Caine announced.

I gathered more snow to build up the first curve's bank, poured a little water over it so it would adhere better, and pounded and rubbed the embankment with my bare hands to make the curve as smooth as possible.

"I want to go down like Caine, on my tummy," Magdalyn instructed.

Dad hesitated before he said, "I'm not sure, honey."

"Oh, come on, just this once," Magdalyn begged.

"All right." He held the sled steady.

Cain began commentating again, "Welcome back to Olympic Hill, ladies and gentlemen. We're about to witness USA's Magdalyn Matthew going for another world record. Two in one day is unheard of in these conditions, but this athlete has the confidence and the courage to attempt such a feat. Can she do it?"

Magdalyn positioned herself on her belly.

"One…two…three…" Dad released her.

My stomached tightened when I realized that her speed was faster than on the previous run. I wanted to scream as the sled sailed over the lip of the first embankment.

The sled skimmed over the snow and curved to the left along the first driveway. With a deafening thud, it came to an abrupt stop as it ran under the back of the parked station wagon.

I staggered through the snow to the sled and pulled it and Magdalyn from under the car. I discovered that her chin had impaled on the old, rusty muffler.

"Oh, God!" I screamed.

I lifted her limp body up into my arms as her chin started to spout blood, covering her face.

"Is she okay?" asked Caine as he ran up to me.

"I don't know." Her eyes were closed. Dad was frozen by the sled course. I pushed past Caine and ran toward the house. "Call 911. Call someone. We need help now."

Caine flung open the door, and Mom was standing there. When she saw the blood, she rushed to the phone. I untied Magdalyn's hood, unzipped the cocoon suit, and peeled back the material.

I held her in my arms, rocking her back and forth.

Sandefjord Natatorium— Tønsberg, Norway, 1979, Locker Room

"Excuse me."

I quickly pushed the stuffed frog back into my bag and turned to find two people behind me. I immediately recognized the Italian diver, Giovanni Pizzini, standing there with a towel wrapped around his hips, hiding behind an older gentleman dressed in a casual jacket, tie, button-down shirt, and a pair of khakis—his coach, chaperone, or interpreter.

"My name is Claude Marini, and this is Giovanni Pizzini," he said in a thick Italian accent.

"Yes, I know Giovanni," I responded.

I looked over Claude's shoulder and smiled at the blond Italian. He looked like a warrior with his Romanesque nose and bushy brown brows.

Claude nodded his head. "Giovanni wanted me to tell you how you dived good today…You understand? My English not too good."

I smiled and said, "You speak very well."

"Thank you…" Claude replied.

"*Gli chiedo se lui sarà a cena con moi?*" interrupted Giovanni.

"*Sì!*" Claude raised a hand to silence Giovanni. "There a dinner tonight for all the athletes and coaches, which I sure you be in attendance."

"Yes," I stated. Hugging my bent knee to my chest, I finished tying my shoestring.

Giovanni spoke as if I could understand, "*Lei sarebbe più tipo di avera la cena con la squadra Italiana stasera?*"

"Would you be most kind to have your dinner with the Italian team tonight?" Claude translated.

"I'd be honored." I nodded to Giovanni and smiled, "*Sì.*"

"*Bravo,*" Giovanni exclaimed and patted Claude on the back.

"*Grazie,* David," Claude said politely. "We see you this night. Please excuse me." Claude backed out of the room.

Giovanni sat on the bench next to me. The towel exposed his left thigh laced with golden fur. I had this urge to run my fingers through the forest, just to see what it felt like.

"*Si colomba ogni bene oggi...*" He paused. He realized that I wasn't able to understand him. He smirked and looked up at the ceiling with his hands rising next to his forehead. "I am sorry...You..." He pointed to my chest, and he began to pantomime his translation. "You dived, is that correct? Dived?"

I nodded.

"Dived good this day, *sì?*" he said.

"Thank you—oh, *grazie.*" I giggled at my attempt at Italian.

"Right, good," he said as he stretched out his arms and leaned in to embrace me, crushing my face into his neck. He pulled back, laughing. "*Sei buffo...*" he pointed his index finger to my chest, "You funny."

"David." I heard my name being called from the locker room's entrance. "Are you in here?"

"Yes," I called back.

"We're heading out, so hurry up."

Giovanni asked, "*Devote partire?*"

I looked quizzically at him.

"You go?" He indicated with his thumb, jabbing in the air toward the exit.

"*Si.*" I nodded my head.

"David?"

I looked up. Mark was leaning against the lockers. "Dr. Don said I had to come in and escort you out."

"I'm coming." I grabbed my duffel bag and hoisted it over my shoulders. Standing, I offered Giovanni my hand, which he took in his. "Thank you, and I'll see you."

Giovanni stood, pulled me into his chest, and quickly kissed both my cheeks.

I blushed red.

"*Arrivederci,*" he said with a bright smile.

I parroted, "*Arrivederci.*"

"All right, break it up," joked Mark.

For a moment I was in utter disbelief. Not more than six months ago, I had first met America's next hope to carry the nation's dominance in the sport of diving. My idol was now my teammate, and he was my escort. I glanced over to Giovanni, Italy's hope of glory at next year's Olympics in Moscow, wanting to become my friend. Not more than two hours ago, I was a "nobody"—just this greenhorn from Aulden, Ohio, who wanted to dive and travel the world. Now I was standing among the best divers in the world.

"*Ciao,*" Giovanni said. He moved from the aisle to allow me to pass.

The entire American team began clapping and cheering as Mark and I exited the locker room.

Patti grabbed me around my waist and nestled close to me. "You did so well."

"And so did you. Who'd imagine we both would be in the top 3?" I said.

"We've got to show these old-timers that the youth aren't just here to play," she joked.

Mark stopped and mocked her, "Keep dreaming, newbies."

We headed out into the afternoon sun.

8 CHAPTER

Athletes and Coaches Dinner—Tønsberg, Norway, 1979

Fashionably late, the American team demanded attention as we stood at the entrance to the banquet hall for the Athletes and Coaches Dinner. Silence replaced the laughing, chattering, silverware scraping against plates, and glasses clinking together. The athletes and coaches from other nations watched as we proceeded to our reserved table.

"David, over here."

Near the center of the room, occupied by over two hundred divers, coaches, and trainers, I saw Giovanni standing and waving for my attention. His golden curls looked like a halo around his beaming face.

"David, come on," the Italian called again as his teammate pulled him back down.

Patti laced her arm around mine and pulled me toward two empty seats at the American table.

"David!" a desperate plea rang over the hubbub.

Mark glanced over to the Italians and politely smiled as he pulled out my chair to sit.

Giovanni caught my eye and lifted his hands up toward the ceiling.

I shrugged my shoulders in defeat.

The Italian, German, and Russian delegates broke out with a roar of laughter as Giovanni disappeared in the sea of athletes eating dinner.

"Have a seat, David," a harsh, deep voice ordered. I glanced over my shoulder to find Dr. Don glaring at me.

I slid into my seat without hesitation.

Patti sat next to me and handed me a napkin, which I automatically placed in my lap. I watched as the other teammates adjusted themselves in their chairs along the long table.

Dr. Don glared at everybody until they were quiet. "We've had a wonderful start to this competition, and I want it to continue. From today's prelims, we qualified five of our six divers into the finals. In the ten-meter women's platform, Megan Gunnels qualified in first place and Patti Lakes, in third. Amy McGill did a good job, but we'll need to focus on consistency."

Amy bowed her head in defeat as we all glanced her way. Patti reached over and took her hand, kissing her knuckles.

Dr. Don looked over to Mark and flashed a huge smile. "Mark, you're exactly where you want to be. Your optional dives will only enhance your chances to defend your world title." He turned to Andy, who blushed with the acknowledgement, "Andy, you've got your work cut out for you. You gave me some new gray hairs with your yo-yoing performance. I literally thought at one moment that you didn't want to be in the finals. But your last two dives pulled you through. You're not out of it, but it's going to be tough to rally back from twelfth."

Andy nodded in agreement.

"Now that brings us to the biggest surprise of all." Dr. Don burned his gaze into my eyes. "I'm not sure what to say. I'm truly at a loss for words." He glanced up at the ceiling and shook his head in disbelief and looked at me. "The fact is this young man has done the impossible. Not only did you qualify for your first international finals in first place, you're almost a hundred points ahead of Hasse and Mark. What happened?" he gestured toward me.

Everyone looked over at me for an answer. Patti reached over and placed her hand on top of mine. "I don't know. It just felt right."

"Bet your ass it was right," bellowed Dr. Don.

The team roared with laughter, and Mark slapped me on the back.

"Excuse me," a voice quieted the table.

Dr. Don found Giovanni smiling from ear to ear.

"Yes?" asked Dr. Don.

"My team, if possible, would like David to join us for dinner... if possible," Giovanni stood his ground.

Dr. Don looked at me then back to Giovanni, "Why?"

"We celebrate him for good dives," Giovanni simply responded.

"We celebrate him here too," countered Dr. Don.

Giovanni's smile faded, "I see." He started to walk away.

He was stopped by a tall and imposing man, whose wild, untamed hair hung to his shoulders like a lion's mane. The man wrapped a huge paw around Giovanni's neck and turned him back to face Dr. Don.

"Donald," the man spoke with a thick Italian accent and such authority that everyone stopped and listened. "Come, it's celebration."

"Who's that?" I asked Patti.

"That's Klaus Dibiasi, the greatest diver ever," she responded with awe.

"Klaus, that's what we're trying to do here, celebrate," defended Dr. Don.

"Yes, we all celebrate. But we mix it up. Have divers sit together and share lives." Klaus flared with his hand, indicating the whole room, "Mix up."

"I don't know. I have to keep my divers focused," said Dr. Don.

"One night. One dinner. One hour," Klaus simply stated.

"Why David?" asked Jack. "Why not Mark or Megan?"

"They are too welcome, all is welcomed. But Giovanni has earlier asked if David could eat with Italian team. No problem, *si*?"

"I don't know. It's against our team philosophy," explained Dr. Don.

"Here's what I do. You let David go to my team table, and I will come to USA team table," Klaus presented a huge smile.

"That'd be awesome," said Andy.

Other divers murmured in agreement.

Dr. Don looked around the table. "What the hell, it'd be an honor to have you with us."

"It has been too long time for us," stated Klaus.

"Way too long." Dr. Don wrapped his arm around Klaus's shoulder and guided him to a seat.

Giovanni grabbed the back of my chair and pulled it away from the table. He offered his hand to me, and I took it. He guided me to my feet and ushered me to the far table. As we approached, the Italians, Germans, and Russians started cheering.

I blushed.

Matthews' Home—Aulden, Ohio, December 1978

"Looks like we're going to have a white Christmas," Caine announced. He bounded from the staircase and landed with a thud. "I'm dreaming of a white," he crooned in his best Bing Crosby imitation but paused a moment to glance out the window trimmed with flickering red, green, and white lights. "Keep snowing, baby, make it all pure and white." He rounded the ivy-draped banister post with such glee that I was sure he had just spoken to his girlfriend whom he kept a secret from everyone.

Caine always sang after his telephone whispers with this girl. Caine would never finish a complete song before transitioning into another, and he had a habit of rewriting the lyrics with colorful overtones.

"My chestnuts roasting on an open fire…" He sauntered up behind me, "Jack Frost flicking on your ear," and he flicked my ear.

"Stop it," I protested and batted his hand away.

"Whaaaaaaat? Is someone not in a festive mood?" he mocked in baby talk.

"Just leave me alone, I'm trying to…"

"What? Finish your precious drawing?" he leaned over me, his stomach forcing my head down.

"Stop it!"

"I'm just trying to see what you're drawing," he said. He reached for the sketch pad.

I immediately threw my arms over to cover it. "Leave me alone," I demanded.

"Ah, come on, let me see." He reached around and pulled the pad from under my arms. "Ah, what's this? A horsey," he said in a patronizing tone, "a cute, little horsey."

I reached for the sketch pad, grabbed it around the spiral wiring, and pulled. It almost slipped from his grasp. "Let me have it," I shouted.

"Oh, is someone getting mad?" He jerked it from me again. "Santa knows if you've been naughty or nice…"

"You're going to wrinkle it," I pleaded.

"Someone's here," announced Magdalyn's voice from the kitchen.

A pair of car lights turned up the driveway, causing us both to look out the window by the stair.

I quickly turned back to Caine and grabbed the sketch pad from his hands.

"I was going to give it back. I just wanted to look at it."

"No, you wanted to make fun of it," I said.

"Why'd you say that?" His attention was still on the car coming to a stop. The windshield wipers continued to wipe across the darkened glass as if waving hello.

"Because you always make fun of me," I said, trying to smooth out the wrinkles on the pad.

"Because you always draw faggotty horses," he replied. "Who's that? That's not Dad's car." He turned his head toward me and joked, "Is it one of your callers?"

The driver's door of the black sedan popped open, and a man in a long coat, scarf, and hat climbed out. He made his way to the back of the idling car, slipped on the ice but was able to catch his balance, and popped the trunk.

The passenger door drew open, and a woman wrapped up in a fur coat, muff, and hat appeared. She seemed to be sending orders to the man, who kept nodding in agreement.

"Nope, doesn't seem to fit the profile to be one of yours," Caine continued to harass.

The man pulled a large garbage bag with a huge bow out from the trunk, set it down on the snow-covered driveway, and closed it. He picked up the overstuffed bag and started toward the front door, pausing for a moment to allow the woman to catch up to him. She took tiny steps to avoid slipping—which was causing her to slip even more in her black patent leather high-heeled boots. She wrapped her arm around the man's for support.

Mom swept in from the kitchen, nervously flapping her hands about her head in the attempt to fluff and reshape her hair into something presentable.

"I wonder who this could be," she practiced her sweet-sounding voice, the one she used when she was greeting people at work or talking to bill collectors on the phone or when she was trying to make a good impression.

"Some man and woman," Caine informed her.

"I wonder what they're doing here tonight." There was a strange tone in her voice, as if she knew the reason for this visitation. She tilted the large plastic Santa face aside and looked through the door's window.

Caine and I watched as the couple struggled up the snow-covered lawn and mounted the steps to the front porch. Mom had the door flung open before they even prepared to knock.

"Well, hello," Mom's sugar sweetness seeped through the sing-song cadence. "What on earth are you doing out on a night like this?"

The man reached Mom first and presented his hand. "Lydia, Lydia Matthew?"

"Yes." She posed by the opened door, one hand playing with the third button of her blouse.

"I'm Reverend Albert Spangler, from the Salvation Army, and this is my wife, Mildred."

"So pleased to meet you," Mom, being ever so cordial, accepted the offered hand.

"We've been informed that there're some children here that were very good this year. So we brought some presents for them."

My body flooded with both fear and anger—fear from remembering a time when Caine and I had to hide in the bedroom closet because Child Welfare was at the door, asking Mom and Dad questions; anger from the fact that Mom must've contacted these nice people to tell them we were too poor to have any Christmas presents, which explained why she'd made sure no presents were sitting under the Christmas tree tonight. She'd had me place the presents in the hall closet earlier today. Her explanation was that she wanted to preserve Magdalyn's belief in Santa Claus for at least one more year.

I couldn't help but think of all the real poor people for whom these presents were truly intended. I quickly scaled up the stairs.

"Come in," Mother said politely.

I positioned myself on the upper landing so that I could listen to what was transpiring.

"Who's this little cutie?" the man's voice carried up to my ears.

"This is our youngest, Magdalyn." I could picture Mom wrapping her arm around her daughter's shoulders and stroking her pigtailed hair, while Magdalyn placed a hand over her mouth and chin to cover the scar from the sledding accident.

"Don't cover your mouth," Mom instructed as she guided Magdalyn's resistant hand down to her side.

"You sure are a cutie," the woman's voice quivered as she saw the *U*-shaped purple scar that resided on Magdalyn's chin.

"What do you say to the nice lady?" Mom instructed.

"Thank you," Magdalyn said. She dropped her head, as if by doing so she could hide her chin.

"You're quite welcome," the woman's voice cooed, "and what a lovely-decorated Christmas tree."

"Oh!" Mom relished. "We've had that tree for years, and the children made all the decorations from stuff around the house."

"It's divine," said the woman.

"And who's this strapping young man?" the Reverend inquired.

"Introduce yourself to the nice Reverend," directed Mom.

"I'm Caine," my brother proclaimed.

Mom quickly added with a giggle, "He's our oldest."

"Nice to meet you, Caine. I'm Reverend Albert Spangler." I imagined the two shaking hands. "So are you the man of the house?"

"Not quite," Caine stated with a laugh.

"My husband's not home yet," Mom added.

"But it is Christmas Eve," protested the woman.

"He's on his way, I assure you." Mom made the statement sound as casual an excuse as possible. "Would you like some coffee?" she asked, playing the perfect hostess.

"Thank you, but no. We better not. We've a couple more places to stop, before the snow gets too deep," the Reverend apologized.

"Is it terrible out?" Mom asked.

"The main roads aren't that bad yet, they were salted pretty well. But the side roads, oh my, now they're a different story. That's where all the problems are," said Mildred. "It was nice meeting you, Magdalyn and Caine."

"Where's David?" I heard Mom asked.

I froze. What should I do? I didn't want to go downstairs and say hello.

"He had to finish his homework," Caine attempted to cover for me.

"Homework on Christmas Eve?" she asked.

"You know how David is, he's an overachiever," Caine replied.

"Tell him to come on down. David," she called up for me. "David, come on down here, honey, for a moment, and meet these nice people. You can finish up later."

There was no way out. I took a deep breath and made my way down the stairs. I paused halfway since Caine was blocking the end of the stairs.

"This is our middle child, David," Mom presented proudly.

"You're the diver?" said the woman with a smile.

"Yes, ma'am, I guess," I fumbled with embarrassment.

"We've heard wonderful things about you." The man with the wrinkled face held his hand out to me. "I'm Reverend Albert Spangler, and this is my wife, Mildred."

"Nice to meet you both," I reached down and shook his hand.

His smile was warm, kind, and encouraging—which made my stomach twist into a knot as I thought about all the goodness he possessed. He gently pulled his hand away.

Reverend Spangler indicated the bag and began delivering a speech that seemed rehearsed. "We know how hard times can be, especially during the holidays. So it's our pleasure to put together a few things for the families who are in need this season." He untied the red bow, fanned open the bag, and handed the ribbon to Magdalyn. "There're things in here for the whole family, even Mom and Dad."

"Make sure you put the turkey and perishable foods in the refrigerator," instructed Mildred before she stopped herself and asked, "You do have a working refrigerator, don't you, dear?"

"Yes, we do," reassured Mom.

"That's good. Make sure you put away the turkey, dressing, pumpkin pie, whipped cream, cranberries, and green beans. Everything's cooked, and all you have to do is warm it up for Christmas dinner tomorrow," the woman said proudly.

Reverend Spangler said, "Under the food, you'll find some presents. Since we had such a short notice to get everything together, they're simple."

"Look, children, there really is a Santa Claus." Mom's eyes filled with calculated tears. "I'm so grateful. Thanks to you, we'll have a real Christmas."

"No matter what, the real Christmas is here." Mildred patted her fur coat above her heart. "God's always here, loving and listening to you."

"Ask and thou shall receive," Reverend shared. "We must be off, Mildred." He ushered his wife out the door as a gust of cold air whipped into the hall. "Good night, and have a merry Christmas."

"Merry Christmas," Mom replied as she leaned out the door and waved. "Thank you, and God bless."

Caine and I watched as the two good Samaritans trekked back through the snow to the car, climbed in, and slowly backed out of the driveway.

Mom closed the door and dramatically collapsed against it, pressing her face against the plastic Santa. Her shoulders quivered as her tears became audible. "There's a Santa Claus, there really is."

She turned and accepted her audience, and then as if she flipped a switch, she wiped below her puffy eyes and pointed to the bag. "Caine, will you carry that to the kitchen, and, David, will you help put the food away?" She walked to the kitchen.

Caine cocked his head toward the bag and indicated for me to take it to the kitchen. I obliged without hesitation. Besides, I wanted to ask Mom how the good Reverend and his wife heard about us.

As I placed the bag on the kitchen counter, I saw that Mom had opened her purse. She slid out a silver card with green pills, forced two pills through the cellophane, and quickly downed them without any assistance of liquid. She stood there a moment, as if waiting for the release from the pills to explode inside her. She opened her eyes and smiled, as if everything was going to be all right. She seemed startled at seeing me there and added, "I have a slight headache."

I overlooked the obvious and started to unpack the bag, placing items packaged in Reynolds Wrap on the counter. I mustered up the courage and said, "So this is really nice of them."

"Yes, it is," she said distractedly as she carefully zipped her purse and positioned it next to the microwave. "Let's make sure there's enough room in the refrigerator."

I opened the brown door adorned with magnets holding Christmas cards and was greeted with overstuffed shelves. A good-sized turkey weighing at least twenty-five pounds occupied the main shelf, with six cans of whipped cream and pumpkin and pecan pies nestled next to it. The upper shelf was filled with sodas, milk, and cranberry sauce. The lower crispers were stuffed with lettuce, cucumbers, peppers, and fresh green beans.

"Where am I going to put this food?" I asked in amazement.

"We'll have to shift some things around or use the refrigerator on the back porch." She pushed me aside and started to rearrange things. "Hand me the cranberries and the dressing."

I handed her the wrapped plates. "How'd they hear about us?"

"I'm not sure. It was definitely a blessing. Now pass me the whipped cream and pies," she ordered.

I handed her the whipped cream and pies. "But we don't need it. Just look at all this food we have."

"We're just blessed, I guess. Now give me the green beans and potatoes."

I handed her the green beans and potatoes. "But what about…?"

"David! That's enough. What's done is done. Leave it alone." She glared at me. "We're having Christmas, and nothing's going to spoil it. You understand? Take the rest to the refrigerator on the back porch."

I nodded and gathered the remaining items.

The door leading to the back porch opened, and Dad came in, red-eyed and smelling of a sweet concoction of cigarettes and whiskey.

Athletes' and Coaches—Dinner, Norway, 1979

Giovanni presented me to the athletes at the table.

"This is Anna Luca and Franco Amarvatti from Italy. Those two are Alexandre Portenov and Vladimir Alleynov from Russia. And Falk Hoffleman and Marta Beck from East Germany. *Ciao a tutti, questo è David Matthew.*"

The athletes gave little waves, nodded their heads, or uttered, "*Ciao.*"

"Thank you. It's nice to meet all of you." I felt overwhelmed. "How do you understand each other?" I asked Giovanni.

"Oh, simple. We mostly speak each other's languages." He pulled out a chair. "Please sit."

"Have you been to Germany?" asked Marta.

I shook my head and sat. I looked over to Marta, and I spoke slowly as if it will help the translation, "No, I have not been to

Germany. I would love to someday. This is the first time I have traveled outside of the US."

"You must come visit," said Marta. "We'll show you everything."

"Sounds terrific," I said, even more embarrassed that she spoke English.

Giovanni sat beside me and gently squeezed my thigh. "*Mangiamo*! Let's eat!"

Before me was a plate of food with some type of meat surrounded by colorful carrots, peas, and potatoes swimming in a cream sauce.

"What is it?" I asked.

"Try it first, and I'll tell you." He took a sip from his wine glass.

I'm not usually very adventuresome, but I didn't want to embarrass Giovanni, so I scooped up a large hunk of meat, wedge of potato, and speared a slice of carrot and a pea or two.

I guided the food into my mouth, closed my lips, and pulled out the clean fork. The flavors exploded against my taste buds. The first familiar taste was salt, a lot of it, followed with a sweetness that infused with the salt, causing a pleasing concoction I had never experienced before.

"This is terrific. What is it?" I asked again.

"It's sheep head," Gianni offhandedly said.

My stomach immediately flipped.

"It's Norwegian tradition. The sheep's head is salted, smoked, and then boiled for a very long time until the meat falls off the skull," explained Giovanni. "You okay?"

My stomach rolled over again. The image of the sheep's eyes, nose, and ears in a huge pot boiling with salt made me nauseous.

Giovanni handed me a glass to drink. "Drink this."

Without thinking, I took a big swig. I gasped for air as my throat burned from the flaming liquid's path.

"Take easy." Gianni took the glass away from me. "You Americans so aggressive. That's meant for sipping and enjoying. It's called aquavit. It's alcohol that's spiced with anise and caraway. Try again." He guided the glass back toward my lips.

I shook my head as I gulped in cool air.

"Come on, just a little. It'll help." He guided the glass closer to my lips.

I blocked the lip of the glass with my palm. "I'm not allowed."

"What?" Giovanni asked.

"I'm not allowed to have any alcoholic beverages." I reached for a glass of water.

"Who says?" he asked.

"Our coaches." I gulped down water, hoping it would quench the burning in my throat.

"They won't know." He guided the glass to my lips again. I glanced over to the USA table, and no one seemed to be watching. I accepted the offered glass and took a tiny sip.

"Let it rest on your tongue." He was encouraging and peaceful. I became deaf to the room's loudness, and I only heard him whispering, "Now let it slowly go down."

As the libation dripped down my throat, the burning subsided and disappeared.

"Good, right?" he asked.

I nodded.

He grabbed my head and kissed my cheeks hard. "Good! Tomorrow I take you walk around city. Okay?" Giovanni flashed a huge smile.

All I could do was respond with, "Okay."

9 CHAPTER

Day Trip with Giovanni—Tønsberg, Norway, July 1979

"Thank you for deciding to join us today and experience my home of Tønsberg," a tall, thin man with prominent cheekbones commanded our small group's attention. "My name is Sven Jorgenson. Welcome. As you can see, we have been blessed with a beautiful morning, a little chilly, but believe me, it will warm up. I would like to introduce you to our tour guide, Tonje Turjorn."

The late morning sun stretched its fingers between the tin roofs of the oldest city in Norway, causing little streams of mist to vaporize. A pungent smell of ocean waters was laced with fresh fish from the bay, and a bit of iciness still hung beneath the shop's eaves and rafters. A group of about twenty divers and coaches had gathered to be taken on a tour of the city. Patti and I were the only Americans. Mark, Megan, and Andy wanted to sleep in, and the other divers had practice for their prelims. I was excited to see a world I most likely would never have the chance to see again.

Patti draped her arm through mine and jostled to get a prime spot in the front of the crowd. I liked to tease her and say that if she were only an inch shorter and had hairy feet, she could be a hobbit like Bilbo Baggins. She never seemed to see the humor. We migrated to the front of the line so she could see.

Tonje Turjorn stepped up beside Sven Jorgenson. She removed her red scarf and allowed her blond curls to bounce around her oval face.

"I'm so glad that you invited me to be a part of such an incredible event." Her English was impeccable with just the slightest Norwegian accent. "I'm humbled to know that I'm standing among the best divers in the world. Thank you for this honor."

Tonje and Sven's lines seemed forced and rehearsed. I scanned the crowd as nonchalantly as I could without being obvious.

"He'll be here, if he chooses. You can't simply will him to appear," Patti sneered from the side of her mouth while still pretending to listen to the Tonje and Sven.

"Who?" I mocked shock.

She mocked shock better than I. "I know who you're looking for."

"I don't know who you are talking about." I tried not to glance away from her.

"Him." She indicated with the jerk of her head.

I glanced over to where she was looking, and there, strolling up the cobblestone street, were Giovanni, Anna, and Franco. Anna was in the middle, with both boys on either side, interlacing arms. They were singing something in Italian as joy ricocheted from them.

I admired how the three enjoyed life at that moment, with a carefree happiness I'd never seen before.

"David," Giovanni's baritone voices bellowed across the cobblestones and caused everyone to look at the trio. He waved his hand high above his head.

"The Italians are here," Rebecca, the platform diver from Great Britain, announced sarcastically. "Now the party can start." Laugher rumbled throughout the crowd.

The Italian trio reached us and bowed, as if we had been waiting just for them.

"You're running a bit late," Sven Jorgenson said.

"But we're here now," qualified Giovanni.

"Yes, we can see that. Please fall in. We must get started," Sven said.

Tonje began her introduction, "Tønsberg is the oldest town in Norway, founded around AD 871. It quickly became an important trading center. We have many places to visit today, such as the ruins of Saint Olav's Church, Haugar Arts Museum, Foynegården, Sem Church, Tønsberg Cathedral, and we cannot miss Oseberghaugen."

Patti gave me an "oh, goodie" face, and I mirrored it back.

Giovanni wrapped his big paw around my neck and pulled me into his hard chest.

Patti relinquished ground and looked off toward the speakers.

Tonje continued, "In 1130, Snorri Sturluson mentioned Tønsberg in his collections entitled *Heimskringla*. According to his writings, the city was founded in 871 before the Battle of Hafrsfjord—which could make Tønsberg the oldest Scandinavian city. But there are disputes as to the actual date of the battle and the authenticity of the city's age. However, archaeological excavations discovered several Viking graves under the monastery. The excavators speculated that 871 may have been the original date of the settlement. We will be visiting those grave sites today on our tour."

"We should start if we want to see everything," politely interrupted Sven. He used his large hands to usher people to the right.

Anna leaned into Patti and asked, "You're Patti Lakes, yes?"

Patti didn't answer but simply nodded.

Anna offered her hand, "I'm Anna Luca. I made the finals in platform as well."

"Yes, I know. It's great to meet you," Patti responded.

Anna huddled close and whispered something into Patti's ear. They both laughed. Anna glanced over her shoulder to Giovanni and led Patti toward the departing group. I wasn't sure what was happening, and then I saw Franco nod to Giovanni and follow the two girls.

I started to go with them, but Giovanni held me back. "Let them become acquainted. We can take our own tour."

"What?" I asked.

"Let me show you Tønsberg. I've been here many times—unless, of course, you would rather go with them?"

"No," immediately flew out of my mouth.

"Well then." He took my hand and led me away.

He ushered me into a small café and pressed his fingers against my lips while the group disappeared around the corner. He walked to the counter and spoke in Norwegian. The waiter nodded and set up two paper cups, while Giovanni swiveled to face me with his hips resting against the glass cabinet filled with gooey pastries. I quickly glanced out the large window and witnessed a gull land in the bay.

"David," Giovanni offered me a cup of the most pungent steaming liquid.

"What is it?" I asked.

"What's it look like? It is arsenic. You Americans, always asking, What is it? What is it?" He walked out to the street.

"Thank you," I muttered. I quickly followed him. The smell of cinnamon and nutmeg reminded me of Christmas.

Christmas—Aulden, Ohio, 1978

Magdalyn snuggled under a blanket on the lounge chair with the doll she'd received from the Salvation Army, watching the broadcasting of *Frosty the Snowman*. Jimmy Durante's raspy voice was narrating how Karen and Frosty were in the North Pole and Karen was freezing. Frosty spotted a greenhouse in the middle of the snow-covered nowhere and decided to let her warm up inside.

I was at the coffee table, busy trying out the new charcoal pencils that the good Reverend had given me. I was shading in another horse grazing peacefully in a meadow, blending in the flank and touching up its mane.

Caine and Dad were in the center of the room, reenacting the Matthews' World Wrestling Championship, squatting and circling each other, waiting for an opportunity to attack. This game had been a part of their controlled roughhouse since Caine was diagnosed with a blood platelet disorder at ten years old. He started getting bruises and nosebleeds, which took forever for the doctors to diagnose. The doctors instructed Caine not to participate in any contact sports. This was devastating to Caine because sports were his world and he was going to be the next Pete Rose for the Cincinnati Reds. After a week of complete depression, Dad started to play with Caine, and they created Matthews' World Wrestling Championships, Matthews' Football League, Matthews' Baseball League, and the Matthews' Summer and Winter Olympics. We all participated in the seasonal sporting events—always trying to own the world record.

I reluctantly partook. I had an issue with eye-and-ball coordination, which made football and baseball difficult, and I had no interest in wrestling. I felt it was ludicrous, and someone was always apt to get hurt.

"Come on, you pansy-waist, you don't stand a chance," Dad taunted Caine.

"Not this time, crater-face, the world championship belt belongs to me." Caine gave a deep grunt, snapped, and grabbed Dad's calf.

Dad quickly responded by anchoring himself around Caine's waist and hoisted the seventeen-year-old upside down.

"Illegal move," protested Caine as he hung dangled above the floor.

"Who says?" challenged Dad.

"It's in the handbook."

"Screw the handbook." He spun Caine in a circle, which caused him to screech. "Had enough?"

"All right!"

Dad lowered Caine so that his head touched the floor and let go of his legs. Caine's socked feet landed with a thud next to where I was sitting, causing me to jump.

Caine laughed. "That was a close call, bro," he said as he diverted his attention toward Dad again. "And now you must pay." He attacked, wrapping his arms around Dad's waist, taking him off guard and shoving him against the lounge chair that Magdalyn was cuddled in, causing her to scream.

The game was becoming more aggressive. "Hey, guys, careful," I said.

"Don't worry about us," Caine grunted. He whirled Dad to the center of the room. "This won't take long."

Caine wrapped a leg around Dad's ankle, causing him to stumble. Dad caught himself against the wall, almost knocking off the aerial picture of our house. Pushing off the wall, Dad staggered forward before falling facedown in front of the Christmas tree, shaking the ornaments and the glass angel on top.

"Seriously, you're going to knock the tree over," I warned.

"You just keep minding your own business," said Dad.

"Yeah, you keep drawing those girly ponies," added Caine.

Dad got up on his hands and knees, preparing to stand, when Caine attacked again, landing on Dad's back. Dad dipped his head and shoulders, Caine flipped forward, and Dad rolled right behind. One of Caine's legs landed on the back of my head and neck, forcing my torso against the coffee table with a crash. His other leg landed on my arm with a thud—forcing the charcoal pencil to snap in two, scarring the sketch with a deep black line that tore through the paper, and pushing the table hard against the wall. Dad rolled into the middle of my back, impaling my sternum against the lip of the coffee table. I felt the pain racing through my head, neck, arm, back, and sternum. In the background I heard laughing. As the laughter grew in volume, the pain resonated in my being, and so did the rage. The room turned red.

"Shit, Jesus Christ, son of a bitch."

I pushed Caine off my shoulder and backed against Dad to free myself from my entrapment. I stood with such intense pain.

Caine was the first to recover and tried to grab my arm, which I deflected with a quick shrug of my shoulder. Dad was on his feet, towering over me with a surprised look etched on his face and his blue eyes darkening.

"It was an accident," said Caine.

"It's always an accident," I ranted. I posed in an attack mode.

"Who do you think you are?" Dad took a step toward me.

"Dad, he didn't mean it," Caine said.

"I think he did. Do you think you're so much better than the rest of us?" His eyes narrowed as he took another step.

"No," I responded.

"So you think you can take me?" His left hand curved around and clocked me above the right ear, causing an instant ringing in my head. "Who made you better than anyone here?" His right hand sailed through the air and clipped my chin, which whipped my head to the left.

"Come on now, we were having fun," Caine tried to stop Dad's aggression.

"This has been a long time coming." Dad grabbed my throbbing chin and held my face in line with his as he inched closer. "Hasn't it, David?"

I closed my eyes and tried to turn my face away.

"Look at me!" he demanded, pulling my face back to his.

I refused to open my eyes.

"Why won't you look at me?" His left opened palm landed on my right cheek, followed by a right palm on my left. "Look at me, you little patsy."

Both cheekbones stung. I tasted a metallic liquid from my lower lip, felt sweat on my temples and nape of my neck, and became nauseous.

"Be a man once in your measly little life, and look at me." His berating was followed by another round of swats to my face.

Caine tried stopping the onslaught. "All right, that's enough." He physically positioned himself between us. "Calm down."

"Don't tell me to calm down in my house." Dad threw Caine across the room.

Magdalyn began to cry hysterically. Mom came rushing in from the kitchen.

I managed to break away and shoved past Mom toward the door. Dad followed.

Mom shouted, "Caleb, that's enough!"

I didn't see it, but I heard her hit the wall. I felt someone grab the back of my shirt and pull the collar taut against my throat. I resisted and forged forward, reaching for the doorknob. The collar cut into the skin as I summoned every ounce of energy. I heard the shirt tear and felt the freedom I was looking for. I was able to turn the knob and fling open the door. I sprinted out into the snow-covered night and down the driveway.

"David, get your ass back in here this instant!" yelled Dad.

I turned left on the road and kept running.

"David!"

I couldn't stop if I wanted to. I wasn't in control of my actions. I kept running and running. Flakes of snow pelted and stung my face. The coldness felt soothing against my bruised cheeks and swollen lip. I could feel blood freezing on my neck from where the shirt's collar sliced me. My cotton shirt absorbed the falling snow and turned wet against my chest, and my feet became numb as my socks slapped against the snow-covered road. I didn't dare stop. I kept running. The glow from the night-light by our silo waned to grayness until I was bathed in darkness. I focused on the yellowish glow from the neighbors' night-light as I made my way past Hawkins' farm on the hill to my left and thought for a brief moment about stopping, but I couldn't direct my body to turn up the driveway. I kept running until the Hawkins' night-light was no longer any assistance.

I followed the road as it sloped down, leading to a small cluster of about fifteen houses, which everyone called Mount Holly. The houses looked serene, warmth pouring through the lighted windows and the chimneys emitting the smell of burning wood. I veered with the road to the left between rows of homes nestled and waiting for the arrival of Santa Claus. I kept running up a steep hill. I slid and kept climbing on my hands and knees to the top. My chest burned from the cold air; my legs burned from the exertion; and my hands burned from the freezing temperature. I couldn't stop. I reached the peak of the hill and kept running.

This quarter-of-a-mile stretch of road was flat and dark with plowed fields on both sides. Nothing provided protection from the whipping and whirling wind. Its howling moan filled my ears. My jeans weighed a ton. My run shifted to a jog.

I turned left on Cook Jones Lane. I could always make my way through the woods and sneak in the back of the barn and stay there for the night, or I could make my way down to the highway and hope someone would give me a lift into town. But what would I do when I got to town? It was Christmas Eve, and everything would be closed. I was lost in my thoughts. I kept jogging.

The fields on both sides of the road were covered with the brown cornstalks that were left unharvest, which bowed from the weight of the wet snow. I was amazed at how the rows and rows of stocks looked identical, like chorus of dancers in perfect unison.

From the field on the left came a guttural growl, deep and foreboding. The stalks started to shake and separate, as if something were forcing its way through them, sending a cloud of brown dust mixed with accumulated snow into the air. I froze. Something inside yelled, *Don't move a muscle.*

The final row of stocks before the ditch parted, and a pair of glowing orbs appeared. The deep growl sounded again. The animal's head was low to the ground, shoulders rounded high, and bushy tail tucked in. It slunk out and sidled its thin rib cage against the last cornstalk.

"Whoa, boy, where'd you come from?" I asked in a soft and soothing tone. "Everything's all right, no one's going to hurt you."

It stepped toward me, lifted its muzzle, and twitched its black nose, gathering my scent. I remember that someone had once told me that animals can smell fear.

"That's right, everything's cool. Are you all by yourself? So am I."

Its brown fur was a combination of light and dark patches masked by a thin blanket of snow. It limped as it held the front right paw close to its chest cavity.

I slowly knelt to get on the animal's sight level. "You're hurt. What happened?"

The wild dog cowered, licked at the wounded leg, and whimpered as if it understood me. I reached my hand, palm facing up, toward it. Its head jerked toward a pair of car lights turning onto Cook Jones Lane. The animal glanced at me, then back to the approaching lamps, and darted back amid the cornstalks for protection.

I leaped into the ditch in hope that the car's driver wouldn't see me. I sank deep into the snow and wrapped my arms around my knees and buried my head against my forearms. I shut my eyes and remained still.

The car slowly crept and then stopped, and the door opened. "Davey, thank God."

Peeking, I saw Mom in the driver's seat.

"Come on now and get in," she said.

I shook my head.

"He didn't mean it," she softly said.

"I don't care, I'm not going back."

"What're you going to do, sit out here and freeze to death?"

"If I have to," I said.

"Come on."

"What? Do what we always do, act like nothing happened?" I buried my face in my arms.

"No."

She started to get out of the car without putting it in park. The car shot forward, jerking her back against the seat. She shifted the gears, and the car stopped. She made her way back to where I was sitting.

"Come on now, I've been searching everywhere for you. You've been out here far too long, and you're going to get sick."

"I can't," I stated.

"Why not?"

"I can't take it anymore. It's always the same thing. I have to pretend that nothing's wrong and act as if everything's okay. I just can't do it anymore."

"Do it for me," she said softly.

"What?"

"I need you. I can't do it without you," her voice started to quiver.

"Then why do you?" I asked.

"Why do I do what?" She fought back the tears.

"Stay."

"Because I love him," she said. "Now, I need you to help me get ready for tomorrow. You're the only one that I can count on." A strong gust of wind swirled snow up and around her. She pulled her collar tighter around her neck.

"What's tomorrow?" I asked.

"Christmas dinner, and everyone's coming. Please, get in the car."

"I thought it was just us."

"It was until your father invited everyone." She knelt down in front of me. "Please come home. It's too cold out here. I'm freezing."

"What's he going to do?" I asked.

"He's not there right now. He drove off somewhere. I'll take care of that. Come home, get warm, and let's look at your lip." She stood and held out her hand.

I didn't make a move.

"Do it for me. I can't take much more. I'm at my wit's end, and I feel like I'm about to break. Please be a good boy and do it for me."

I found myself automatically crawling out of the ditch and climbing into the warm car.

* * *

The back door opened, and someone stumbled in, running into the chair next to the door. Since my room was on the landing above the kitchen, I was always aware when someone was coming or going or talking. I heard the familiar creak of footsteps on the stairs and the exasperated exhale. I closed my eyes and feigned sleep as someone arrived on the landing. Someone sat on the side of my bed and pushed back the hair from over my eyes. Fingers caressed my cheek and lightly brushed across my swollen lower lip.

"I'm so sorry, son," Dad whispered. "I never meant to hurt you. I don't know why, but I just get so angry with you. I'm so afraid for you and the direction your life is taking." He leaned down and kissed my cheek. His perfume of whiskey and cigarettes lingered as he rose and made his way back downstairs.

I let out my held breath and listened as he went in to the kitchen to make a cup of coffee. When I heard the clinking of the spoon stirring his coffee and sugar, I got up and crept downstairs. Lights twinkled on the Christmas tree as Mom and Magdalyn slept on the pull-out couch.

I was sitting in the shadows on the stairs when Dad came back into the living room. He placed his coffee cup on the side table and sat on the edge of the pulled-out couch. I never understood why my parents chose to sleep in the living room when they had a nice bedroom down the hall, but my dad would always answer that it was the center of the house and that he was able to hear everything and if there was ever any emergencies, he could be there quickly.

He removed his boots and swung his long legs on to the mattress. He wrapped his large arms around the sleeping child and kissed her forehead, "Good night, my sweet Maggie."

"What time is it?" Mom asked half asleep.

"Not too late," Dad whispered.

"Where were you?" She rolled on her side to face him as he cradled Magdalyn in his arms.

"Shhh, you're going to wake my Maggie," he whispered.

"She's almost ten years old," she hissed.

"She's only eight." He smiled as he brushed the sleeping Magdalyn's bangs from her forehead.

"She'll be ten next month, Caleb."

"She's still my Maggie," he declared. He kissed her cheek. "I've been thinking. I think we need to do those treatments that Dr. Shultz suggested for her chin."

"Which one?" Mom struggled as she positioned herself sitting up.

"The good one, the one that'll erase the scar for good," he said softly.

"It's too expensive. We can do the shots, the doctor said that the cortisone shots will be just as effective," she droned on as if she was tired of repeating herself.

"But the shots are extremely painful," he said.

"But we can do them in stages." She took out a cigarette and lit it, taking a drag but not completely inhaling. She blew out a large white puff of smoke.

"Right, and if we do the reconstruction, it'll be over with in one operation." He lightly touched her chin.

"If it takes correctly. I don't want her to have to undergo any more surgeries," Mom stated with finality. "And we don't have the money."

"We can find the money for the reconstruction."

"Where?" Mom snapped.

"We'll find the money, and besides, that's what insurance is for," he said.

"There's no way. And why do you always coddle her so much?"

"She's my beautiful baby Maggie."

Mom got up with a huff and ran her hands through her hair. "I better get the presents so that there'll be a Christmas in the morning. We wouldn't want to disappoint the *beautiful baby Maggie.*"

As I crept back to my bed, I heard her open the hall closest, pull out the wrapped presents, and situate them under the tree.

"Caine, Cainey, wake up," I heard Magdalyn's excitement. "Santa Claus came and brought lots of presents."

"Did you get David up yet?" asked Caine.

"No, not yet," her voice was shrill.

"Well, you better," said Caine.

"Okay."

Tiny feet came running up to my bed, and the mattress shook. "Davy, get up, Santa came."

"It's too early, just five more minutes," I moaned.

"Come on," she urged.

"All right. All right." I stretched and rolled onto my back and saw her face next to mine. "I'm getting up."

"You better. You don't want to disappoint Baby Maggie," Caine chuckled. He leaned against the door frame that separated the two rooms.

"Hurry up," Magdalyn pleaded. She tugged on my hand.

"Go ahead and I'll be right down," I sat up in bed, feeling the aches from the previous night.

Magdalyn laughed and pointed at me. "Nice hair." She ran down the stairs.

"Thanks." I felt my hair sticking out in all different directions.

"What's the matter, sporting morning wood?" Caine chuckled. I shot him a look of disgust. "Don't give me that look, it happens. Hey, don't take too long." Caine grotesquely jerked his hand back and forth. "Remember to clean up after yourself."

"I'm getting up," I said.

"I bet you already are!" He punched me in the shoulder, leaped down to the small landing, and darted down the main stairs with a banshee yell.

I stood and patted my hair down and discovered that Caine was right. I adjusted myself and stepped toward the staircase when I felt my head throb and a sharp pain shoot down my spine. I grabbed the banister with both hands as the room spun. I took a deep breath and found my balance before I started the descent.

"Look, Davey, look," Magdalyn screeched.

Beneath the Christmas tree was an avalanche of presents flowing out to the middle of the living room.

"Santa did come, he did," Magdalyn exclaimed. She held her hand out for me. I managed down the remaining steps, trying to cover the pain, and took her hand. "You sit over here, David." She guided me to an area by the television. "Caine, you sit there." She pointed to the lounge chair. "And I'll pass out the gifts," she said with authority.

Day Trip with Giovanni, Norway, 1979

I sat next to Giovanni on a bench overlooking the bay.

"Drink it slow. It is meant to savor and enjoy, not to gulp. Like this." He lifted the paper cup to his nose and inhaled. His eyes shut, and a slight hint of a smile crept across his mouth. He guided the cup to his lips and barely sipped. He remained still as the liquid traveled down his throat and dispersed throughout his veins. He cocked his head and looked at me out of the corner of his eye. "Now you try."

I squared my back against the bench and lifted the paper cup to my nostrils and took a slow and even inhale. The coffee had a strong, acidic aroma with a hint of cinnamon, nutmeg, and something else that had sweetness to it. I sipped cautiously. At first it was hot and tasteless, but as it cooled, a nutty butter flavor exploded and bathed the inside of my mouth.

"Good, yes?" Giovanni asked.

I nodded and savored the experience.

"See, there are pleasures in the things you take time with. No need to rush everything in life," he said.

He placed his arm around my shoulders. It was so nice, sitting next to him and sipping coffee. I kept my eyes closed to remember every detail. His hand wrapped around the nape of my neck, and his fingers caressed the fine hair.

"Wait a minute." I leaned forward to see his face. "Your English is very good."

"So?"

"When we met in the locker room, you had a translator, and he told me you didn't speak English very well." I waited for a response.

He took another sip, smiled, and shrugged his shoulders.

"You played me."

"Look at the clouds above the bay."

I looked at the bright-white and dark-gray clouds stretching across the center of a huge yellow ball resting above the bay.

Giovanni leaned in close to my ear. "I want to show you something." He stood and offered me his hand.

We followed the cobblestone road as it wound its way north, passing little store fronts that looked like something from *Hansel and Gretel*. I had little time to take in the sloping roofs and vibrant colors, before Giovanni released my hand and swept us through a steamed-up glass door to an anteroom, where the heat from within pressed hard against us and kerosene filled our noses.

In the far side of the room, an artist was blowing through a long metal tube with a bright-red glob on the other end morphing into a shape. After a long exhale, the artist placed the orb back into a fire pit furnace and pumped a pedal on the floor that operated a large bellow that fanned the flames. He pulled the orb out and laid the pole on a bench and started rolling it. The soft orb rotated as the gravity's pull reshaped it. He took a leather towel in the palm of his hand and wrapped it around the orb, forming it into an oblong shape. He repeated this several times to manipulate the soft glass. The orb turned a rosy pink as it cooled.

A woman came rushing over to Giovanni and hugged him.

"Anje." He hugged her back. They traded kisses on each cheek. "Anje, this is David Matthew. He's from America." Giovanni introduced me to her.

"Hello," Anje said. "Come, let Jorgen work in peace." She escorted us back to the front of the store where the glass vases and figurines were on display. "You win meet, yes?" Anje asked Giovanni.

He smiled, "We finished preliminaries, and finals are tomorrow."

I saw a small glass vase in the window and wandered over to look at it while Giovanni and Anje caught up with each other. I was afraid to touch the vase; it was so delicate-looking. The bottom half was a clear, see-through teal. The color darkened toward the top into a blood-red.

Giovanni joined me. "You like?"

"It's beautiful," I replied.

We looked at each other for an awkward moment.

"Come, we have to get back to the pool. Practice starts soon. Bye, Anje."

"Bye, Giovanni. Bye, David." Anje waved as we left the store.

Dr. Althea Warner's Office—Dayton, Ohio, August 2016

Sitting in the small waiting room, a middle-aged woman came in, looked at me, and exited. There was a knock on the other door in the hallway to the office and followed with murmuring.

Althea came into the waiting room and closed the door. She sat next to me.

"I don't have you scheduled for today."

I quickly pulled by calendar out and showed her where I wrote the time on the date. "This is the second Tuesday since I was last here."

"Oh, I see what happened. I didn't think you were going to come back, so I erased you and booked someone else," she explained as she looked at her schedule.

"Why would I not show up?" I asked.

"It is something that I have become used too." She looked at her schedule. "How about tomorrow?"

"I'm not available."

"Let's set it up for next week then, same time."

"Fine."

Althea got up and walked back into the office and closed the door.

I left the office space confused and made my way to the parking lot. As I reached for the car door, I glanced back up to the second-floor window and saw Althea watching me.

Is this some type of test? I climbed behind the wheel and turned the ignition. As I shifted into drive, she was still watching.

10 CHAPTER

Practice before the Finals—Norway, July 1979

I was stretching with the team before our scheduled practice when Patti came rushing in and sat next to me.

"Where'd you disappear to?" She pretended to stretch her hamstrings.

"Nowhere," I simply stated.

"Well, you sure weren't with the tour group," Patti said.

"Oh, Giovanni wanted to get some coffee, and when we came out, the group was gone. We didn't know which way you went, so he showed me his favorite places."

"Did you have fun?"

"It was fun."

"Time's wasting while you two are here chatting." Jack was right behind us.

The Italian, Russian, and German teams were finishing up their practice. Giovanni was on the three-meter, laughing with Franco. They had a sense of ease and love for the sport—so different from the seriousness and pressure I was feeling from the American coaches.

Giovanni skipped down the metal plank and positioned his toes on the edge. He gracefully swung his arms through and performed a beautiful inward two-and-a-half somersault in the tuck position. He ripped through the water without a splash. Everyone in the arena applauded.

A voice echoed over the PA system, "The practice time is open to group B, which is Canada, Norway, and United States. Italy, Germany, and Russia's practices are over. Please clear the boards for group B."

Uneasiness sprouted in the pit of my stomach, a feeling of doom and lack of confidence. Was I beginning to feel the importance of being at the world championships?

Do I belong here?

Group B divers bounced the boards, and the vibrations on the frame made me nervous and dizzy. I felt like I was going to fall, so I grasped the railing harder until my knuckles turned white.

"Matthew, you're up," a voice called from the deck. I looked over and saw Dr. Don standing there with his hands on his hips.

I adjusted the fulcrum and took a practice bounce. My balance was off, and I almost fell. I shook my head and walked back to my starting position. I tried to focus on the end of the board, but my breathing was erratic, and my heart was pounding. I started down the board, hurdled, and flung myself into the air. I got lost while spinning, and I came out too early. I landed with a loud smack on my stomach. I floated on the water's surface, stunned, embarrassed, and feeling like a fool.

"Do it again," Dr. Don shouted when I reached the side of the pool.

I pulled myself out and noticed red welts immediately forming on my chest, stomach, and thighs.

"Matthew, you better focus," Dr. Don yelled.

Mark handed me my chamois. "It's all right, shake it off. You can do this."

"I feel funny, dizzy, and edgy." I looked at Mark with fear in my eyes.

"You're still shaken from passing out. Maybe you should've stayed in instead of sightseeing." Mark grabbed the back of my head and pressed his forehead against mine. He looked into my eyes. "This is only practice. This doesn't mean anything. Take one step at a time. You are all right. Now get up there and do this dive like you always have."

I climbed the ladder and adjusted the fulcrum. My pride was more bruised than my chest, and I was petrified for the first time in my short diving career. I had smacked before, but not in such a high-profile place. I was only grateful that the media were not permitted in the natatorium during practices. I tried to clear my head, but I looked toward Mark.

"You got this," he reassured me and held out his hand for me to slap it.

"Any day, Matthew," shouted Dr. Don.

I walked down the board, hurdled, and swung my arms through. I spun three and a half times and sliced the water like a knife. I broke the surface to applause from the other athletes.

I rushed to the locker room, feeling embarrassed.

"David?" Giovanni was finishing getting dressed.

I froze when I saw him, not sure where to go.

"Are you all right?" He lightly touched the raised bruises on my chest. "What happened?"

I shook my head and looked into the mirror. The bruises were changing from a red to a deep purple and outlined in white.

"Here, put this ointment on it." Giovanni pulled a small jar from his bag and offered it to me.

I stood there.

"Turn." He guided me to face him. He gently rubbed the ointment on my throat, chest, and stomach. "It stings a bit, but it will help you heal faster."

I didn't react to the stinging sensation.

"There, that should do it." He put the jar back into this bag. "I want to give you something." He removed a small box from his bag. "It's not much, but I wanted to show gratitude for spending the day with me." He stood, arms stretched, offering the present in the palm of his hand.

I slowly reached for it. "You didn't have to do that. I enjoyed spending the day with you," I admitted.

"I know. You glowed today. Not so sad." He handed me the box.

I opened it, and nestled in a sea of cotton was a small glass figurine of a diver.

"Jorgen made it. It reminds me of you." He helped me remove the diver from the box and held it up so the refractions of red, yellow, and blue danced in the light as it spun.

"It's beautiful," I whispered.

"Like you," Giovanni whispered before kissing my cheek. "You remind me of my younger brother. He always had a sad face."

"Is he a diver too?" I asked.

"No longer. He was national champion, but he didn't believe in his talents." His eyes welled.

"Why did he stop diving?" I hesitated, feeling there was something more to his brother's story.

Giovanni forced a smile and squeezed his eyes shut to fight back any tears. He held up his hand and took a deep breath. When he opened his eyes, they glistened as liquid collected in the corners. "He took his life last year, before the Swedish Cup. He was so sad."

"I'm sorry." I wanted to hug him.

"You remind me of him. Hiding secrets. Ricardo, that was his name. Ricardo tried to tell me, many times, but he never finished." He pressed the heels of his palms against each eye, wiping them of tears. He looked at me a long time, before pushing a strand of hair from my forehead. "You look like him. I saw the same look in your eyes at the registration." Another tear rolled down his face. "I must go. Glad you like the glass diver." Giovanni left without another word.

Did I really remind him of his brother? What was he trying to tell me? Have I been misinterpreting his kindness and friendship? Was I just a way for him to feel better about his brother?

"That was some wipeout, dude," Andy said. He patted my chest. "You are going to bruise. I think I would've cried."

"Leave him alone, he's fine," said Mark.

I wasn't fine! I wanted to scream.

New Year's Eve—Aulden, Ohio, 1978

"Let's do it again."

"All right. This'll be the last time," I said. I bent over the portable record player to restart the 45.

"What are you kids doing?" Mom asked. She came into the bedroom wearing a silky pink floral formal dress. "Would you zip me, David?" She turned and pulled her hair to the side to reveal her bare back.

"Sure."

Chanel Number 5 perfume rose from her skin. I had to pull the material on both sides together to guide the zipper up, and Mom had to cinch back her shoulder blades. I managed to get the zipper fastened and closed the hook at the top of the dress.

Mom turned around and held out her arms for our approval.

"Mommy, you look like a princess!" Magdalyn proclaimed.

Mom smiled and looked over at me.

"You look beautiful," I confessed.

"Thank you. Do you think I should wear the pearls?" she asked as she held the stand up to her neck.

"That seems too much. What about your gold cross with the diamond?" I advised.

"You don't think it's too simple?"

"It's just right."

"Yes, yes, the diamond," Magdalyn encouraged, jumping up and down.

"All right, the cross it is." She cupped the strand of perils in her palm. "What were you two doing?"

"Singing," Magdalyn boasted.

"We're working on a show for New Year's Day," I explained.

"Show me," Mom encouraged.

"Yes, yes," Magdalyn pleaded while she clasped her hands together and held them under her chin.

"It's not finished," I said.

"Show me what you have," Mom said. She leaned against the door's frame.

"I don't know. Where's Caine?" I tried to deflect the attention to something else.

"He went over to Zachary's house. They're having a get-together to bring in the New Year."

"Magdalyn and I are on our own tonight?" I asked.

"Come on, Davy. Let's show her, it'll be fun." Magdalyn pulled at my arm.

"I can see if we can get Tammy to come sit with you," said Mom.

"I'm too old for a babysitter, Mom," I protested.

"Davy, let's show her our song." Magdalyn collapsed onto the floor and started pounding her hands and stomping her feet.

"You better show me, or who knows what'll happen. What's the song?" asked Mom.

"'On Top of the World,' by the Carpenters," Magdalyn announced. She released my arm, clapped her hands, and jumped up and down.

Mom clapped her hands with the pearls still cupped in one palm. "I love the Carpenters."

I threw up my hands, "All right, all right."

Magdalyn squealed with excitement.

"Get in place, and remember to wait for the vocals," I ordered.

Magdalyn rushed to her rehearsed position next to the bed while I picked up the arm of the record player and aligned it with the beginning of the 45. Static bled through the tiny speakers as the needle glided through the threading of the record. Silence. The first chords rang clearly through. Magdalyn and I turned our backs to the audience, and as the vocals started, we flipped our heads and looked over our shoulders.

"Such a feelin's coming over me." We turned completely around, facing the intended audience. "There is wonder in most everything I see." We flashed an opened hand, palm outward, arching from our heart to over our head. "Not a cloud in the sky." We looked up and pointed to the sky, "Got the sun in my eyes," pointed to our eyes. I glanced over to Magdalyn and saw her beaming. "And I won't be surprised if it's a dream," this called for another flair of spirit fingers over our heads.

"Honey, what tie do you think I…" Dad came in from the bathroom and froze with two ties dangling from each outstretched hand.

I stopped in mid choreography, arms extended above my head, fingers wiggling, and my best musical theater smile plastered on my face.

"What's this?" he asked, staring at me.

"We're performing," explained Magdalyn as she demonstrated a high kick.

"Performing?" he asked as if he hadn't heard correctly. He never broke the glare at me.

I lowered my arms and bent to turn off the record.

"They're just having fun, Caleb," Mother said.

"Doing all that cheery queer stuff?" He imitated the motions I was performing, with his hands over his head and shaking the ties he was holding on to. "I think you might want to add a little more of this." He placed his hands on his hips and shook them back and forth.

"Stop it," Mom laughed.

Magdalyn said, "That's not part of the dance, you silly bones."

"Maybe it should be." He glared at me again.

"But it's not," Magdalyn corrected.

I sank down on the side of the bed, arms folded against my chest, and focused on my dingy socks.

"Do it again, and show me," he said with a sweet affectation to his voice. Mom playfully slapped his shoulder. "No, I'm serious, I want to see it," he demanded.

"Okay, yeah," Magdalyn jumped with elation and turned to me. "Let's do it."

"You can do it, I'll sit this one out," I said.

"No, you have to do it too," Magdalyn pleaded as she pulled on my arm to stand up.

"Not this time, you go ahead," I tried to be polite.

"Please!" she whined.

Dad chuckled, "What's wrong, stage fright?"

"Maybe later," Mom interjected. "Caleb, we must be getting out of here. We're going to be late." I wasn't sure if she was really worried about the time or if she thought this was a way to save me from any further humiliation. Whichever the underlying reason, I was grateful.

"We'll keep practicing and show you when you get home." Magdalyn pirouetted like a ballerina.

"You do that, my precious baby girl," Dad said. He bent down and wrapped his arms around her and kissed her reddened cheeks. He swept her up into his arms and swung her out the door.

Mom looked at me for a moment and then smiled. "How do I really look?" she asked.

"Stunning," I said. I tried to smile.

"Thank you," she whispered. She leaned in and kissed my cheek.

"There's nothing so pretty as my Magdalyn in the Morning…" Dad sang from deep within the living room in his best Bing Crosby croon.

"It's not morning, you silly bones," I heard Magdalyn retort.

"There's nothing so pretty as my Magdalyn anytime of the day."

Mom rolled her eyes and exhaled heavily. "Even before the accident, he doted on her, but now it's all the time. I don't know how much more of it I can take." She turned on her heels and walked down the hall, passing the entry to the living room. "We're going to be late," she said as she continued toward the back door. "David?" she called as she reached for the door's handle.

I rushed to the kitchen. I got a glimpse of Dad and Magdalyn dancing in the living room.

"The Paragon's telephone number is on the notepad by the telephone. Call if you need us," she instructed.

"Yes, ma'am," I said.

"Let's go, we're going to be late," she bellowed, accentuating each word.

"I'm coming," said Dad. "I don't see why we have to go to some shindig to celebrate the New Year when we could simply stay here and celebrate." He stalked into the kitchen, tying his tie.

"Because I want to go out," Mom said. "And besides, you promised me."

"It's such a waste of time," Dad continued to complain.

"Here we go again, every time we're invited somewhere, I get my hopes up and then you crash them. I want to go to the party. I'm going to go with or without you. You're not going to ruin this night for me because you want to stay home." She pulled open the door and exited, slamming it in its hinges.

"I better go, just to keep peace. See what you have to look forward to when you get married?" He shared this for my benefit and went out the door.

"Are they fighting again?" Magdalyn peered around the doorway to the kitchen.

"No, no, they're excited about getting out on their own. So what do you want to do tonight?"

"Let's watch the ball fall." Magdalyn pirouetted and bowed.

"Okay, do we want to watch a movie or something before the ball falls?" I asked.

"Yeah, and have popcorn and ice cream and soda pop." She continued to dance into the kitchen.

"Sounds good to me. You get the soda out of the refrigerator, and I'll start the popcorn," I suggested.

Magdalyn flung open the refrigerator door and immediately asked, "Where's the soda?"

"On the bottom shelf," I replied. I opened the cupboard and rummaged through the various flavors of cake mixes and Jell-O boxes to reach the Orville Redenbacher microwavable buttered popcorn.

"Root beer, Coke, orange, or diet?" Magdalyn asked. She hung on to the door as it swung.

"I'll have a diet," I replied. I pulled down the red box with Orville smiling on the front.

"I think I'll have root beer." She pulled out the cans and placed them on the kitchen counter, flung closed the refrigerator door, and climbed up on a stool.

"Good choice," I said, opening the box and pulling out an envelope of kernels. I unfolded it, placed it in the microwave, and turned the dial to set the time. "Keep your ears peeled, and listen when the kernels stop popping," I suggested.

"I always do," she replied.

"I know you do."

I sat on the stool next to Magdalyn and pulled the tab to her root beer. "Do you want a glass?"

"No." She adopted a sophisticated attitude and swiveled back and forth on the stool. "I think I'll drink it out of the can, like Daddy does."

The popcorn started exploding inside the microwave, staccato at first and then rapid machine gun fire.

"This is fun, isn't it?"

"Yes." Her eyes squinted, and she turned her head slightly. "I think the popcorn is done."

I glanced over to the microwave. "But there's still some time."

"Believe me. I know when the popcorn's done. It's not popping anymore, if you're not careful, you'll burn it."

"All right, all right." I pressed the microwave's lever, and the door popped open, allowing a buttery odor to escape the confined metal box.

"Be careful, it's going to be hot," Magdalyn advised.

I didn't hear her in time, and I pulled the swollen bag out scorching my fingers, "Oh, shit!" I shook my hand in the air and then licked my fingers.

"I warned you, and you didn't listen," she commented. "And you said a bad word."

"Don't tell on me," I begged.

"I'll think about it." She took on a superior air, as if she had to contemplate the possibilities of retaining a secret or telling someone.

I carefully opened the popcorn bag. A white cloud of steam rolled out. I poured the contents into a big red bowl and placed it in front of Magdalyn.

She grabbed a handful and guided it to her mouth. "Oh, so buttery," she said through a mouthful.

Someone knocked on a window. We both looked at each other and then toward the kitchen window, which was black with night.

There it was again, a rapping against glass. We both looked toward the dining room windows, and Magdalyn and I let out a horrific scream, and I wrapped my arms around Magdalyn. There in the middle window were two scary faces, glowing from a flashlight beaming up grossly accentuating the chin, nostrils, cheekbones, and hollowing out the eye sockets.

"We've come to get you," one of the faces said with a deep demonic voice.

Magdalyn shook with fright as she yelled again in my ear. The faces disappeared as the flashlight was turned off and the window went black, reflecting the image of Magdalyn and me huddled together on the stools.

Rapid banging made the back door shake. Magdalyn screeched again, broke away from me, and fled into the back bedroom.

I watched as the doorknob turned. The door slowly creaked open a bit before being flung open, banging against the dining room chair. Squatting in the doorway were Caine and Zachary, laughing.

"You should've seen your face," Caine droned. He rolled on the floor, holding his sides from aching with laughter.

I just sat there, not sure if I should get mad or laugh myself. I think I peed myself a little.

Zachary Spence stood tall in the door frame, face turning red from trying not to laugh. His preference for dark ripped T-shirts, tight straight-legged jeans, ratty black knitted toboggan hat, and a long, black wool overcoat was his signature look. He stood there, just nodding his head like a toy dog on the dashboard of a car, bobbing up and down and side to side.

Caine pulled himself off the floor and pounded the kitchen countertop, causing me to jump a bit, "Did you shit your pants?"

"No," I said, feeling a surge of anger.

"I bet you did." He glanced over to Zachary. "Looks like he shit himself, don't it?"

Zachary just nodded his head.

"You scared the crap out of Magdalyn."

"Lighten up, buttercup, we was only joking." Caine started down the hall. "Maggie, where are you?" He said in a creepy Jack Nicolson voice from *The Shining*.

"Check the closet in the bedroom, in the back," I called after him.

Caine called as he entered the room, "Magdalyn it's only me. Where are you?"

"Go away," her muffled voice sounded.

I looked over at Zachary, who was still standing in the doorway. "You can come in if you want." I felt like I was inviting a vampire into the house.

Zachary grinned and lowered his head shyly. He stepped into the room and closed the door.

"You can sit down. Do you want a soda and some popcorn?" I asked.

He simply nodded his head and moseyed to the empty stool next to me. As he lifted and swung his leg to position his thin butt on the stool, his knee brushed my thigh. As he settled, he pressed his thigh against mine again and left it there. I felt the urge to move, but something ruled against it. I allowed his thigh to rest against mine. I even added a bit of resistance. He put more pressure as he reached for the popcorn.

"Magdalyn, where are you?" Caine's voice rang.

"Coke," Zachary softly mumbled.

"What?" I automatically leaned in toward him, getting a strong whiff of his musk, cigarettes, and a sweet herbal scent—which made me wonder if they had been smoking weed in the silo.

He nodded his head and repeated, "Coke."

"Oh, you want a Coke to drink."

He grinned sheepishly as a strand of brown hair escaped from behind his ear and cascaded over his eyes. He carefully guided the hair with his long, thin fingers and anchored it again beneath the toboggan hat.

"Magdalyn, I'm getting closer. Where can you be?" Caine's announcement elicited a muffled giggle from Magdalyn.

I swiveled in the stool, causing both of my knees to brush along the length of his thigh. I opened the refrigerator and was greeted with a wave of coolness. I grabbed the Coke can and fought the temptation to hold it against my forehead and cheeks. I presented it to him.

"Thanks."

"Not a problem." I climbed back on to the stool and swiveled myself around, calculatingly, to make sure my knees skimmed along his thigh again—which they did perfectly—and he didn't seem to mind because he didn't move or even flinch.

"It's good," Zachary stated. He licked the butter off his fingers. His eyes went half-mast as his lips closed around his thumb, rolling his tongue around the perimeter of his digit, and savored it. He opened his eyes, caught me looking at him, and just smiled. "You got something on the corner of your mouth."

I attempted to wipe it away.

He pointed to his own mouth, "You missed it. It's right about here."

I tried to mirror his actions.

He giggled. "Nope, you still missed it."

"Are you sure? Where is it?"

He leaned in and studied. He licked his thumb and reached over and rubbed the corner of my mouth. Then he let his thumb graze my bottom lip. The simple touch set me on fire inside.

"Did you get it?" I asked nervously.

Zachary shook his head and said, "It won't come off."

I started to reach for my mouth, when Zachary grabbed hold of my hand. Without saying a word, he leaned in closer and pressed his lips against mine. I froze, not sure what to do. He pressed harder and parted his lips. His tongue slipped into my mouth and explored. The warmth and wetness was intoxicating, and I slide my tongue into his mouth. He pulled my head closer and opened his mouth wider. Time stopped, but his tongue and lips continued to explore. I thought I was going to explode.

"There you are, I found Magdalyn," Caine triumphantly proclaimed.

Zachary gently slid away, pulled the tab on the Coke can, and took a swig.

Magdalyn released a high-pitched screech as she came running down the hallway and shimmied herself between Zachary and myself.

"I'm going to tickle you," Caine teased. He lumbered down the hallway like a creepy old man. "Tickle, tickle, tickle."

"No!" shouted Magdalyn. She confronted Caine with a pointed finger. "You scared the shit out of me with your shenanigans."

We all hooped and hollered. Caine crumbled to the floor again. Zachary let out a giggle.

"You said a bad word," I informed her.

"I did?" she asked, all red-faced.

"Yes, you did. You said 'shit,'" I was using my parental voice.

"Now we're even," she retorted. "I won't tell if you don't."

"Deal!" I agreed, and she high-fived me. I looked at Caine, "What were you two doing? Mom said you were over at Zachary's house."

"We were, but we had to come back to get something, which reminds me—" He turned and ran upstairs.

"How could you be over at your house when you were outside our house, scaring the shit out of us?" Magdalyn directed toward Zachary.

"Maggie, that's enough of the bad language," I scolded her.

"Why's it okay for you guys to say it and not me?" she asked.

"Because we're older." I tried not to smile.

"That's not a reason, you silly bones. And besides, the only time anyone listens to me is when I say shit. Shit. Shit. Shit." She accentuated each with a stomp of her foot.

"All right," I said, "I see your point. But it's still not a good reason to go around saying *shit*."

"Ohhhhhh! You just said it. You said it, you said it." She ran up to me and pointed her finger. She quickly turned to Zachary, "You haven't answered my question."

"You better give her one, or she'll not let you off the hook, and I'll be hearing about it all night."

Zachary doggedly nodded his head, removed his knit cap, and ran a hand through his hair. "We saw your parents' car still here, so we parked behind the silo until they left."

"Was that all you were doing up at the silo?" I questioned. Zachary just gave a crooked smile and replaced the cap on his head.

Caine came running down the stairs with a game under him arm. "Got it, let's blow this popcorn stand." He patted Zachary on his shoulder and made for the back door. Zachary swiveled in the stool, grazing my thigh with his knees.

Caine opened the door, "Let's go, Zachary, before anyone misses us."

Zachary moved fluidly toward the exit, causing his coat to billow out behind him. "Thanks for the popcorn and Coke," he said as he grinned.

"Not a problem," I said.

Caine shoved him out and followed, slamming the door behind.

Magdalyn and I rushed to the dining room window and watched as they climbed into the red Torino. Caine fired the engine and spun the wheels, shooting gravel and snow into the night sky. He flew down the second drive, hardly slowing before merging onto the road, squealing the rubber against the wet cement, and disappearing behind the edge of the woods.

"Well, it's just us now." I looked at Magdalyn. I was still reeling over the kiss and how soft Zachary's lips were.

What initiated it? What did it mean, if it meant anything? Will it ever happen again? Isn't he straight? What would Caine say?

"I'd say so," Magdalyn said. "Let's get this party started."

"What?" I asked.

"Let's party." She jumped up and down, clapping her hands.

* * *

The phone screamed, jarring me awake. Magdalyn was cuddled next to me on the couch, and some Frankenstein movie played on the television. We must have fallen asleep after the New Year's ball fell in Time's Square.

The phone continued ringing.

"All right, I'm coming." I pulled myself out from under Magdalyn's head and ran to the kitchen.

"Hello?" I said.

"Is this the Matthews' residence?" asked a deep, firm voice.

"Yes." I wondered who it could be.

"Mr. Matthew?"

"No, he's not here right now."

"Is Mrs. Matthew there?" the voice asked.

"No. May I take a message?" I asked.

"To whom am I speaking?" the voice was stern.

"David, their son," I replied.

"David, when do you expect your parents back?"

"May I ask who this is?"

"Officer Remfer, from the police department."

"Is everything all right?" I started to wonder what could've happened for the police to call.

"When do you expect your parents to come home?" his voice sounded impatient.

"They're at a party, I can try calling them."

"Do that."

"What should I tell them when they ask why you called?"

"I'd rather speak to them myself."

"I have to tell them something," I insisted.

"Is Caine Matthew related to you?"

"He's my brother. Why, what's wrong?" I started to imagine him lying in a ditch, thrown from the Torino, with blood gushing from his forehead.

"He's fine. We have him here at the police station," he stated in a matter-of-fact manner.

"Why's he there?" I continued to press.

"There's been an accident."

My mind went back to the Torino, picturing it wrapped around a telephone pole.

"Is he hurt?" I was afraid to ask.

A noisy, raucous echo rang through the phone, sounds of scuffling and a woman yelling, "It ain't my fault, you have no right to treat me like this. I wasn't doing nothing."

Another voice shouted, "Just shut up and sit down."

"Simpson, I'm on the phone here!" growled Office Remfer. "Kid, what'd you say?"

"I asked if Caine was hurt."

The woman was still screaming in the background. "I'm the victim here. I called you about that scum wad, and here I am, and he's got nothing coming to him. I want a lawyer."

"Get her out of here! Place her in number 5 until she sobers up," yelled Remfer. "Your brother's fine," he said.

"Is the car totaled?" I asked.

"What?" Office Remfer asked.

"His car. Was Caine's car totaled?"

"No, this wasn't a car accident." Remfer must have pulled the phone from his ear; his voice sounded distant. "Charlie, did you file the break-in over at the O'Bryan farm? Good, could you get me a copy?"

"Please just tell me what happened," I asked.

"There's been an accidental shooting, and your brother was there. He tried to save the boy that was shot but wasn't able to," Officer Remfer's voice sounded detached.

"Who?"

"Zachary Spence. Why don't you give me the name or the number where your parents are?"

I felt numb. I didn't know how to react. Accidental shooting, and Caine was there. He tried to save the boy, Zachary Spence. I glanced over to the stool where Zachary was sitting only hours before, resting his thigh against mine. I replayed the kiss in exact detail. This couldn't be real. *What do I have to do tomorrow? I need to practice my hurdles and takeoffs. I need to do my dry-land exercises…*

"David. David," the voice echoed from the receiver.

"Yes," I mumbled.

"Give me the number where I can reach your parents?"

"Sure." I looked down at the pad and found my mother's writing. The numbers were blurry, and I wiped my eyes. "It's 898-0034. They're at the Paragon."

The phone went dead.

Before I could set the receiver back into the cradle, an icy liquid filled my veins. I walked back to the living room and sat next to a sleeping Maggie. My mind was racing with the officer's words and how it seemed impossible about Zachary. I got up and started to pace and tried to think of something else, but I needed to hear my parents' voices. When I got to the kitchen, I dialed the number, but the fear of speaking the words I heard would make it real. I disconnected. I felt overheated and nauseous, and all I wanted was to hear Mom's voice. I dialed again.

What am I going to say?

"Hello, this is the Paragon Banquet Hall. How may I help you?" a sweet voice answered.

"Hi…my parents are attending a party there, and I need to speak to them."

"What are your parents' names?"

"Matthew, Mr. and Mrs. Matthew." I was professional and to the point.

"Wait just a minute. They're getting ready to leave."

I heard the receptionist call them over.

"Hello?" It was Mom, her voice was shaky and nervous.

"Mom?"

"David, is everything all right?"

"Yes, no, I don't know. The police just called, an officer…"

"Officer Remfer. I just spoke to him."

"So it's true?"

"What?"

"About Zach?"

"It seems so." There was silence on the phone.

My stomach dropped. "Oh, God," my voice cracked.

"Stop it. I need to pull it together. You can't fall apart now. I've to go. We're heading to the police station. Take care of Maggie." The phone disconnected.

"I will."

"Why are the police calling?" Magdalyn asked. She leaned against the refrigerator and rubbed her sleepy eyes.

"Some message for Mom and Dad," I said.

"Is everything all right?" she asked.

"I think so. We'll have to ask Mom and Dad when they get home."

"What time's it?" She yawned.

"It's late."

"I'm tired." She rubbed her eyes.

"Let's go watch some television and wait for them." I took hold of her shoulders and steered her back into the living room as I swallowed the lump forming in my throat.

She climbed up on the couch and put her head down on the pillow. She was asleep in no time. I wished I were able to that.

* * *

What was that?

A muffled squeaking, sounding something like a mouse in pain, woke me up.

It stopped. I must have imagined it. No, there it was again.

Heaving sobs were coming from Caine's room. I flung my legs over the side of the bed and crept to the doorless frame that separated our rooms.

The pale light from the window revealed him in a fetal position, wrapped in his blankets, and his pillow over his head.

"Caine?" I whispered. His body stiffened and the sobbing stopped. "Caine, you okay?"

"I'm fine," he retorted from beneath the pillow.

"You don't sound fine."

He pulled the pillow from his head and glared at me, the light from the early morning revealed his swollen eyes. "What do you think?"

"Want to talk about it?"

"What's there to talk about?" He sat with his back against the wall and cradled the pillow against his chest. I just stood there. "What?" he barked at me.

"I'm sorry," was all I could say.

"For what?" His defensiveness came across cold and harsh.

"For what you went through." I felt a tear slip from my eye close to the door frame. I hoped that he didn't notice.

"No big deal." He slid back under the covers, pulling them high over her shoulders, with his back toward me.

"If there's anything I can do…"

"No, there's nothing you or anyone can do but leave me alone."

"All right." I nodded and went back to my bed.

"Dave?" Caine called.

I froze with one knee on the mattress, "Yep?"

"Could you come here?" His voice was weak.

"Are you sure?"

"Yeah."

I walked back and peeked around the door frame. He looked like a scared little boy, not the seventeen-year-old who thought he was a grown man and knew everything.

The growing glow of the early morning was sneaking in through the windows, streaming the floor with blue ribbons.

"Can you sit with me?"

"Of course." I stepped though the pools of blue lights and sat on the edge of the bed.

No one said anything.

Without thinking, I wrapped my arms around his head and pulled him into my chest. He allowed it, which amazed me. I felt him shake as if he was about to erupt, and then he did—heaving long sobs of agony and pain. I pulled him tighter to me to keep myself from crying. He wrapped his arms around my shoulders and squeezed.

He suddenly pulled away. "I'm sorry." He wiped his eyes with the back of his fist. "This is stupid. It's so stupid."

"Do you want to tell me about it?" I asked.

"I don't know. I do, and then I don't," he hesitantly said.

"Just tell me what you want to tell, and if you don't want to talk about something, then don't." I was looking at the lines in my palms, trying to remember what Dad said about how all the lines create the illusion of the whole hand.

"You won't make fun of me?"

I shook my head.

"You won't tell anybody?" He grabbed my hand and squeezed it. "Promise me, you'll not tell anybody…ever! There are things I haven't told people about tonight." His eyes darkened to almost black as he pleaded with me.

I pulled my hand away and rubbed it against my chest, "I promise."

He sat there in silence and then shifted over to the far side of the bed. He patted the open area indicating for me to sit next to him.

Caine started speaking quickly and in a low tone, as if he didn't he'd never get it all out. "As you know, Zachary and I were back here before the party. We were going to meet up with some girls but remembered they were away for the holidays. So we came back here and parked the Torino behind the silo so that Mom and Dad wouldn't see us. And Zachary had some…" He lifted his hand with his forefinger and thumb pinched together to his lips and inhaled.

"I knew it." I slapped my thighs with my hands.

"I didn't want Mom or Dad to know. So we waited until they left and then came to get the game," he explained.

I pictured Zachary sitting on the stool, pressing his thigh against mine, kissing my lips, and drinking the soda. He was stoned.

"We went back to Mike Watson's house where we were going to have the party," Caine continued.

I glanced over at him. "I thought the party was at Zachary's house."

"It was going to be, but his mom decided not to go out so we switched it to Mike's. Anyway, Mike and Steve Carson were already on their second six-pack when we got there. We all grabbed a beer and went up to Mike's bedroom. His room was such a mess that we decided to play in the hallway. Zachary and I were setting up the game while Mike disappeared. I was situated in front of Mike's bedroom door, while Zachary was across from me in front of the bathroom. Steve was next to me.

"Then we heard Mike behind me. 'Hey, guys, look at this,' he said. He was showing off his new shotgun he got for Christmas. He was proud of it, lifting it up and looking through the scope. 'Put that thing away,' Steve said. 'Want to hurt someone?' Mike laughed and said, 'It's not loaded, stupid ass. You think I'd have a loaded gun in the house?'"

Caine stopped a moment and looked toward the glowing window.

He continued, "Steve stood up and went to Mike to convince him to put the gun away, but Mike talked him into looking through the scope. 'Wow, that's powerful. What's the accuracy?' 'All right, that's enough,' Mike said. 'Wait a minute, I want to check something,' Steve deflected. 'Come on now, hand it over.' Mike was getting impatient. I sat up and turned to them because they were acting like kindergartners. They both were pulling and tugging at the shotgun. And before I knew it, a white light flashed, and a stream of air brushed past my ear, followed by a wet sucking sound and a dull thud as something hit the floor." Caine's eyes widened in terror.

"It was like a movie in slow motion, as I turned and saw Zachary lying facedown on top of the Battleship game. He wasn't moving, yet there was this horrible wheezing sound. I rolled Zachary over and there was all this blood gushing out of his chest, and he had this slight smile on his face." Caine's hands started shaking, and tears streamed from his eyes. "I tried. I did everything I knew how. I couldn't stop the bleeding, and there were so many holes where the buckshots entered." His shaking became more like a rocking as he stared at his hands. "Blood everywhere. On everything. I tried CPR, but every time I did compressions, his chest oozed more blood, and when I gave him mouth-to-mouth, I knew he wasn't getting any air. But I kept trying. I was still trying when the paramedics arrived. I remember someone grabbed my shoulders and said, 'That's all, buddy, you did all you could, let us take over.'"

He looked at me. "I tried."

"I know you did."

His lower lip started quivering. "Hold my hand." I took his wet palm in mine, and I didn't mind. I wasn't going to let go until he told me to. "But he was already gone. I knew it. I saw him die."

"It wasn't your fault."

"No, I mean I saw…"

"What?"

He rubbed his face. "You won't believe me."

"Just tell me."

"No. I was hallucinating. I had to be." He rubbed his eyes.

"What is it? I want to know."

"I saw this…he had this thread…there was this golden thread…" He stopped and looked at me. "You can't tell anyone about this."

"I swear!" I promised.

"I saw this thread, a gold thread coming out of Zach's chest." Caine started pounded on his chest. "It was coming out of his chest and travel upward to the ceiling. In the corner…" Caine looked up at the ceiling and pointed with his finger. Zach was floating there." He paused as if he could see it again, then quickly, he sunk down into the bed. "This is fucking ridiculous."

"No, it's not." I reached and placed my hand on his shoulder.

He shrugged it off. "Leave me alone. I want to be left alone."

"Come on."

"Come on, nothing. I must be fucking crazy."

"No, you are not."

"How can you be so sure?" He sat up, staring at me. "You weren't there. You didn't see what I saw, or thought I saw."

"So you saw Zachary in the corner of the ceiling. That's a cool thing."

Caine looked at me, his mouth was partially opened. "Are you kidding me?"

"No." I tried to make my voice steady. "I believe you saw him."

"Are you fucking crazy?"

"Maybe."

Caine chuckled and nodded his head. "You are a bit crazy."

"So tell me what you saw."

He paused. "You can't tell anyone."

"I know."

"I saw Zach, floating there. He had this big smile, watching the scene below. I knew. I knew then that it was too late. But I didn't feel so bad because he seemed happy. He was glowing, as different colors flashed out across the room. It was beautiful." He looked at me with a pained expression, and the blue morning light added to the eeriness of the moment. "Then I realized that I'd never see him again." Caine shimmied himself down and placed his head on his pillow. "Will you stay with me?"

"Sure." I lowered myself next to him.

He searched for my hand, wrapping his fingers securely around mine. He leaned over and kissed me on the cheek. "Thanks for being my brother." He laid his head on my chest, and I stroked his hair until he fell asleep.

11 CHAPTER

Sandefjord Natatorium, Tønsberg, Norway, July 1979—Introduction of Finalists

I stared at my palms, trying to remember what Dad said about the lines in the hand. The lines are never straight, and they should not always connect, leaving the viewer to subconsciously make the connections.

"David?" Mike Drake, the AP photographer from England, pointed his camera at me.

I forced a smile.

The shutter clicked several times. "Thanks, and good luck." Mike quickly moved toward the Russians to capture their images for posterity.

"Ladies and gentlemen," a voice filled the stadium up to the rafters. "Welcome to the finals of the men's 1979 three-meter Springboard World Diving Championships."

I felt someone grab my elbow and guide me to my feet.

"David, why aren't you answering me?"

"What?" I focused on the stadium filled with thousands of people laughing, chattering, and taking pictures.

"David!" Dr. Don grabbed my jaw and forced me to look at him. "You have to focus! Now!" he said harshly.

"Yes, sir." I was distracted as thousands of thoughts rushed through my mind, like trying to catch butterflies without a net.

Dr. Don's stern eyes glared at me. "You've got to listen and do what I tell you."

Television cameras were on the five and seven-and-half-meter towers, aiming at the three-meter springboards.

"Are you paying attention?" Dr. Don desperately placed his hands on both sides of my face.

"Yes, sir," I replied.

"I want you to come to me before and after each dive for instructions." I felt his hands rapidly slap both of my cheeks. "Wake up!"

I backed away, covering my face. "I'm awake."

"I got it, Coach." Mark put his arm around my shoulders and led me away. "We've got to get lined up for the introduction."

"What?" I asked.

"They introduce the finalists to the audience after we march in. It's all part of the showbiz." Mark guided me through the mayhem of the competition's preparations of milling divers, coaches, judges, reporters, and photographers.

We were in slow motion as everything else sped around us. The blurring of colors made me dizzy, causing my stomach to flip and churn. I was going to vomit.

Mark said, "It's going to be all right. Just do what I do."

"Dive well, boys," someone said.

"Thanks," replied Mark.

"Mark, may I get a picture of you and David?" someone asked.

"Sure." Mark guided my chin toward the camera. "Smile, David." He leaned his head against mine for the pose.

"Thanks."

"No problem," responded Mark. He started leading me again.

Megan and Patti ran up and wrapped their arms around both of us.

"Group hug," shouted Patti.

Megan said, "Make us proud, boys."

"We will," said Mark. He broke the hug and escorted me into a hallway where all the finalists were gathering.

"Dive well." Giovanni placed his hand on my shoulder.

I wanted to hug him, but I couldn't move, so I just nodded.

"Dude, you okay?" Andy stopped us.

"He's fine," Mark replied.

"You look like you're going to hurl any minute," said Andy. "You're white as a ghost!"

"Andy, stop it. He's fine," stated Mark.

Mark placed me at the end of the line next to where Norway's Hasse Havdvent. I glanced back at Giovanni, who winked at me.

Mark said, "We'll walk into the arena in a line, all you have to do is follow Hasse. We walk in reverse order in which we finished in the prelims." He gently wrapped his hands behind my neck and rested his forehead on mine. "You'll be fine, just remember to breathe."

This was all happening too fast. I needed one more day, one more day to find my balance and feet again. A vice was crushing my lungs, keeping me from getting a deep breath. My hands trembled, and I wasn't able to control them. If my stomach twisted one more time, I knew I was going to hurl.

The fanfare started.

"Here we go." Mark left me behind Hasse. "Wave and smile, that's all you have to do, and breathe."

The line weaved through the hallway, along the perimeter of the fifty-meter swimming pool, and toward the diving well. The line came to rest on the median between the two pools.

The announcer's voice boomed over the speakers, "Ladies and gentlemen, your finalists for this morning's competition—from the United States, qualifying in twelfth place, Andrew Kirkland."

I looked down the line. Andy stepped forward and waved to the crowd.

My heart pounded like a drum. I was numb and felt like I was underwater. I didn't hear the announcement of the next few divers.

"From Italy, Giovanni Pizzini."

I applauded and watched him wave to the crowd.

"He is currently in third place, from the United States of America, the current defending world champion and three-time US National champion, Mark Bradley."

The arena exploded with admiration.

"Currently in second place, your two-time Norwegian national champion…" The crowd erupted, making it difficult to hear Hasse Havdvent's name. It didn't keep him from waving eagerly and blowing kisses to people in the stadium.

"And now, currently in first place and making his first appearance at the World Games, from the United States of America, David Matthew."

I stepped forward, waved to the crowd, and stepped back in line.

"These are your finalists for the gold medal in springboard diving." The fanfare started again.

Hasse guided me back the way we entered.

"Let's go. Let's go," shouted Jack. "Andy, you're up first, give me your warm-up." Andy quickly removed his warm-up and rushed to the three-meter.

"David, make sure you're stretched out. You must be ready to dive when they announce Giovanni," explained Jack in my ear.

I removed my warm-up and did some side stretches.

Patti wrapped her arms around my waist and whispered in my ear, "You can do this. I know you can. Just one dive at a time."

"Ladies and gentlemen, the finalists will perform six optional dives, and the scores will be added to the preliminary scores. The first diver from the United States of America is Andrew Kirkland. He will be performing an inward two-and-one-half somersault in the tuck position."

Andy adjusted the fulcrum and stood at attention until the whistle. He walked down the plank and pivoted on his toes. He lifted his arms, took a moment, and compressed the board downward.

I wasn't able to keep focused. My mind worried about my first dive—a dive I had just learned a few days before nationals.

* * *

I dried my shins with my chamois, more a superstitious habit than a necessity, and besides, all the great divers did it. Tossing the knotted cloth down to the edge of the pool, I located my starting mark, positioned myself, stood at attention, and took a deep breath.

"Let's go, David, we don't have all night," called Trevor.

I glanced down to where Trevor was standing on the pool deck with his hand cupping his forehead like a visor. Something inside me wanted to please him, to make him proud of me. If only I was able to be like Icarus, sprouting wings to fly high enough into the air, so that I could perform the needed revolutions and slice the water like an arrow. But unlike Icarus, I didn't want to fly so high that the heat from the lights on the ceiling melted the wax that held my feathers together.

With a moment of uncertainty, I hollered, "Can you call me out?"

"Of course," Trevor reassured.

"Were my lead-ups good enough?"

"I wouldn't let you up there if they weren't," he encouraged. I watched as he shifted from one foot to the other. "Do it just like on the low board, take your time and get a high hurdle, get your arms through narrow, keep your head in line, and don't pull with your chest. Look for your spot twice, kick your toes toward the ceiling, and reach for the bottom of the pool with your hands. Keep your stomach tight, and don't arch your back. You'll be fine."

"Go for it, Davy," echoed Jake Wilde, the captain of the swim team, from the far end of the pool. He stood there dripping wet, swimming goggles donning his head like a crown, and a towel draped over his left shoulder like a toga. "Ya got this, Monster!"

I focused on the end of the metal plank. I visualized the perfect dive, walked down the springboard, propelled myself skyward, and drew my knees tightly toward my chest. I spun through the air. I saw the water flash by twice. I kicked my feet toward the lights, reached my arms over my head, and stretched for the bottom of the pool. The water swallowed me, and I torpedoed toward the bottom. I pushed off the pool's tile flooring and sped toward the surface, where I was greeted with a deafening screech from Jake. He was jumping and swinging his towel over his head like a lasso. Trevor stood there with a huge, crooked smile. He opened his hands to the heavens and cocked his head to the side.

"Way to go, Monster," shouted Jake. "It looked like a ten to me." He waved and exited to the locker room.

I swam to the edge of the pool where Trevor stood. As I pulled myself out, he pulled me into his body. His chest rumbled as he said, "I'm so proud of you." He squeezed me tighter in his bear hug.

I was intoxicated. I was actually getting high on his adulation. I didn't want him to unclasp his arms even though he was crushing my ribs. But I wanted to be angry with him. I didn't want to forget about the incident at Ohio State. I wanted him to remember it too. What did it mean? Will we ever talk about it, or do I have to continue to pretend it never happened?

* * *

I adjusted the fulcrum and took my position on the metal plank. I tried breathing deeply while the scores were being read for Hasse. The crowd was going crazy, and it seemed to be a long time before they quieted.

"David Matthew from the USA will be performing a reverse two-and-one-half somersault in the tuck position." The whistle blew.

My heart pounded because of having only performed this dive in one competition. *What happens if I smack like I did in practice?* I felt this pressure to make Dr. Don proud. I felt like I needed to make the USA proud of me. I felt like I needed to prove that I belonged here.

"You got this, David!" shouted Patti from the sidelines.

I looked over at her encouraging face.

Taking my starting position was the last thing I remembered. My muscle memory took over as I walked down the board, spun in the air, entered the water, and pushed off the bottom of the pool.

I broke the water's surface to a deafening thunder of applause. Patti was jumping and clapping. I swam to the side, pulled myself out, glanced at the scoreboard, and waited.

"Poing?" asked the announcer. "8.5, 8.5, 8.0, 7.5, 8.0, 9.0, 9.0."

The scoreboard revealed the places. The top 3 were the same, with me leading by a large margin; Hasse, second; and Mark, only five points behind in third. The really big change was Andy moving up to eighth place.

I walked over to Dr. Don.

"Good, nice reach. That's the way to nail the entry. I want you to keep this up." He patted me on the back.

Patti ran up with a towel held out and wrapped me in it. "That was awesome."

"Five more to go!" was all that I could say.

I sat and started to think about the next dive, but my mind was uncooperative. My head started filling with images that had nothing to do with diving.

Aulden High School, Aulden, Ohio, 1979

The afternoon's sun bled through the windows and spilled onto my desk. The final bell for the day was about to ring. It seemed that exactly at this time every day, Mr. Happy came alive. It'd start out as a warm sensation, which quickly developed into an uncontrollable, full, and painful erection. Mr. Happy had a mind of its own and started pushing hard against the cotton lining of my underwear.

Why did I have to wear these jeans today?

Ms. Winthrop lectured, "In the spring of 331 BC, near the City of Nineveh, Alexander the Great marched into Mesopotamia. It was here that Alexander and his army met up with Darius, again. Both were ready for the last stand." Ms. Winthrop pushed her turquoise-colored bifocals up on the bridge of her thin nose. The excitement of retelling the Hellenic-period battle oozed from every pore, causing a glow to her angular face.

She clutched one hand on the history textbook like a Bible. "Alexander's tactical genius and stratagem was too much for Darius and the Persians. The Persian pride was broken, and Darius ran away, again, leaving his army behind to save his own…"

"Ass," interrupted Jake Wilde, the captain of the swimming team.

Everyone broke up with laughter and hoots.

"All right, all right," Ms. Winthrop held up her hand to discourage any further outbursts. "Victory was Alexander's, and he was hailed as king and liberator."

A liberator—that was what I needed. The flow of blood southward was backed up because of the position I was in. Usually, if I adjusted my hips slightly back in the chair, Mr. Happy would find a way to adjust around and move to a more comfortable position. But it seemed to be lodged against the seam of my zipper and felt like it was going to snap in two.

Ms. Winthrop crossed to her desk and sat on the corner. "Now, this city was filled with palaces and a royal treasury that held great wealth. This ended Alexander's financial troubles."

The pressure I was feeling was monstrous, if only I could give Mr. Happy enough room, but my jeans were too tight. I slid my hips forward to see if that would help. *No!* I quickly retracted. That position tightened the crotch's denim. I shifted my hips back in the wooden chair. The further I wiggled my hips back and rested my arms on the desk, rounding my back as much as possible, the more relief I found.

The bell rang, setting off every student in the room. I chose to remain in place until everyone had exited.

"Another boner, Matthew?" teased Jake. He slapped me on the back. "You're killing me, man. You're such a monster." He stepped up next to Liz Fields and kissed her on the mouth and said, "Matthew's sporting another woody."

"Stop it." Liz hit Jake's chest, laced her other arm around his back, and hooked her thumb into his back belt loop.

"Don't be late for practice, you monster," Jake said as he and Liz headed for the exit.

"Hey, everyone, listen up," called Ms. Winthrop over the clamor and bustle. "Have your projects ready for tomorrow. Remember, it can be a short story, a poem, or an essay about Alexander."

Moans and groans erupted from the exiting crowd.

"Do we have to?" questioned April. She gathered her books and pressed them against her cheerleading sweater.

"Yes, you have to," Ms. Winthrop responded.

April stopped in front of Ms. Winthrop's desk, shaking her head so her ponytail bounced. "Ms. Winthrop, I just don't understand the assignment."

Ms. Winthrop leaned back on her desk supported by both hands, "What's there to get?"

"I just don't understand why it's so important to write a paper on this Alex guy who died like ten thousand years ago and no one really cares about anymore."

"It's important because it's an assignment that you'll be graded on," explained Ms. Winthrop.

Relief. Mr. Happy went back to sleep. I stacked my books and saw Christie still sitting at her desk, watching April's display of procrastination.

"But it isn't fair," April continued. "We had sectionals last week, and I forgot to take my book home over the weekend." April twirled a strand of hair in front of her left ear.

"I'm sorry, life isn't fair. The deadline's tomorrow."

April huffed and spun out of the room.

"David, may I have a word with you?" Ms. Winthrop asked as she maneuvered herself behind her desk to sit.

"Sure." I watched Christi gather her books and exit the room. I went to Ms. Winthrop's desk.

She removed her bifocals. "I wanted to talk to you about the Alexander project."

"I won't be here tomorrow. I'm leaving for a meet in the morning, and I didn't want it to be late, so I turned it in yesterday."

"I realized that. Your poem about Alexander and Hephaestion took a very interesting and original look at their relationship." She shuffled some papers and pulled mine out. She flipped the cover page. "I especially liked, 'Orange-fire fingers interweave the eastern sky / While the phantom of darkness slinks / For shelter in the west,' and…" she quickly turned to the final page, "'Speeding through the damp morning hour / I pause enough to look back / I see a gold thread trailing behind / Wrapping itself around Alexander / And attaching to my fevered body / Like a spiderweb entrapping its meal / Alexander and I are finally one.' What made you think about writing from Hephaestion's point of view?"

"I don't really know. I had this dream, and it felt so real," I explained.

"Well, whatever it took, I'm pleased by it. I was hoping to have your permission to enter it into the Scholastics Writing Contest. Would you mind?" she asked.

"Do you think it's good enough?" I asked.

"I wouldn't ask if it wasn't." She replaced her bifocals. "What do you think?"

"Sure, I guess."

"Good. I'm glad."

"Thank you, Ms. Winthrop."

"Thank you for writing it, David."

A rush of approval filled my head, and excitement rushed through my veins. I couldn't wait to get to the pool to practice.

"May I be excused, Ms. Winthrop?" I asked.

She smiled and said, "You may."

"Christi?" My palms were sweaty, and my mouth was extremely dry as I stopped next to her gathering books from her locker.

"Hi, Dave," she said.

My heart raced because she knew my name. *Just say what you have practiced.* "The dance is next week, and I was wondering if you're going."

"I don't think so," she said.

"Why not?"

She closed her locker door, rubbed her swollen belly, and gave me a "what do you think?" look.

I nodded with understanding. "Well, I was thinking." The nerves strangled my voice, causing me to speak two octaves higher and crack.

Christi chuckled.

"Iwouldlikeitifyouwouldattendthedancewithme," I said as quickly as I could.

Her eyes widened. "What?"

"Do you want to go with me? To the dance, I mean."

"That's what I thought you said." Her eyes filled with pain. "Like this?"

"I don't care. You're as beautiful as ever."

I felt my face burn. It didn't seem to be a problem for me about her condition or the fact that no one knew who the father was. What was important to me was that I liked her and wanted her not to listen to the rumors flying around school. It would also help with my struggle against the gay rumors. I wasn't sure what the hell I was or wasn't, but I knew that this could do some damage control. Besides, I loved to dance.

"You're so sweet." She touched my cheek. "That's the sweetest thing anyone has said to me since all this happened."

"We'd have fun," I stammered.

"I don't know, David. Let me think about it," she said.

"Great. Good. That'd be terrific."

"Thanks, David." Christi started for the exit without looking back.

I walked in the opposite direction, past the posters announcing the dance, graduation, and yearbook orders. I glanced at the trophy case that was crammed with past football successes and made my way to the back entrance that led to the awaiting buses.

As I pushed open the back door, I saw three guys huddled and smoking by the garbage bins.

"Hey, is that you, Matthew?" the one in the ball cap asked.

"Looks like it," said another.

I should've gone out the front door. I walked past them without saying a word.

"What's wrong, too good to talk to us?" said the guy wearing the ball cap.

I kept walking with my eyes fixed on the buses lined up in the semicircle driveway.

A hand grabbed my shoulder and forced me around.

"I'm fucking talking to you."

I realized that it was Calvin Landis, who was kicked off the football team for smoking marijuana, and two of his friends.

"I'm late for the bus." I shrugged his hand off my shoulder.

"I'm sure the bus will wait for the world-class diving pansy," Calvin stated. The other boys laughed.

"I've got to go." I backed away.

"When I say you can go." Peter and Stan got behind me. One knocked my books out of my hand, while the other pinned my arms.

"Let go!" I shouted.

"We will…when we're done." Calvin nodded, and one of the boys kicked me behind the knees so my legs collapsed and I fell to the ground. "Look, boys, the queer's on his knees."

"Why are you doing this?" I felt gravel poking my kneecaps.

"Just want to know if it's true, all the rumors I keep hearing." Calvin stepped in front of me, pressing his crotch close to my face.

I turned my head away.

"Now, be a good boy." He grabbed my ears and forced his crotch against my face. "I think he likes it, boys." He rubbed his crotch hard, slicing my lip with his zipper.

"Stop it!" I shouted. The buses engines drowned out my plea.

"Get him up."

Peter and Stan grabbed each arm and pulled me up.

"Aw, looky, his lip is bleeding." Calvin rubbed my lip and shoved his blood-covered thumb into my mouth. "That's right, suck that thumb."

I pulled my head away and clamped my mouth shut.

"What's wrong, am I being too aggressive?" whispered Calvin in my ear, "Do I need to say pretty things first?" causing the other boys to laugh. "I heard you've been checking out my ass. Is that true?"

I shook my head.

"I can't hear you," Calvin stated.

"No!"

"What's wrong with my ass? It's a good ass." He turned and shook his hips. "I heard you wanted to touch it. Do you want to touch it?"

"No."

"That's not what I've heard. Go ahead and touch it. You're allowed."

"I don't want to." I heard the buses' gears shift and start pulling out of the driveway.

"I know you do." Calvin nodded, and Peter forced my hand on Calvin's butt. "Like it, don't you? Nice and firm, huh?"

"Please stop." I pulled my hand away but couldn't stop the tears from collecting in my eyes.

Calvin turned and pressed his nose against mine. "That's going to be the only time you ever get to touch my ass."

I felt his fist, like a hammer, plummet into my stomach, forcing all the air out. I crumpled over, while the other two supported me.

Calvin grabbed my shirt and flung me into the metal garbage bin. I felt the connection of his knuckles against my jawbone and was quickly transported into a darkened world.

* * *

"David." Someone lifted my head. "Oh, shit. Are you all right?"

I didn't know who was talking. I tried to open my eyes, but one was swollen.

"Liz, we need some help over here!" the voice called. "David, what happened?"

"What? What are you talking about?" I pulled myself into a sitting position with my back against the garbage bin.

"I didn't see you get on the bus. I was going to ask if you wanted a ride to practice."

"Jake? Is that you?"

"Yes, buddy, it's me."

"What's going on?" said Liz as she came rushing up. "Oh my god!"

"We need some help. Get a teacher or the principal," instructed Jake.

"No, don't," I shouted. "There's no need to." I tried to stand, but my head spun, my jaw ached, and my abdomen couldn't support me. I fell, and Jake caught me.

"Stay seated," Jake instructed. "Who did this?"

"I must've fallen or tripped or something…" I held my head in my hands. "It was an accident."

"No one falls like this." Jake took a towel out of my bag and placed it against my bleeding lip.

I pushed the towel away. "I don't want any problems. I'll be all right." I gathered my books and slowly stood with the assistance of the garbage bin.

"Why are you protecting the person who did this?" asked Jake.

"Why do you care?" I asked.

"Because I'm your friend," he said.

I stopped and looked at him. "You are?" He nodded. "But you make fun of me all the time."

"I'm only teasing, that's just my way."

I started shaking. "I'm scared, Jake. I'm really scared."

"I know, buddy."

"I didn't do anything to them. I don't even know them. I'm not sure why they hate me so much." I couldn't hold the tears any longer.

"I don't know, man. But I'm going to find out." He pulled me into his chest and held me. I lost control and started hyperventilating between sobs. "It's okay. Everything is going to be okay."

"Are you really my friend?" I asked with my face next to his neck.

"You betcha. I've always been your friend. Even Liz is your friend." He caressed my aching head.

"That's right, David," Liz said as she stroked my back.

"Can you take me home?" I asked. "I don't think I'll be able to practice today."

"Sure. Liz, can you drive?" asked Jake.

Sandefjord Natatorium, Tønsberg, Norway, July 1979

The whistle blew. I shook my head and walked to the end of the board in a trance. I couldn't picture the dive in my head, and yet I was calm.

As I positioned my toes on the edge, raised my arms, and compressed the board downward, and I forgot what dive I was doing. It was too late to stop. I cut off my reach and rotated too slowly. I kicked toward the ceiling, only to feel a gush of water against my arched back.

"Poing?" asked the announcer as I swam to the side of the pool. "5.0, 4.5, 5.5, 6.0. 6.0, 5.0. 5.0."

"David," called Dr. Don.

I shuffled to him with my arms hugging my chest because of the cool air.

"What was that?" His eyes burned into mine.

"I'm sorry," I said.

"Don't be sorry. I need you to focus on what you're doing. Get out of your head." He dismissed me by looking at Jack sitting next to him.

"Yes, sir," I mumbled. I scurried to my area, and Patti handed me my towel.

"Hey, it's okay," she said encouragingly.

The audience applauded as the scoreboard displayed the rankings. I was still leading by fifty points. Mark moved into second. Hasse fell to third by only two points, and Andy moved into sixth place behind Giovanni and Alexander from Russia.

Everything felt like it was unravelling, like I was spiraling down a bottomless vortex. I tried to find something to ground me, to keep me from falling apart—someone or something that proved anything was possible.

Alden, Ohio, 1978—The Tornado

"Oh my god!"

I glanced up from my sketch pad to see what Mom was commenting on. We were stopped at the traffic light on the corner of Woodman and Dunabe Court in Kettering, across from the Woodman Bowling Lanes—the squeal of the brakes from a semitruck that came to a stop next to us on our left.

"Look how yellow everything is, it's like an old postcard," Caine said as he flipped around in the front passenger seat to look at me. The afternoon seemed dark, and the shadows made Caine's face seem hollow and evil as he glared at me from over the back of the seat. "Another queer horse," Caine spouted.

"Caine! I hate that word," Mom corrected him.

Ignoring Mom, Caine asked, "What's with these horses? Why not draw a football player or better yet a baseball player pitching the final strikeout? You should draw Pete Rose hitting a home run—now that's something I'd like to see, not those pretty ponies that girls draw."

"That'll be enough. Now turn around," Mom ordered and tried to guide him with her right hand while her left hand gripped the steering wheel.

Before Caine gave in, he grabbed my pencil and took it with him as he spun and dropped his back hard against the seat.

"Mom, Caine took my pencil," I cried.

"Shut up, both of you." There was a sharp tone to her voice, tinted with worry.

"But, Mom, I was trying to finish…"

"Listen to me, and do exactly what I say. Fasten your seat belts now!" Mom's voice was filled with urgency, and yet she pronounced each word slowly and separately.

"But Caine took my…"

"Do it. Now!" Her voice cracked.

I defiantly tossed the sketch pad on the seat next to me. I looked outside at the yellowish green tone and noticed how still everything appeared. There was no wind, and nothing seemed to be moving. I didn't even see a bird in the sky. The greenness darkened and turned almost a burnt orange and then dark gray. A sheet of rain raced toward the car, drenching everything in its path; an even darker curtain of black clouds followed. Pellets of rain splatted against the windshield and scattered into pools. The raindrops fell faster and harder, making it difficult to see in front of us, even though the windshield wipers were on high. The Renault shook as the wind battered against us. Objects rushed past the windows at speeds that made it difficult to identify them.

"Are your seat belts fastened?" Mom yelled over the increasing noise.

"Yes," I replied.

"Mine won't snap closed!" Caine panicked.

The Renault rocked side to side, and I screamed. The windows shook, battered by marble-size hail, dinging and pinging against the metal exterior and the windshield.

"What's happening?" Caine asked as the noise swallowed his voice.

My ears hurt, as if my head was going to explode. And at that moment, the side windows shattered, sending shards of glass through the air.

"Get down on the floor!" Mom ordered.

"I can't. There's glass everywhere," Caine shouted.

The windshield was sucked up and out of its framing, leaving the wipers in place. Caine yelled and disappeared.

"Caine!" I screamed, thinking he was taken by the wind.

The back window flew off and slammed into the car behind us, shattering against the car's hood. Wind whipped through the Renault like a vortex, rocking and shaking the small frame. I was pushed back against the seat as the wind and debris whipped through. To protect my eyes, I covered my face with my hands. As the wind picked up, a deafening hollow sound grew like a speeding freight train. The Renault's front end lifted and dropped violently. Twisting metal screeched, and tree branches snapped, adding to the cacophony. The small car spun to the left, where I knew the semitruck was. I squeezed my eyes tighter and awaited the impact. There was none. The Renault came to a halt, in the oncoming lane facing in the opposite direction.

Through my parted fingers, I watched the black twisting cloud skip and hop down the street, causing everything in its path to burst apart and send items spinning in the air.

It was over.

"Is everyone okay?" Mom's voice shook. "David?" she initially looked for the rearview mirror, which was no longer there. She turned to look at me. I sat there with my mouth and eyes wide open.

Caine appeared over the back of the seat. His face was cut and scraped, and he had this huge smile. "You look like a fish with your mouth hanging open like that."

"I thought you were sucked out the window," I stammered.

"Not your lucky day," he joked.

I laughed.

Caine and I looked at Mom. She was sitting there, staring forward, her hands strangling the slightly bent steering wheel, and hairdo adorned with shards of glass, leaves, and twigs.

"Wow, look!" Caine said in amazement.

I glanced out to see the semitrailer, lying on its side in somebody's yard. It had to have been picked up and tossed over the Renault to have ended up there. Its trailer was twisted and ripped open, scattering hundreds of pairs of shoes. The driver climbed out of his side window. Some people stood in a windowless building, looking at the destruction. Others milled about the street, picking up articles or helping people who were injured. It looked like a bomb exploded.

Mom shifted the car into drive, maneuvered down Woodman Avenue, swerving other vehicles, tree branches, garbage cans, and people. There was no windshield, but the twisted wipers kept their motion. People were yelling for her to stop, but she kept driving in the direction of home.

We didn't speak.

The storm's path was evident as we veered onto Wilmington Pike. The trees were stripped of their green foliage, and branches snapped like twigs. Lounge chairs and furniture were everywhere. An apartment building was missing its roof. Live power lines were sparking and dancing against the curbs. A ranch-style house was gone except for the bathroom. Mom kept driving at a steady pace.

She pulled into our driveway and honked the horn. Dad rushed out with a look of horror. Mom stopped the car next to him, turned off the ignition, and kept nodding her head. She was amazing. She was brave and determined to go against all the odds to get us home safe and secure. She was a hero.

Sandefjord Natatorium, Tønsberg, Norway, July 1979

I positioned my toes on the end of the diving board. I couldn't hold my balance and had to step back onto the board. I was spiraling out of control. I tried to push all thoughts aside and only think about the back one-and-a-half somersaults with two-and-a-half twists. *Relax!*

I repositioned my toes on the end and started to raise my arms. My weight shifted back, and I didn't have the time to compress correctly and ride the board into the air. I cut off the lift and got into the twist too early. I lost my bearings in the air and was not quite sure where the twist ended. I guessed. I committed. I reached for the water, which came too quickly. I stretched for the bottom of the pool to only find that I entered at almost a forty-five degree angle.

"Poing?" asked the announcer.

It was a distance to swim to back to the side of the pool since I went too far out.

"5.5, 5.0, 5.5, 5.0, 5.5, 6.0, and 5.0."

I glanced up at the scoreboard. Mark had taken the lead by 21.45 points ahead of me. Giovanni moved into third, while Hesse fell to fourth. Andy moved into fifth place.

I rushed to my camp area and buried my head under the towel. I was losing it. I was letting everyone down. I had to find a way to focus and clear my head.

"David," Dr. Don's voice was stern yet held a sense of care. He motioned for me to come to him. I reluctantly obeyed.

"Giovanni Pizzini from Italy will be performing a front three-and-one-half somersaults in the tuck position," stated the announcer.

Giovanni glanced down at me, tapped his chest, and winked. The whistle sounded.

"This is do-or-die time." Dr. Don looked sternly into my eyes. "You really need to rally back and nail this dive. Get your arms up, over the board, and throw them down narrow. Don't rush."

The crowd erupted. I had missed Giovanni's dive. I automatically walked toward the diving boards.

"David." Giovanni climbed out of the water and made his way next to me. "Where's the happy boy I spent the day together with? Remember, this may be only time to come to World Games, don't waste it with nonsense."

I ran my hands through my hair.

"Mark Bradley, USA, will be performing a reverse one-and-one-half somersaults, with two-and-one-half twists," said the announcer.

"Do what you came here to do. Dive. Enjoy each dive as if it was your last." Giovanni hugged me.

The audience erupted; Giovanni and I glanced at the scoreboard.

"8.5, 8.5, 8.0, 9.0, 9.0, 9.5."

Dr. Don stood and cheered.

"Now you do it," said Giovanni as he turned me toward the springboard.

I stepped on the bottom rung of the ladder and waited for Hasse to dive. My pulse slowed; my head stopped spinning; and my breath returned deep into my lungs. The arena was hushed, but I could hear humming from the pools' generators and the shifting of the spectators. The springboard banged back against the stand as Hasse sprung into the air. The crowd reacted as Hasse missed his dive.

"Poing, 4.5, 4.5, 4.0, 5.0, 5.0, 4.0. 5.5."

I scaled the ladder and adjusted the fulcrum. My legs felt sturdy and strong.

"David Matthew, USA, will be doing an inward two-and-one-half somersault in the tuck position."

I knew I had this dive. I waited for the whistle and walked to the end, positioned my toes on the edge, and masterfully pressed it down. I felt the board propel me into the air, causing me to spin fast. I sliced the water and sped to the bottom.

I could hear the roar from the crowd before I broke the surface of the water.

"Poing, 10, 9.5, 9.0, 9.5, 9.5, 9.0, 10."

Patti and Megan were hugging and jumping up and down. Mark whistled with his fingers in his mouth. Giovanni threw his fists into the air. Dr. Don sat there, nodding his head.

I glanced at the scoreboard. Mark led by ten points. I remained in second, with Giovanni in third and Hasse in fourth. Kirk held fifth.

Before I knew it, I heard, "David Matthew, USA, will be performing a front one-and-a-half somersaults with three twists."

"David, you are up," Patti urgently said.

How did we get through all the other divers? I seemed I just finished my last dive only a few seconds ago. I threw the towel off my shoulders and rushed to the three-meter. I scaled the ladder and set the fulcrum as quickly as I could manage. I stood at attention, and my mind went blank.

I looked at the announcer, "What is the dive?"

"A front one-and-a-half somersaults with three twists."

I took a deep breath and started my approach. My hurdle was strong, causing the Maxiflex board to fling me higher than I had ever been. I initiated the triple twists. The surrounding colors blended together as I twisted like a top. I piked out hard and reached for the water. I was too high. I overrotated. I felt the water slap against my calves, causing me not to go very deep.

I swam to the side and hurried to my area without talking to Dr. Don. Patti sat there in silence. I buried my head under my towel and screamed inside my head, *Why do I have to always fuck up? When is it going to be my turn to win?*

"Why are you hiding?" said a deep voice. "You have nothing to be ashamed of."

Dr. Don squatted next to me, pulling the towel from my face. "You didn't come see me after the dive, so I came to you. I want you to look at the scoreboard."

My named appeared in third, behind Mark by ten points and Hasse by five points. Andy had moved into fourth, and Giovanni fell to fifth.

"Who would've thought that a sixteen-year-old nobody from Aulden, Ohio, would be sitting in the bronze-medal position, going into the last dive of the World Games? Not me! Not until I met you. You're special, David, you really are. And no matter what happens, you did well." Dr. Don rubbed my head. "Have fun on this last dive." He walked away.

Aulden, Ohio, June 1979— Caine Drives David to the Cemetery

"Dave, you up?"

"What time's it?" I rolled over and found Caine leaning over my bed.

"It doesn't matter. Get up and come with me."

"Why?" I stretched my arms over my head.

"Just do it, peon. Meet outside in the Torino. And hurry, but don't make any noise." He left the room.

I threw on a shirt, jeans, tennis shoes, and quietly made my way down the stairs. I halted when I heard snoring. Magdalyn and Mom were snuggled under the pull-out couch's blankets, while Dad lay on top of the covers with his boots still on.

I hung close to the radiator and slipped into the kitchen. As I reached for the back-door knob, Dad coughed. I kept going.

Lightning bugs ignited the fields, flickering yellow flashes in sync with pulsating bass emitting from Caine's Torino parked by the silo.

"Hurry up," Caine said as I opened the passenger door.

I slid onto the leather seat and slammed the door after me.

Caine flashed me a look, "You don't need to slam it so hard."

"Sorry."

Without a word, Caine shifted into drive, and we were off.

Did I finally become Hutch to his Starsky?

Caine fishtailed as he pulled a hard left onto County Line Road. I glanced back to see if we had left any tread marks. The smooth ride became bumpy from the road's gravel and potholes.

"Heehaw!" Caine screamed as the Torino sprung into the air and flew from launching off a bump in the road.

I grabbed the dashboard in anticipation of the landing.

It was a rough one. The Torino's springs caused the car to bounce several times before the tires reconnected to the road. Caine laughed like a hyena.

"That was awesome, let's do it again," I said.

"What? I thought you'd pee your pants," he said.

"That shows how much you know me."

Caine stopped the Torino alongside an old Civil War cemetery's gate.

"Why are we stopping here?" I asked.

"I want to show you something."

He pointed out the window toward the full moon illuminating the tombstones. Through the clearing of the trees, the sky was a circus with aerial performances from a dozen bats. They were zipping and darting in all directions and never colliding with each other.

"That's awesome," I said.

"They're blind," Caine said.

"How can they…?" I asked.

"Sonar. They send out these waves and can sense if something is near them so they don't run into it."

"That's so neat," I said.

Caine became somber. He ran his fingers along the steering wheel. The illumination from the console threw a bluish light on his face. "These last few months have been tough."

I didn't know what to say or how to react.

"You're the only person I've been able to talk to." He stopped to gain control. "I still have nightmares. I keep replaying ways that I could've saved Zachary, and it keeps ending the same." Caine looked at me with red, swollen eyes. "But you're the only one that doesn't keep asking me to relive that night. You never forced me to tell what happened, and yet you let me tell you when I was ready." He wiped his nose with the back of his hand. "I guess what I'm saying is, Thanks."

"Not a problem." I looked at the bats darting past the limbs of a huge oak tree.

"Whew," he took a deep breath. "I also know it hasn't been easy for you either. I don't understand or pretend to try to understand what's going on in your life. You're gone all the time, traveling across the country to meets, and we don't seem to have any time together." He paused. "I can't begin to comprehend why those cars pull up to the house and you always go with them, even when I can see the anger in your face. I don't pretend to understand why Dad's always gunning after you and Mom's always babying you. We're so different, and yet we grew up under the same roof." He folded his arms across his chest.

"I want to let you know, I was jealous...at first. You were the golden child who could do no wrong. Going here and there, being on TV and the radio, everyone talking about you and asking, 'Are you David-the-diver's brother?' I was angry, but I wasn't able to realize that there must have been some kind of cost. I knew there was the sacrifice on the family's part, and we all had to pull together to get you to practices and meets. I wanted to believe that people were helping us because you're this famous diver, but…I started noticing how different you were when you came back from those 'dinners.' You weren't yourself. You never spoke about it, so I thought you were okay with everything. I don't know, and yet there's a part of me that doesn't want to know. I don't think I could handle it."

I resisted looking at him and kept focused out the side window, feeling ashamed.

"Hey, I didn't mean to hurt your feelings," he apologized.

After a long and awkward moment, I lied, "You didn't."

"You're my brother, my only brother, and I feel I let you down," he said.

I finally looked at him. "How?"

"I didn't protect you. I saw your pain, but I was so caught up with my own stuff. I should've stepped in to stop things, to find out what was going on and help you. I should have found out who that asshole was that beat the hell out of you at school and killed him."

"Who told you that?"

"Christi."

I glanced at him. "How do you know Christi?"

"It doesn't matter. She heard about incident the following day at school and told me, but she didn't know who it was or why they did it." He nodded his head. "I have a suspicion why they did it."

I was embarrassed and felt dirty.

"Whatever the reason, I should have cracked some skulls."

"You couldn't," I felt my voice tighten.

"I have a mean right hook." He held up his fist and swung it. "Anyway, I should've done something. I'm sorry."

The car became silent as we both watched the diving bats.

"I want to give you something, and you have you take it." Caine reached into the glove compartment and pulled out an envelope. "I want you to take this with you to Norway. I want you to focus on your diving and put everything else out of your head. You're leaving tomorrow, and I want you to win." He handed me an envelope.

Inside was a thick wad of money. "I can't take this."

"Why? I'm your brother. That's what families are supposed to do—help each other and not go look for it somewhere else."

His statement stung me; maybe he knew more than I thought he did. "But…"

"Just take it."

"I don't know what to say."

"'Thanks' will do," he said, looking out the windshield. "Shhhh, look."

A raccoon was climbing the wooden fence, followed by two cubs. They awkwardly scaled the fence, wagging their behinds. Once on the other side, they glanced back with their masked faces and scampered into the shadows of the cemetery.

"Thanks," I said.

"What?" Caine looked at me.

I held up the envelope.

He reached over and squeezed the nape of my neck. "Don't tell Mom. I told her that I was taking some time off from work to think about college, so I wouldn't be able to give her any money until next week." He stopped short and glared into my eyes. "I don't care if you're orange or purple or pink, you're my brother, and I love you."

The words burned through me, and I ached. "I love you too."

"Don't cry about it," he punched me in my shoulder. "All I ask is that you beat some Russian butts over there."

Sandefjord Natatorium, Tønsberg, Norway, July 1979

"David Matthew, USA, will be doing his final dive, a front three-and-a-half somersault in the tuck position."

My nerves flared up again as my belly smack in practice replayed itself in detail. But it didn't unnerve me. I touched the bruises that were yellowing on my chest, stomach, and thighs. I felt like a warrior, confident and strong. I belonged here, and it was time to show everyone. I realized that this experience was once in a lifetime. Everything that Dr. Don, Giovani, Patti, Mark, Dad, Mom, and Caine have said and done showed me that anything was possible.

The whistle sounded.

I was in control and focused. The hurdle was high and powerful, and the compression of the board was smooth and easy. The recoil sent me toward the ceiling, and my spins were fast. I clearly saw the water and stretched for the bottom. I sliced an entrance without a splash. It felt good.

As I broke the surface of the water, the stadium was dead silent. No one was moving. As I swam to the side, I felt everyone's eyes on me. Patti stood by the pool with a shocked expression.

Maybe my dive wasn't as good as I thought it was.

Everything was in slow motion and garbled. As I went to my camp, Dr. Don watched me; Mark's hands covered his mouth; Giovanni was silent; and Andy and Megan wouldn't look at me.

I grabbed my towels and bag and rushed to the locker room, throwing everything on the bench as hard as I could.

I took a stance, looked at the ceiling, and asked, "Why, God? Why can't I win?" The rage rushed up from the pit of my stomach. "When is it my turn? When do I get to be special?" I started shaking as my face burned and my eyes blurred. "Why do I always come so close and then have it taken away from me?" I pounded the locker door with a closed fist. "Haven't I paid the price? Haven't I done everything that was asked of me? Why can't you ever let me win?" Hot liquid ran down my cheeks as I pressed my face against the cool metal of the locker. "Why do I always let everything go? Why can't I be worthy enough to win?"

A large gasp, followed by a thunder of cheers and claps, rang from the pool area. All I could imagine was that Mark defended his title or Hasse had made history in his home country. I knew I should be happy and excited, but I could've performed better, I could've been more prepared, I could've been more focused.

"Here you are. Why you hiding in here?" Giovanni smiled as usual. "Why your face so red?" He took a step closer, "David, why you crying?"

I quickly wiped my face, "I'm not crying."

"Yes, I can see. You should be happy." He placed his hand on my shoulder.

"I know, but I wanted to win. I didn't think I really cared about winning until it was all over and then I realized that I really did want to win. I never identified with that feeling before," I said.

Giovanni laughed.

"Please don't laugh at me," I asked.

"Why not? You being ridiculous. You are so much like my brother." He leaned against the locker, facing me. He looked deep into my eyes and then chuckled again, "You don't know, do you?"

"Know what? How I totally embarrassed myself out there? I wasn't able to hold it together, and I melted under the pressure!" I pounded the locker again.

He grabbed my hand to stop it. "You must see for yourself."

I felt the blood drain from my face. "What?"

Giovanni just smiled and nodded his head. "Pull yourself together, and go look at the scoreboard."

"Giovanni," a voice called from the door, "*dobbiamo andare.*"

"*Sarò lì!*" Giovanni called back. "I must be going. I wanted to find you to congratulate you and say good-bye."

"Are you leaving?" I asked.

"Yes, I go back to Italia now, since I'm not diving platform. I must prepare for wedding."

"Whose wedding?" I asked.

Giovanni smiled broadly, "Mine."

"What?" I was confused.

I thought he liked me. I must have misunderstood his affections for me. I was sure he was the one, the love of my life. He understood me, he was kind to me, and yet he never pressured me with sex. I had this whole fantasy of moving to Italy and being with him forever.

"No." I wanted to keep him here.

"I brought you something." He pulled a small plastic box from his duffel bag. "I want to give this to you." He handed it to me.

The plastic box protected a silver medal.

"I won this at our Olympic trials last month. I want to give it to you to bring to Moscow Olympics and give it back," he said.

"Giovanni, I couldn't," I said.

"You can, and we'll be friends forever," he smiled.

"But I thought you…" I couldn't finish, maybe because I was embarrassed for assuming that he felt for me the way I was feeling for him.

His eyes revealed pain and compassion. "You're my little brother. I love you like a brother." He wrapped his arms around me and pulled me into his chest.

"Giovanni!" a voice rang from the door.

"*Si, io vengo*," he called back. "I have to go. I am so proud of you. Promise me to make the USA team, and we'll meet up in August in Moscow next year." Giovanni kissed both of my cheeks and ran out of the locker room.

Dr. Althea Warner—Dayton, Ohio, August 2016

It felt strange to be sitting on the couch in Dr. Althea's office again after the time off. I wasn't sure I was coming back, since the unconventional way we last parted.

"I'm not sure I can explain," I started. "The only way I can explain it is it was dark, like a dark cloud. Since I saw you, I got really sick with a viral infection in my lungs. I went to the hospital and was given horrible meds. I got stomachaches and gained twenty pounds. When the medication was completed, I was still sick. I went back to the doctors, and they prescribed stronger prescriptions, but I wasn't able to afford them since my insurance refused me, it was too close to the last prescriptions."

"What did you do?" asked Althea.

"I got over-the-counter medicines and went home to bed." I shifted my weight on the couch. "I'm not sure if it is because I am digging into my past, but I started to feel extremely worthless. The pressures from school were mounting, and when I went to speak to the department head, she informed me that I was behind on the pacing guide since I have had been sick. I tried to share with her my frustrations, and she informed me that we were not friends."

"Wow, that's harsh." Althea wrote on the clipboard.

"While in the meeting, my aunt texted me and said she was in from New York and asked if I was coming to see her. I explained that I wasn't aware of her visitation. She told me that she was coming to take 'her' sister back to Rochester to have 'her' sister's teeth fixed. I quickly texted that I thought it was a wonderful thing. Then she called me. I couldn't answer, being in the meeting, so it went to voice mail. Later, when I was in the car, I listened to the message, and she said, 'Like I tell my boys, if you can text, you can talk.' The whole time Mom was in New York, my aunt sent passive-aggressive updates on her condition."

"You didn't know anything about it?" asked Althea.

"No, I had no idea, which made the whole situation weird. I felt guilty that I wasn't a good-enough son. Everything kept coming on. My book was turned down, and I was stressing to make the deadline for my PhD predissertation, creating lesson plans in order to catch up the two weeks I missed for being sick, and I was taking everything out on Jake. I felt like I was a walking time bomb, waiting to explode at any minute. I couldn't move forward or backward. My chest constantly hurt. I felt hopeless. I said good-bye to the puppies and was ready to make my exit."

"Did you make a plan?"

"That's the thing, I didn't. I just felt that it would be better for everyone that I was away. I realized that I hated myself and how I had allowed my life to get to this point. I hated teaching and going to the school. I understood how our friend Sam must have felt before he decided to end everything. How lonely and empty he must have been." I rubbed my palms together. "I thought about how to withdraw my savings from my 401(k) and stocks so Jake could pay the house for a year. That's when I stopped—when I thought how unfair this was to Jake. He didn't ask for this. How unfair it would be when he found my body. How selfish. It would ruin his life. So I fell to the floor and cried as hard as I could."

"How are you feeling now?" Althea's face was drained of color.

"Better. I still hate teaching and going back to the school. I get nauseous and feel panicky every morning, especially on Sundays. I still have bad days, and I feel like I want to get the pain and anger out, but I don't know how."

"You were taught not to share your frustrations. You were taught to always be a good boy and not rock the boat," Althea said.

"And there are days that I feel terrific. I started the AdvoCare 24 Day Challenge, and I feel healthier than ever."

"What is that?" she asked.

"It's a lifestyle change. It focuses on cleansing your body for ten days with vitamins and protein shakes, and then fourteen days of learning how to eat properly, while continuing the supplements and shakes. It is fantastic. I have not needed any medication for my lungs since I started. I'm not saying that AdvoCare cured me. I'm saying that becoming more aware of what foods I'm putting into my body has helped."

"So are you feeling suicidal anymore?" asked Althea.

"No, not to the extent I was during the black days. It was over-whelming with all these past thoughts starting to reveal themselves to me. I found that I was punishing myself for allowing everything to happen. I felt extreme guilt and shame. I felt like I lost myself along the way. I became this 'yes-man' and worked so hard to hide my pain and anger. I can't even make a decision on where to go to dinner. Jake will ask, and I'll turn it back and ask him because I know it'll be easier to adapt to what he wants, and besides, every time I make a suggestion, he doesn't want it."

"Did you ask for help?"

"I did. I reached out to friends, but they were too busy. I'm not good at sustaining friendships. I isolate myself too much. And the people I did speak to, the conversation always ended up being about helping them."

Althea placed the clipboard on the floor and leaned in to me. "What do you want to do now?"

"I want to fix myself." I gave a nervous chuckle. "I'm scared about what I will find out and why I choose not to remember certain aspects of my life. But I want to be here for a long time."

12 CHAPTER

Tonsburg, Norway, Calling Home, July 1979

"Who is this?"

The familiar voice seemed groggy, yet it cracked like a whip as it traveled from a farmhouse in Ohio along the transcontinental wiring under the Atlantic Ocean to a pay phone in Tønsberg, Norway.

My mouth went dry as I listened to the faint buzzing emitting from the phone's earpiece.

"David, could you look this way?" called Mike Drake. He flashed perfect white teeth as he held his Kodak camera to his eye and adjusted the focus. "Smile," he coaxed.

I followed the order.

"Who the hell is calling at three o'clock in the morning? Hello!" a voice filled the telephone.

"Dad?" a mousy voice squeaked from my throat.

"What? I can't hear you!" he shouted. I imagined him pulling the receiver from his ear in frustration and then staring at it as if he were able to remedy the bad connection from sheer willpower.

I heard another faint voice, "Caleb, what's wrong?"

I immediately sensed it was Mother, and I prayed that she'd take the receiver from him.

"Nothing's wrong. Someone called, and I'm taking care of it."

I pictured him pulling out a cigarette and placing it between his lips. I heard the scratch of the match and saw the flame ignite in my mind's eye. He deeply inhaled, and I imagined the end of the cancer stick sizzling red. He exhaled as his voice rang through loud and clear.

"Who the hell is this?"

"Dad, it's me, Davy," I said.

"Who?" he demanded.

"Your son!" I was perplexed, because I wanted this call to seem full of celebration. The little phone booth became a gathering hub, with competitors, reporters, and photographers.

Jack, the assistant coach, stood by my side.

"Who's he talking to?" asked a reporter.

"He's talking to his parents in the States," Jack tried to quiet everyone.

"David?" Dad's voice was filled with disappointment.

"Yeah, it's me," I shut my eyes tight.

"What the hell are you doing, calling at this ungodly hour?"

"David!" called Mike. I glanced over to him. "Can you hold up the medal?" He indicated that I should hold it next my face.

I had almost forgotten that the weight of the medal hung from around my neck on a red, white, and blue ribbon. I pinched the heavy gold plated medal between my thumb and forefinger, lifted it to my cheek, and absentmindedly smiled. Cameras' shutters clicked as lights flashed in my face, causing momentary blindness.

Patti Lakes came squealing across the lawn, pushed herself through the circled crowd, threw her arms around my neck, and kissed me—which caused another ambush of flashing bulbs and clicking shutters.

"I'm so proud of you. I knew. I just knew you could do it," she screeched like a high-pitched owl.

"What the hell's going on?" The essence of my father's hardness pulled me back to reality.

Without thinking, I uttered, "I won."

"What? I can't hear you. Speak up, or I'm going to hang up."

"I won!" I relished in the golden moment, while Jack escorted Patti to the side to become an observer with Mark, Megan, and Andy.

"You what?" This rhetorical question was followed by a long silence.

My heart sank as I feared that he had hung up.

"Dad?" I bit my lower lip.

Rendezvous with Dad—Middletown, Ohio, 1978

The night sky seemed almost blue-black as the downtown lights refracted off the low ceiling of cumulus clouds. Rain glistened in the parking lot and danced amid Mrs. Baumgartner's van's headlights. The two yellowish beams reached out, illuminating each of the cars parked in precise alignment. Mrs. Baumgartner came to a stop behind Old Blue—Dad's dented and scratched-up car. But Dad wasn't in the car.

"That's it, isn't it?" Mrs. Baumgartner asked with a note of concern in her voice.

"That's it," I offhandedly replied as I gathered my duffel bag and made sure that I had my schoolbooks. I didn't want her or anyone in the van to see that I was worried about where he was.

"Do you want us to wait until he shows?" Mrs. Baumgartner asked.

"No, that's all right. I'm sure he just went inside to use the bathroom or something. I'll be fine." I popped open the side door and stepped down to the wet pavement.

"Remember to tell your dad that I won't be driving next week," said Mrs. Baumgartner. "We're going on vacation, so you'll have to make other arrangements. The following week, we'll be back on schedule." Mrs. Baumgartner smiled in the rearview mirror, revealing lipstick smeared on the lower edge of her front teeth.

"Sure will. Lily, you be good," I said.

"I will," she smiled and waved. "I miss you."

"Make sure you buckle up," I playfully ordered her.

"Yes, Davy."

"Help your mom drive home," I said.

"You are silly, Davy, I can't drive. Not yet. Soon!" she responded.

"No way, you'll never drive," announced a sleepy Bobbie from the back row of seats.

I closed the door and walked to the driver's window. I waved and said, "Thanks."

Mrs. Baumgartner rolled down the window. "Are you sure you don't want us to wait?"

"It's fine, thank you."

"All right then. Good night." She released the brake and rolled away.

I watched the van pull out of the parking lot and turn right onto the highway. Larger pellets dropped from the sky, landing heavily on my shoulders. I stood in the parking lot, wondering what I should do as the rain flattened my hair to my head. *What if something terrible had happened to my dad?* The parking lot of the Motel 6 was not the best place to be making a rendezvous with Mrs. Baumgartner.

What if this isn't my dad's car?

I walked to the passenger side, wiped the window with the palm of my hand, and looked in. It was his car, all right. Sitting on the seat was my world history test with a score of 94 percent and a happy face in red ink. I tried the handle, but the door was locked. My mind started racing.

Where could he be? Did someone kidnap him? The kidnappers could have forcefully hit him over the head with a wrench or a crowbar. He could be bleeding in the trunk of some maniac's Ford and driven to some undisclosed location to be dumped and forgotten. What if he abandoned the family? What if he couldn't take it anymore and decided to stage this elaborate hoax to make everyone think that he was abducted and killed so that he could start all over without the problems from home?

Lightning flashed, followed by a deep rumble of thunder. The sign to the Motel 6's bar flickered, "Cujo's," in red neon. All I could think of was Stephen King's novel.

What if he had been attacked by a rabid wild dog and gnawed to death. Stop it, I shouted inside my head. *There's a simple explanation. I'll just wait here for him.* The storm was overhead, dowsing the parking lot. I glanced back at the entrance. I felt my stomach drop. *No! He wouldn't. He's probably had to use the bathroom. I'll just go inside and check.*

I pulled the metal door, causing it to screech on its hinges. I looked in. I couldn't see very well except for the bluish cloud of cigarette smoke. The place was empty, except for the pool table in the far corner and a pinball machine that was flashing hues of red, white, and blue. I closed the door behind me and stepped down the two steps leading to the main attraction, a wooden bar with six barstools. The bartender squinted, as if trying to determine my age. His thick arms were inked with a dragon on one and a rose on the other and a half-smoked stogie drooped from his lower lip.

He removed the stub of a cigar and pointed toward me. "What can I do for ya?" His voice rumbled deep from within his chest.

"I'm trying to find someone," I meekly answered.

"Ain't we all?" He chuckled at his joke. "Check it out, not much to choose from. Who ya searching for?"

"My dad," I said.

"Oh, is that right? Pretty boy's looking for a daddy. You must be in the wrong place, we ain't got those types in here." There was mockery in his tone.

In the far corner, opposite the flashing pinball machine, a man sat at a table—hunched over a beer and squeezing a cigarette between his fingers. I recognized him immediately. The waitress, a buxom redhead was very close to him, leaning in with her back arched and whispering something in his ear. When she finished, she rounded her back and coquettishly giggled, biting the tip of her manicured nail. He laughed and looked at her. From the angle I was at, it looked as if he might have kissed her. My heart dropped to my stomach. I slowly walked toward the duo.

"Kid, you can't be in here," the bartender snarled.

I growled, "That's my dad."

I stood there for an eternity, until the redhead glanced up from under her heavy mascara lashes, "See what the cat dragged in."

The color in Dad's face drained before he dropped his head.

"I'll leave you two for a minute," she said, drawing every word out in a fake Southern accent. She draped her hand on my father's shoulder, leaned to my dad's ear, and said, "You didn't say how pretty he was." She picked up her tray and started to leave but stopped. "Do you want a Coke or Sprite or something, sweetie?"

I just shook my head while my eyes stayed glued on him.

The waitress strutted to the bar.

"What?" he asked defensively.

He was cheating on Mom.

"So this is your dirty little secret?" I shook my head, turned on my heels, and marched out of the place.

"Come back soon, kid," the bartender waved without looking up.

I didn't even acknowledge him. I was too focused on getting outside.

"David!" I heard a faint call from the depths of the bar and the screech of the chair being pushed back.

I banged through the metal door, crossed the parking lot, and leaned against the wet car. I didn't care about the rain or the cold. As I replayed what I thought I witnessed, I realized it might have been innocent enough. I really couldn't make out if they were kissing, but it was the idea of the whole thing.

How often has he talked to this woman? How well does he know her? It was my fault because this is the rendezvous with the Baumgartner so I could go to practice. If I didn't dive, this would never have happened.

Dad banged out of the door with fire in his eyes. He glared at me as he forged to the driver's side, rain danced off his head and shoulders.

"What's wrong with you?"

It must have been a rhetorical question because he didn't wait. He unlocked the door, leaned over the top of the car, and then his eyes pierced through the falling rain.

"What the hell was that?"

I just lifted my arms as if to say, "You tell me."

"Get in," he demanded.

I waited for him to clamber into the driver's seat, reach across, and manually pull the door lock tab up so I could open the door.

I climbed in, threw my bag onto the backseat, slammed the door, and crossed my arms in front of my chest. I focused straight ahead.

"Fine."

He shoved the key into the ignition and rotated with such force that I thought it might snap in half. The engine sputtered and coughed to life. He forced the car into reverse, arced out of the parking space without looking, and stopped abruptly, throwing me forward and then back against the headrest. He shifted into drive, glanced over at me, and shook his head. He floored the gas pedal, causing the tires to spin and squeal against the wet pavement until the treads found their traction and jerked forward. He didn't look before merging onto the highway.

The fan belt's monotonous whirl and the wind's whistle against the window harmonized with the motor's roar; otherwise, the ride was silent, neither of us willing to speak. I tried to think about other things.

What do I have to do tomorrow? What time is practice? How much homework do I have to do when I get home? There is the Bible lit paper, math problems, and the new unit in history to read.

His anger grew as the oncoming traffic's beams illuminated his face. His left hand gripped the steering wheel, while his right hand vibrated on his thigh with tension. His breathing was irregular, and his driving was erratic, which could have been due to his indulgence, anger, or both.

At any moment, I anticipated the back of his right hand striking my cheek. I imagined the car skidding into a 360-degree spin, flipping down and over the ditch, and landing in the cornfield.

What if no one witnessed the accident or could see the car lying on its roof amid the cornstalks? We would remain there all night, unable to move due to broken bones and skull fractures, and we would eventually bleed to death.

The *tick, tick, tick* of the turning signal made me look over to Dad. He veered off the highway onto a ramp that led to a side street decorated with neon lights for McDonald's, Wendy's, and Bob Evans's restaurants. I thought we were stopping for gas, but Dad drove past the BP and Shell stations. He continued as the two lanes merged into one; the lights faded behind us; and we became bathed in darkness, except for the dim glow emitting from the dashboard. Dad's eyes remained focused on the road ahead.

I wasn't sure where we were heading. I had never taken this route before. We continued as trees walled us in and the road turned into a gravel path. He pulled off onto the shoulder and put the car into park. He just sat there, staring out the windshield, as the car idled.

Finally, he said slowly, "I know what it may've looked like to you. But it didn't mean anything."

I leaned against the darkened window, feeling the pane's coolness kiss my forehead. I was wishing that I was home in my room, far away from here. I wasn't prepared to deal with this. I just sat there, hoping that it would end soon.

What's tomorrow? Friday. What do I have to do tomorrow?

"Sometimes I need to talk to someone. Candy listens," he continued his confession.

"Candy?" I looked at him speculatively.

Defiance tightened the corners of his eyes. "Yes, Candy's her name."

"How many times have you talked with this...Candy?"

"Watch your tone," he ordered. I cowered closer to the door. "It's not what you're thinking."

"What am I thinking?"

He was taken aback for a moment. He squinted and clenched his fist. I thought, *This is it*. I prepared myself for the impact, maybe an openhanded slap or an upper cut with his closed fist. I tried to relax my neck so the blow wouldn't be too costly. I waited. It didn't come. Instead, he lifted his hand and gently caressed my cheek with his rough knuckles. He ran his fingers through my hair.

"Someday you'll understand."

He traced his large thumb roughly over my lower lip. I smelled residue of burnt tobacco.

"You're something else, so sensitive, so emotional. You need to toughen up a bit. You need to be more of a man. I sometimes look at you and I'm not sure who you are. Where'd you come from? Where'd that blond hair come from? How are you ever going to make it out there?" He dropped his head and looked at me from under his dark brows. "You're too pretty to be a boy. It's amazing how pretty you are. You have a pretty mouth."

I tried to move away without him noticing. I could smell the whiskey and cigarettes as he leaned in closer and spoke.

"What was God thinking when he made you?" he roughly pulled back the flesh on my cheek.

"Dad, we need to get going. Mom will be waiting." I tried to gently push his hand away.

"What's the rush? Can't I spend some time with my son?"

"Sure, but it's getting late. I've got homework, and I need to start a research paper."

He grabbed me behind my neck and pulled me to his mouth. His aggression surprised me. He pressed his mouth against mine, parted his lips, explored me, and bit my lower lip—hard. He withdrew and with disgust shoved me away. I felt the door's handle jab me in the lower back. He gripped the steering wheel and banged his head against it.

"See what you made me do! The way you look at me." His voice was harsh and filled with disdain.

I huddled against the door's frame, shocked and stunned. I couldn't move. I wanted to fling open the door and run into the woods. I wanted to disappear. I wanted not to exist. I felt ashamed as I tasted blood and felt the swelling of my bruised lip.

A strange high-pitched, squeaking sound filled the car, like a wounded animal or a puppy whimpering. Dad hunched over with his arms wrapped around the steering wheel. I don't know why, but for some reason, I felt sorry for him. I placed a hesitant hand on his shaking shoulder.

"Dad, are you all right?" I spoke with a softness that even surprised me.

"I don't know what that was all about," his voice broke.

"It was nothing," I said.

"What the hell's happening with the world? Everything's going to hell in a hand basket." He shook my hand off his shoulder, propped his chin on the back of his hands, and stared forward.

"It's all going to end, you know, the world as we know it. All this running around is nonsense. Everyone's rushing around, going here, going there. You've got to be at a certain place at a certain time. Everything runs on a schedule that 'The Man' devised. Who does all this benefit? I'll tell you, the rich, the wealthy, the upper class—it's all about the little people doing all the work for the big shots, but no one cares what happens to the little people, they're easily replaced."

The dashboard's light revealed his narrowed eyes.

"They're watching. They know what you're doing. They could be watching us right now." He stopped suddenly and looked up at the black sky. "They have informants, you know. For all I know, you could be one. You could be on their side," he looked at me accusingly.

"Dad, no, I'm not," I said.

"How do I know?" His eyes grew wide, like two silver dollars. "They're after me, son. I just know it. They don't want me to finish The Luper. If The Luper gets out there, there'll be hell to pay, because it'll cost the government a lot of money. The little people wouldn't have to pay such high gas prices. They'll probably want to kill me."

"Dad, no one's after you. We'll protect you," I tried to sooth him with a soft voice.

"I don't know. I just don't know anymore," his voice grew.

I put my hand on his shoulder again. He turned and collapsed in my arms, crying hysterically. I wasn't quite sure what to do. I wrapped my arms around his large back and rocked him.

What's tomorrow? It's Friday. What do I have to do on Friday? I have morning practice, school, afternoon practice, and I have to start the research paper for Mr. Chambers.

He pulled pull away, took a deep breath, and shifted the car into drive. It crept back onto the road, crunching the loose gravel. He floored the gas pedal, and nothing more was said.

We arrived at the house after ten—almost an hour late. I gathered my bag and books and reached for the car handle.

"Tell your mother I had to go get some cigarettes. I'll be back soon," he said.

"I thought we got some cigarettes on the way to the rendezvous…"

He cut me off, "Just do what I asked you."

"Yes, sir." I pulled on the latch, and the door creaked open. I felt his hand on my arm.

"Don't mention anything to your mother. She wouldn't understand. Let's keep this as our secret." He forced a smile.

"Okay, no one needs to know."

"That's my boy."

When I got out, he backed down the driveway and disappeared into the night. I watched the red taillights until the edge of the woods masked them.

Calling Home—Tonsburg, Norway, Phone Booth, July 1979

I waited for Dad to give some type of response, but nothing came. I knew he was still on the line because I heard him take a drag on his cigarette.

"David." A voice pulled me back to the phone booth and the crowd grew larger. "How do you feel at this moment?" A reporter shoved a tape recorder under my chin. Jack tried to politely push the device aside.

I leaned into the silver box with a red light and said, "I don't know exactly. I'm not sure it has completely sunk in yet."

"Wait a minute." Caleb's voice grew on the other end of the phone. "This is crazy. This is the worst joke anyone has ever pulled. My son would never win the World Games." With that, the call was disconnected.

I knew instantly that he had hung up this time. I had no doubt. Numbness flooded my veins. I became deaf. I became blind. All I could comprehend was that I was standing at this phone booth in Tønsberg, Norway, with all these people surrounding me, taking pictures and asking questions. I knew the conversation with my father was too short. If I hung up the receiver, they would want to know what the reaction from home was. So I pretended that the conversation was still alive.

"Yes, can you believe it?" I spoke to the dead line. "I can't either…I know, I know, it's amazing. We just finished, and I'm wearing the medal right now. I had to call you and tell you, I couldn't wait."

I lifted the medal and looked at it as my eyes filled with hot liquid. I read the inscription that ran around the edge, "Fédération Internationale de Natation Diving Association," with a figure of a diver flying in the middle with, "Tønsberg, Norway 1979," inscribed on the bottom third of the award.

"I'm overjoyed…Thanks. I love you too."

I turned to hang up the receiver as I noticed the sun sneaking behind a large gray cloud. I wiped my eyes, planted a smile on my face, and turned back to the press as the cameras clicked like machine guns. The flashes made my eyes see red spots, as Patti snuggled in to pose.

Dr. Althea Warner—Dayton, Ohio, August 2016

"What is the Luper you keep talking about?" Althea asked.
Before I could respond, she stood and went to her desk.

"You just have to try this chocolate I found the other day at Trader Joe's." She glanced over her shoulder. "It's divine." She pulled out a bag from the drawer. "It is dark chocolate and sea salt. Oh, it is so good."

She sashayed over, handed me a piece, and repositioned herself on her chair. She held the piece of chocolate in the air, as if she was making an offer to the gods, and said, "You are going to heaven after one bite." She looked at me and waited, with anticipation in her eyes.

I nodded and took a bite. The bitter chocolate was accented by the sea salt and was decadent. I forced a smile. "Nice."

"Do you really like it, or are you just saying you do?" Worry weighed down the corner of her eyes.

"No, it's good. I like it."

Her shoulder released. "I'm glad, because I love it." She popped the whole piece into her mouth and leaned back into the chair, relishing the flavor.

I glanced up at the clock on the tower and discovered there were only a few minutes left.

"So this invention of your father's, the..." She licked her fingers.

"The Luper." I placed the rest of my chocolate on the Kleenex resting on my lap.

"What was the purpose of this creation?" she asked as she took the clipboard to take notes.

I shifted on the couch. "I don't know all the details, but it was an engine that ran on water instead of gasoline."

"And this was why the government was after him?" her brows furrowed.

"He thought that it would be a solution to the gas crisis, and for that, the government wanted to silence him."

"Your dad was crazy."

I chuckled despite myself.

"He was. Did he have the invention patented?" she challenged.

"I'm not completely sure, but I know he said that he was wait-ing to hear from a patent lawyer."

"I feel from what you have shared that he was disillusioned. He was actually projecting his infidelities onto The Luper. Don't get me wrong, if he had a patent on it and he was in the position to mass-produce this invention, the government may have raised an eyebrow. But since the prototype was in the basement of your house, it is likely that it didn't get very far in production. And if this sit-uation with Candy was ever consummated or just platonic doesn't matter. You father hid secrets and asked you to keep them for him as well. He abused you."

She stood, dropping the clipboard to the floor, and walked to her desk.

"It angers me that a parent or person in power usurps the trust of innocent people to keep their indiscretions at bay." She dug her hand into the bag of chocolate. "Chocolate?"

"No, thank you."

"Suit yourself." She placed another piece in her mouth. "Oh my goodness, it doesn't get any better than this," she spoke with her mouth full. "But what gets me even angrier is that his son accom-plished an amazing feat, and he couldn't even acknowledge it. He hung up on you. I would have been so proud, no matter what time the call came in. Oh, I am livid. You have to excuse me."

The church bells rang, and her eyes darted to the window.

"Our time is up. Same time next week?" She slid behind her desk.

"Sure." I gathered my things.

"Here, take some of this chocolate with you."

13 CHAPTER

Dayton International Airport—Dayton, Ohio, August 1979

The sweltering August heat suffocated anything that tried to take a deep breath. Sweat soaked my shirt as I pulled my luggage closer to make room for a heavyset woman.

"Thanks." She plopped down, sending a waif of odorous air in my direction. "Hot enough for you?" She adjusted herself on the bench.

"Stifling," I said.

She studied me, "Aren't you that diver from Aulden, the one that was recently in the meet in Europe?"

I smiled.

"You are. Oh my goodness, this is crazy. You won the gold medal, didn't you?"

I nodded.

"I read it in the newspaper. This is so amazing." She looked around to see if anyone noticed us.

"Are you just getting back in town?"

I smiled again.

"You are just getting home." She leaned in, "Do you have your medal with you?"

I nodded.

"Can I see it?"

I reached down my shirt and pulled out the medal. I had it around my neck for safekeeping.

The woman squealed with excitement. "That's beautiful," she said as tears collected in her eyes. "Your parents must be so proud."

I shrugged.

"Hey, pretty boy, how much?" a voice rang from a car that pulled up in front of us.

I slipped the medal back behind my shirt.

Caine grinned from ear to ear as he leaned across the passenger seat of his Torino.

"That's no way to speak to him. Have some respect. He is a champean of the world," the woman chided.

"It's okay, that's my brother." I gathered my luggage and bags.

"Are you being for real?"

I nodded.

"You should be so proud of him," she shouted to Caine.

"Extremely proud."

He popped open the passenger door and helped guide the luggage to the backseat. I fastened myself in and shut the door.

"Not so hard."

"Sorry," I apologized.

Caine shifted in to drive. "Have a wonderful day," he called to the woman and waved.

She waved back and started to say something, but Caine merged with the oncoming traffic.

As he veered on to the highway, he broke the silence in the car, "Yeeeeeeehaaaaaaw. Where is it? Where is the medal?"

He searched his right hand over my chest and thighs, causing me to curl up into a ball, laughing.

"All right, stop," I batted his hand away. "Give me a sec."

"I have to see it."

I pulled myself up in the seat.

"What's taking so long?" He reached over and pinched my tit.

"Ouch," I slapped his hand away, "that hurt."

"'Cause you're taking too much time."

"All right." I guided the medal out from behind my shirt.

"Shit, no." He grabbed and pulled it toward himself, trying to get a better look, tugging me with it. "It's heavy."

"And it's still around my neck."

"Oh, sorry." He let go, flipped the turning signal, and veered right to pass an old pickup truck.

I removed the medal from around my neck and placed it in his palm.

A smile grew on his face. "You showed those commie bastards, didn't you?" He slipped the ribbon around the rearview mirror so the medal dangled between us, sparkling with the sun. He turned on the stereo, and Freddy Mercury belted out "We Are the Champions."

We both cracked up.

"This is nice," I said.

"Just like Starsky and Hutch. But I'm the one that gets the girl." He pointed his finger at me.

"That's cool." We laughed again. "Thanks for picking me up."

"Not a problem, how else were you going to get home, by the bus?"

"Dad or maybe Mom?"

"What? Am I not good enough for you?"

"Oh, no, it's just that one of them always picks me up."

"Things are different."

"How so?"

Caine grew silent as he manipulated the Tornio into the right lane to exit the highway.

"They're fighting more than before you left. I'm not sure why, but it's crazy. Magdalyn's crying all the time. Oh, while you were gone, we inherited a felon into the family."

"What?"

"Yeppers, your mother is a full-fledged felon now."

"No way."

"Way," Caine nodded while focusing on the traffic ahead. "Mom has some sticky fingers."

"I don't follow."

"Well, she went to Big Bear to get her paycheck and more of her 'girls.'" Caine laid on the horn. "Come on, Grandpa, decide which lane you want. They really need to start taking fossils' driver's licenses away. They're a danger to society."

"The one she works at?" I asked.

"Aren't you listening? *Worked* is the appropriate word. Anyway, Mom was in the card section, and for some reason—'accidentally'—she put a card into her purse, which was in the pushcart. She goes on and shops for another forty-five minutes, getting her 'girls' and toilet paper, dog food, and some other items. Goes to the checkout counter and starts to pay, when the cashier asked if she intended to pay for the card in her purse. Stupidly, she said, 'What card?' She was escorted to the back and asked to empty her purse. When the card was discovered, she was shocked at how it got in there. The security guard said, 'Lydia, you put it in there. We have an eyewitness.' She panicked, I guess, and swore that she meant to pay for it. She was fired on the spot and has been banned from Big Bear for life."

"Unbelievable," I said.

"Well, believe it, all for $1.75. She is a marked felon now."

"Was she prosecuted?"

"No, they didn't want the publicity. But it was the last straw for Dad. He went on this tirade about how he's been working so hard to bring home the bacon and there's no need for Mom to embarrass the family like this and stormed out of the house. He's hardly ever home now. I just wish they'd get divorced because they aren't aware how messed up they're acting and how it's affecting Magdalyn."

"Do you think they'll get a divorce?" I asked.

"I don't know. It just seems like the logical thing to do."

"Oh, I almost forgot." I pulled out an envelope and handed it to him.

"What's this?" he asked.

"I didn't use all of it. I'll get the rest as soon as I can."

"Don't worry about it. It was a gift." He reached over and opened the glove compartment to stow the envelope inside, when a dark knitted toboggan cap fell out.

"Is this yours?" I held the cap up.

He snatched it out of my hand. "It's Zachary's. He must have put it there."

We rode the rest of the way in silence.

Alden YMCA, Alden, Ohio, August 1979

It felt great to be back. The timing and recoil of the springboard felt familiar as I soared into the air, looked down my left arm, and performed a front dive-half twist. A crowd of people watched behind the glass panel separating the pool from the waiting area. Caine was talking to three girls at a table. I smiled and waved as I climbed back up the three-meter ladder, went to the end of the springboard, turned, compressed down, and propelled myself into an inward one-and-a-half somersault in the pike position. The crowd applauded as I broke the water's surface, and Caine gave me two thumbs-up.

"There he is, the newly crowned world champion."

Trevor stood on the deck by the office.

I hoisted myself out of the pool and gave him a big bear hug, lifting him off his feet.

"Woo, Tonto. Put me down."

Trevor stepped back and held his arms out to the side. The front of his shirt was soaked, clinging to his chest.

"Sorry," I said.

"No problem." He brushed the front of his pants, as if by doing so he could somehow dry them. "You did it. You actually did. Deb called and was screaming over the phone with excitement."

My face burned. "I thought you were gone this week?"

"I had to come see you before I left. I want to introduce you to someone." He placed his hand on the back of my neck and guided me, at arm's length, to the office.

A petite brunette with large silver eyes smiled.

"David, this is Tracey. Tracey, this is the new world champion, David Matthew."

"He taught me everything I know," I joked.

"Not everything." His eyes sparkled as he sheepishly grinned. "You taught me a thing or two."

I tried not to blush and offered my hand to Tracey. She grabbed it with both of her hands and squeezed.

"It's a pleasure, and congratulations," she gushed.

"Thank you." I gently pulled my hand away and turned to Trevor.

"I wanted the two most important people in my life to meet," he said.

I nodded.

"We're getting married," Trevor gleefully announced.

My world collapsed under my feet. I recovered and bobbed my head from Trevor to Tracey, back to Trevor, and then back to Tracey. "Trevor and Tracey, that's so cute, T and T."

Tracey giggled. "You never said how pretty he is," she directed it to Trevor.

"Yep, he's a pretty boy." Trevor slapped me on the back.

Silence filled the space.

"I'm going to go to the snack bar and get something to drink and give you two some time to catch up. Do either of you want something?"

"I'm good, what about you, David?"

I shook my head.

"Okay, I'll be back." Tracey leaned in and kissed Trevor on the lips. "Love you."

"Love you too," Trevor responded.

"See you soon." She gave a cute, little wave and went down the hall.

Awkwardness filled the room.

What is this? I thought I was your "cocksucker"?

"Isn't she something else?" Trevor asked as he sat in the chair behind the desk.

I hesitated to look at him.

"Here." He threw a towel at me. "You're dripping."

I looked at the towel. *This is all I get? What about the time in Columbus and all those other times you pretended to be drunk? Am I just a convenience? I thought you were different.*

"Sit," Trevor indicated to the empty chair next to the desk.

I lowered myself, hugging the towel against my chest.

"I can't believe how lucky I am in finding her."

I felt my heart rip apart. "She seems great."

"Why don't you wrap that towel around you? You're turning purple."

You want me to cover up? "I'm good."

Another silence filled the air. I watched the swimmers doing laps. Trevor's hand landed on my knee, causing me to jerk.

"Why so jumpy?" His smile was captivating as he replaced his hand on my knee.

I stared at his hand, recalling Dad's suggestions of when drawing a hand, not to connect the lines completely and which way the hair grows.

"So tell me all about it. What was Norway like?"

"It was neat, old, and smelled like *fish*." *Do you get what I mean? What do you want me to say?*

"Good, good." His hand slipped further up my thigh. "So how do you feel about how you dove?"

I remained focused on his hand. "I could have done better."

"But you won!" He chuckled, squeezed my thigh, and sat back in the chair. "How does it feel to be the freakin' world champ?"

I didn't respond. I kept looking at where his hand left a warm impression on my thigh.

"I wanted to make sure I spoke with you before I left." He paused, causing me to look at him. "Since I'm getting married, I won't be able to coach you anymore."

"Why?" I asked.

"I just think it would be better that I don't."

I searched his eyes for the real answer. "Why?"

"Well." He broke the eye contact and rubbed the back of his head.

I leaned in to inhale his musk.

He got up and walked toward the door.

"I've taught you everything I can."

"You made me, you created me." I stood next to him, dropping the towel onto the floor.

He glanced over his shoulder at me. "You did it all by yourself. I only guided you."

"You believed in me." I stepped closer.

He turned and looked me up and down. His lips looked inviting, and I wanted to taste them. He stopped me, gently pushing my shoulders back, and walked behind the desk.

"I'm getting married, and things will not be the same. I won't be able to be at all the practices and travel to meets. You need to start focusing on the Olympic trials next spring." He opened a folder. "Harold Hall contacted me, and we had a meeting."

It was like someone punched me dead center in my stomach.

"He and I agreed that you need the very best coaching in order to get prepared."

"But you are the best coach for me," I defended.

"No, I was lucky getting you to this point. I'm no Dr. Don," Trevor said.

"You know me and how I think." I leaned against the desk. "You changed me and gave me confidence."

"No, you had all that inside."

"But you were that one that found a way to bring it out of me." My throat started to tighten up.

"I just forced you to wear a Speedo, and I needed Deb to tell you." He wrapped his arms against his chest.

"Don't do this to me."

"I'm not doing anything to you." His lip quivered.

"I need you."

"No!" His word slapped me across the face. "You don't *need* me. What you need is the best coaching staff in the country. I have given you everything I can."

"Why are you doing this?"

"Because I..." he stopped himself. He looked down and took a deep breath and then looked up, "Because I care about you. I'm too close."

"No, no, you don't mean that. We're a team, a good team. I couldn't have gotten to where I am if it wasn't for you." My eyes burned.

He smiled and slowly said, "And now it's time to move on."

"No, no, no," I reached out to him and rounded the table. He countered to keep distance between us.

"Harold Hall has everything arranged. He has contacted Dr. Don, and you're going to go practice at Mission Viejo."

"No."

"It will be only until the Olympic trials. Then depending on the results, I may be able to coach you then."

"No, I don't want to go." I crumbled to the floor.

He lifted me up to my feet. I wrapped my arms around him and buried my face into his neck.

"Is everything all right?" Tracey asked as she entered the room.

"Everything is fine," said Trevor.

I pulled myself away from him and walked toward the pool. I stopped and said, "I'm so happy for you two." I forced a smile. "Trevor, thank you for everything, and I mean, everything." I walked onto the pool deck.

"David, don't leave," Trevor called.

I didn't even look back. I knew I couldn't. Everyone had decided what seemed to be best for me, and I had no say. I waved and kept walking toward the locker room.

Matthews' Home—Aulden, Ohio, August 1979

Caine stopped the Tornio at the back door. "End of the line."

I unfastened the seatbelt, and Caine grabbed my hand. "Is everything all right? You haven't said a word since we left the pool."

I forced a nod, "Everything is fine."

"If you say so, Hutch."

I felt a smile grow on my face.

"I have to get to work if I want to keep my job. If you want to talk later, let me know."

I gathered my bags and luggage. "Thanks, Starskey." I climbed out of the car and shut the door.

"Not so hard."

"Sorry."

Caine backed out of the driveway, whipped onto the road, and peeled out, leaving tread marks and a cloud of dust.

Bear greeted me with a bark. He was chained in the backyard.

"Hi, boy."

I opened the back door and put my luggage and bags on a chair.

Mom stood at the kitchen sink, busy removing her "girls" from their packaging. She popped the pills, drank some water, and threw her head back. She leaned over the sink like she was about to vomit—eyes shut and mouth open.

I watched in silence for what seemed an eternity, wondering if she was going to be okay. She lifted herself up, looked out the window, and wiped her forehead with the back of her hand.

"Hi, Mom," I said.

She looked at me and cocked her head.

"It's me, David."

She nodded. Then suddenly, she was herself again. "Yes." She put the box of diet pills back into her purse and flung the strap over her shoulder. "I don't have much time. I have a meeting with the office manager at Dr. Shultz's to see if they'll hire me."

"That's good," I said.

"Yes, it is. We've been basically living there while Magdalyn's getting the cortisone shots to her chin. That's where she is now. Caleb took the day off to take her. God forbid I take her. No, he has to take a sick day to take her." She waltzed around the counter. "How do I look?"

She was dressed in a wide-legged, blue polyester pantsuit, a white blouse with the collar perfectly placed over the jacket's lapels, and a matching scarf tied around her neck.

"Very nice."

"Are you sure? I have to make a good impression. I really need the money." Her hands fluttered around her hair, trying to put flya-ways back in place.

"You look great as always," I said.

"That's sweet of you." She grabbed the keys off the counter. "Your dad should be bringing Magdalyn home soon. Now, when she gets here, she's going to be groggy. Make sure she takes a nap. She may fight you on that, but the shots make her irritable if she doesn't sleep. Her medicine is on the side of the table. Make sure she has two tablets as soon as she gets home. Only give her the codeine if the pain is too much, and redress the bandages." She stopped in front of me as she reached for the doorknob. "How was your little trip?"

"It was good."

"That's nice." She kissed me on the forehead. "Harold Hall wants to have dinner with you tonight." She looked at her wrist-watch. "I have to go. We'll catch up later." She opened the door. "I want to hear all about it." She was gone.

I stood there as if a tornado had whipped through the kitchen.

"Welcome home, kiddo," I said out loud to the empty house. "We are so proud of you."

I gathered my bags and luggage to take upstairs. As I passed the living room, I saw a bunch of first aid material on top of the table next to Dad's side of the pulled-out couch. I dropped my bags and luggage at the foot of the stairs and went over to examine. There were three different sizes of bandages, a roll of gauze, tape, antibacterial cream, and pill bottles. The bottles were labeled with "Tetracycline," "Penicillin," and "Tylenol with Codeine."

Something was sticking out of the table's drawer. I discovered a newspaper article with the title, "Local Makes Good at World Games." Under the title was a picture of me soaring through the air and a caption, "David Matthew, sixteen years old, surprises the world by winning the gold medal today in Tønsberg, Norway," byline was Mike Drake, AP, London. Another picture of Patti hugging me inside the phone booth was at the bottom of the page.

I refolded the paper and placed it back in the drawer.

Humble Inn, Aulden, Ohio, August 1979

"This way," the maître d' said. "Please watch your step."

I followed Harold Hall down three steps into the main dining room of the Humbler Inn. The room was mostly lit by candles on each table. Couples scattered around the room at intimate round tables.

"Hal, how are you tonight?" a gentleman asked.

Harold stopped and greeted the couple as if he was running for political office, "James. Good to see you. This must be your lovely wife, Marcia." He offered his hand to the woman, who daintily placed her fingertips into his palm. He lifted her hand to meet his lips.

"What a pleasure," the woman cooed.

Harold placed his hand on my shoulder. "Let me introduce you to my friend. This is David Matthew."

"You won the gold medal in Europe recently," the man said.

"He won the World Games in springboard diving," Harold added.

"Oh," the woman said in a pretense surprise, "are you going to the Olympics?"

"I have to qualify at the trials," I said as politely as possible.

Harold smiled. "Please excuse us, the maître d' is waiting." He guided me away and whispered in my ear, "They are the Rosenfelders, very wealthy and love to invest in the arts."

We positioned ourselves in the chairs the maître d' offered.

"Any wine tonight? We have a nice Pinot Noir."

"Yes. Bring us a bottle, we're celebrating." Harold looked at the menu. "Also, can you bring us some calamari?"

"Of course. Your waiter this evening will be Adam." The maître d' placed the napkins in each of our laps.

"This is amazing," I said as I looked around the room.

"I like this place because you can talk." Harold folded his hands in front of him. "So let's talk."

I nodded.

"I've been doing a lot of thinking. Since you won the World Games, you are going to be in the running for the Olympic team. And we have to make a plan. So what I have been thinking is that we get you out to California and work with Dr. Don until the Olympic trials."

"What about Trevor? He knows me, and..."

"He's no Dr. Don. Dr. Don coached you to a gold medal in Norway, not Trevor." His eyes flickered in the candlelight.

"But..."

"Don't get me wrong. Trevor has done a fantastic job, and he'll be compensated. He'll receive the rest of this year's pay and a bonus gift for the wedding."

My mind spun. *Did Trevor sell me out?*

"Hello. My name is Adam, and I will be your server tonight."

He poured a small amount of wine into Harold's glass. Harold lifter the glass, sniffed, swirled the wine, sniffed again, tasted, and nodded. Adam filled both of our glasses halfway. A busboy brought an ice bucket and a stand to place next to Harold, in which Adam placed the bottle and wrapped a napkin around the neck.

"Our specials tonight are filet mignon and blackened swordfish. I will give you a moment." Adam departed.

"Trevor even agreed that you need to work with the best." Harold lifted his glass and said, "To you and the Olympic trials."

I reluctantly lifted my glass, and our glasses clinked. I watched Harold as we both tasted the wine. I remembered Giovanni's instructions to sip the wine and let it rest on my tongue before swallowing.

Harold replaced his glass on the table. "I have spoken to Dr. Don, and he's willing and excited to have you work with him to prepare for the trails."

"What about school?" I said as I watched the liquid in the glass catch the candlelight.

"You'll go to school there while prepping." Harold leaned back in the chair. "If you don't make the Olympic team, you can always come back and finish at Aulden High."

"The way you put it makes Aulden seem like a jail sentence," I tried to joke as I put the glass down.

Harold leaned in and placed his hand on top of mine. I resisted the urge to pull it away and looked around to see if anyone noticed.

"It's all right. No one cares." He squeezed my hand. "I want you to have the best. You deserve the best. There's only one shot at making this Olympic team, and I want you to have every possible opportunity to make that dream come true."

"What about the cost? Mom and Dad can't afford this," I said. I noticed the black hairs laced on the back of his hand.

"Don't worry your pretty little head about it. It's all taken care of." He squeezed me again and leaned back in his chair, withdrawing his hand to take another sip of wine.

When was anyone going to ask me what I wanted?

"Dr. Don has agreed to send me the bills, and I will make sure they're taken care of. I have several people that want to help. We're starting a fund at the bank so people can donate there, no money can go directly to you in order to keep in compliance with the AAU and FINA rules. Now here's the exciting news, Dr. Don wants you there by the end of the week. You'll be able to get acclimated and enrolled in school before the season starts. A friend of mine, Joe Walker, has agreed to let you live with him. He owes me since I helped him get into paralegal school at USC. He's house-sitting in Hollywood. You'll be living with the rich and famous."

"But…"

"Dr. Shultz, by the way, thinks the world of you, has agreed to continue Magdalyn's sessions, and also has offered your mother a position in the office—which took a little more persuading since her event at Big Bear. So as you can see, everything is arranged. All you have to do is show up, practice hard, and make the Olympic team." Harold held out his hands and smiled.

"What will it be, gentlemen?" asked Adam.

14 CHAPTER

Washington, DC, March 21, 1980

"May I?" asked the waiter. He stood to my right and removed the plate with the half-eaten chocolate truffle cake.

"It was very good, just too rich for me," I apologized.

"Yes, sir." He turned to another waiter and handed him the plate and floated to Patti's right. "May I?"

"Please. Thank you." Patti shifted to her left to provide more room and leaned against my shoulder. "This is heaven. I can't believe we're at the White House. And any minute, President Carter is going to be addressing us."

"It's amazing," I whispered.

I smiled at Mark, Megan, Dr. Don, and Jack. My heart filled with pride as I glanced around at the accomplished swimmers sharing our table: Tracy Caulkins, Rowdy Gaines, Nancy Hogshead, Stephen Lundquist. The table next to us was occupied by world-ranked gymnasts: Bart Conner, Jim Hartung, Kathy Johnson, and Julianne McNamara. The table on the other side had the well-known track-and-field representatives: Donald Page, Mary Stanley, Edwin Moses, and Jan Merrill. Every table was filled with national and world champions representing their respective sports. These were the best American athletes with the best chances of Olympic gold in Moscow this summer. It was such an honor to be included with such Who's Who among American athletes.

The waiters continued sweeping through the room, removing the dessert plates and offering coffee. This type of dinner held in the state dining room was usually set for the medalists after each Olympic Games, but to have one with athletes that have not even been named to their sport's Olympic team was unexpected.

The diving Olympic trials weren't scheduled until June; the gymnastics team was to be named in May; and the swimming and track-and-field trials were to be held the beginning of July. We were all invited due to the results of the 1979 national, international, and world championships.

In Tønsberg, Norway, Mark won the platform and took the silver medal behind me on springboard, and Megan was a double gold medal winner, with Patti winning the silver on platform. Andy couldn't make it because of a prior commitment, but his presence was felt as he completed the USA's sweep with his bronze medal on the men's three-meter springboard.

The room hushed as the secretary of state, Cyrus Robert Vance, stepped up to the podium with the president's seal in front.

"Ladies, gentlemen, distinguished athletes, and coaches, it is with great pride that I present to you the president of the United States, Jimmy Carter."

Everyone stood and applauded.

Patti squeezed my hand as she cranked her head to get a glimpse of the smallish man walking into the room. She gasped and pointed, "There he is."

The man with a huge smile walked to the podium. He nodded to all sides of the room, stepped back, and started to applaud his guests. He continued until all the athletes and coaches quieted down, and his hands were the only ones clapping.

I couldn't help but remember my father's theory of connecting President Carter with Caesar and Hitler. The ghostly image of the skull flashed through my mind, as I tried to get a sense of any essence of evil from the peanut farmer standing before us.

President Carter tapped the microphone. He motioned with his hands for everyone to sit.

"First of all, it's a real honor for me to be here with all of you famous people. I have a great admiration for you in this time of challenge and disappointment." President Carter's Southern voice magnified throughout the dining hall.

Patti squeezed my hand tighter.

"This is a sad time for all those in our country who are involved in amateur athletics. This past week, as you know, a tragic airline accident occurred in Warsaw, Poland, and twenty-two members of the US amateur boxing team were killed. Our whole nation was reminded of when we lost the ice-skating team in 1964. Our nation is reminded of the value of a human life and also reminded of the sacrifice that goes into the training for championship sports. This team was overseas to do its best. They were full of spirit and full of determination to exhibit their own prowess and achievement and also represent their country. And they represented us well. And I personally feel the loss, which I know you all share." He wiped his eye. "Let's have a moment of silence for these incredible athletes."

Everyone glanced over to the empty table that was set for the boxing team. Some bowed their heads, while other placed a hand over their hearts.

During the silence, I noticed the chandeliers glowing with actual white candles, as well as the sconces on the walls and the centerpieces on each table. The soft glow brought warmth to the boxing team's hushed tribute. Washington, Lincoln, and Kennedy glanced down from oil paintings as if saying silent prayers. The tables were adorned in white linen and bouquets of red, white, and blue roses.

The silverware glowed gold, as the crystal gold-rimmed stemware sparkled. Peace filled the hall. I couldn't help but think of Zachary Spence, how we sat beside each other, pressed our knees together, kissed, and shared a laugh. It was strange to think I was never going to be able to share that moment of him with anyone and how strange it felt to know he was gone forever.

The president continued, "When we are confronted with stark tragedies such as these, we have to stop for a moment and put our own lives and our own principles, our emotions, our own commitments, back into perspective. This is one of those times. And that's why I've asked you to come to the White House to meet with me to discuss a very serious and very vital matter—one that does directly involve human lives. Thousands of human lives already lost in Afghanistan, and many more hundreds of thousands of lives that could be lost, unless our nation is strong enough and is willing to sacrifice, if necessary, to preserve the peace of our country."

"Oh my goodness, what's he trying to say?" Patti whispered in my ear.

"I'm not sure." I tried to listen to the president, but the athletes' murmuring was making it difficult to hear.

"The Olympics are important to the Soviet Union. I can't say at this moment if other nations will not go to the Summer Olympics in Moscow. Ours will not go," explained President Carter.

Gasps echoed throughout the beautiful dining hall. I felt the floor was ripped out from under me. I wasn't sure I had the drive, stamina, and finances to continue at this level for another four years. *What if this was my only chance to compete at the Olympics?*

Although President Carter's earlier State of the Union announced the possibility of a boycott against the Russians for their invasion of Afghanistan, we all thought that he was going to recant his announcement at this dinner.

The president held up his hand to quiet everyone.

"I say that not with any equivocation, the decision has been made. The American people are convinced that we should not go to the Summer Olympics. The Congress has voted overwhelmingly, almost unanimously, that we will not go. And I can tell you that many of our major allies, particularly those democratic countries who believe in freedom, will not go."

"This can't be happening," Megan said as tears rolled down her cheek. "What if I can't last another four years?"

Dr. Don wrapped his arms around her shoulders. "We'll figure it out."

"No, we won't. It's over. It's really over," Megan buried her face in her napkin.

The president resumed, "I understand how you feel, and I thought about it a lot as we approached this moment, when I would have to stand here in front of fine, young Americans and dedicated coaches who have labored to become among the finest athletes in the world, knowing what the Olympics mean to you, to know that you would be disappointed. It's not a pleasant time for me." He took a napkin and dabbed his forehead. "You occupy a special place in American life, not because of your talent or your dedication or your training or your commitment or your ability as an athlete, but because for American people, Olympic athletes represent something else. You represent the personification of the highest ideals of our country. You represent a special commitment to the values of a human life, and to the achievement of excellence within an environment of freedom, and a belief in truth and friendship and respect for others, and the elimination of discrimination, and the honoring of human rights, and peace."

Megan walked out of the room. Jack quickly followed her.

Giovanni's smile rushed into my thoughts when he handed me his silver medal and said, "Bring this back to me in Moscow, and we'll be friends forever." How am I going to return it to him now? Would Italy boycott or not?

President Carter took a deep breath and looked around the room, waiting for everyone to settle. "This is obviously a difficult decision for me to make. It's much more difficult on you. We have many kinds of awards and types of recognition. I'm not an outstanding ten thousand–meter runner."

There was a polite laughter from the track-and-field table.

"But I've been honored by election to the highest elective office in our country, and there will be a difference—not just a subtle difference—between a gold medal that you might win the last part of August in international games that will not equal an Olympic gold medal. I understand that. But there will be an additional award that I will help to emphasize within the bounds of my capacity and authority and influence and status as a president, and that is a special recognition to you that you not only prevailed in a superb international competition of a world championship quality but that you also are honored along with it, having helped to preserve freedom and having helped to enhance the quality or the principles of the Olympics and having helped in a personal way to carry out the principles and ideals of our nation and having made a sacrifice in doing it."

The waiters entered the room, carrying small wooden boxes on trays and placed one in front of each of the athletes.

"And I hope that at least in the minds of some of you, the medal you might win in competition and the recognition of a grateful nation will at least partially make up for the sacrifice that you'll have to make this summer in not going to Moscow for the Summer Olympics." President Carter forced a smile. "I'm very grateful that you came, and I hope that you will help me, and I hope that you will agree, if possible. But this is a free country, and your voice is yours, and what you do and say is a decision for you to make. But whatever you decide, as far as your attitude is concerned, I will respect it. And I will appreciate this opportunity for me as president to meet with you to discuss a very serious matter as equals, as Americans who love our country, who recognize that sometimes we have to make sacrifices and that for the common good, for peace and for freedom, those sacrifices are warranted. Now, if you will excuse me. Thank you." He stepped away from the podium.

"Mr. President, Mr. President," people started standing and calling to ask questions.

Cyrus Robert Vance quieted everyone. "Please, please, this is a very difficult decision for the president. Please remain seated."

The hubbub was respectful, but the athletes were in shock with disbelief; some returned to sitting, while others remained standing.

I wasn't sure how to react. The politics surrounding and influencing sports were new to me. Yet I felt sad deep inside, for the boxers, Megan, and that we weren't going to the Olympics. I felt a different type sadness, more like disappointment, that I wouldn't get to meet up with Giovanni and that I might never get to go to any Olympics.

I opened the box placed before me. A golden medallion with the US presidential seal and the engraving of "1980 USA Olympic Team" nestled against a purple velvet cloth.

"It's pretty, isn't it?" Patty asked.

I nodded. "What do we do now?"

"We look forward to the 1984 Olympic Games in Los Angeles," Dr. Don said.

"Yes, but what about in the meantime?" I asked him, trying to hide the pain behind the question.

"We continue practicing and perfecting our sport as we have been," Dr. Don replied. "I've been doing some thinking. I'd like to have you and Patty stay in Mission Viejo permanently and let me coach. If you'd like to, that is?"

Patti nodded.

"That'd be awesome," I said. "But what about Mark?" I asked.

"Mark needs to finish his college commitments at Ohio State, and when he's graduated, he'll be joining us," Dr. Don said.

"What about our schools?" I asked.

"Both of you will finish high school in California. Then we need to get you admitted to USC or UCI for college. I don't want to break up our little family."

The word *family* resonated in my head and caused me to slump against the back of my chair. The image of Caine sitting in his Torino next to the cemetery flashed in my face. His words echoed in my ears, "I love you."

"What's wrong?" asked Dr. Don.

"I'm not sure if that'll happen. My parents..." I shook my head. "They aren't going to let me remain in California because of the cost."

"You'll be on scholarship," Dr. Don said.

"Scholarship? What do you mean?" I asked.

Mark chuckled and grabbed my hand under the table. "Dude, you are the current world champion, just say yes!"

"I want to. I really do, but..." I said.

"But nothing. Say yes!" begged Patti as she grabbed my other hand.

I pulled my hands from both of them and covered my mouth as if I was trying to stop any words from rushing out. Finally, I asked, "Can I make a call first?"

"By all means," responded Dr. Don. "Mark, will you take him? I'm sure they'll permit him to use the phone at the receptionist's desk."

"Not a problem," Mark said.

"Hello?" The voice interrupted the first ring.

"Caine?" I asked.

"Yep!" his voice seemed sharp and distracted.

"It's, me, Davy," I said.

"Is everything okay?" He chomped down on something crunchy, like potato chips.

"Everything's fine." Athletes were milling around in the dining hall, some were going to the coat check to get personal items, and some heading down the long hall to the exit.

"You want to talk to Mom? Dad's not here." Another noisy crunch crackled through the receiver.

"No. No, I was hoping to talk to you," I said.

"Me? Are you sure?" He licked his fingers.

"I'm absolutely sure."

"Okay, what's up?"

"Who you talking to?" Magdalyn asked Caine.

"Davy," said Caine. "Now be quiet, I can barely hear him."

"I want to say hi," Magdalyn said.

"Caine, I don't have much time…" I tried to explain.

"Hi, Davy. What cha doing?" said Magdalyn.

"Hi, Maddie. Let me talk to Caine, real quick. I can't talk long."

"Where are you?" she asked.

"I'm at the White House," I said. "Now let me talk to Caine."

"All right, hold your horses." She pulled the phone away, and her voice sounded far away. "He's at someone's house named White."

"You're calling from where?" Caine clearly asked into the receiver.

"Caine, I don't have much time. I'm calling from the White House."

"The White House? The president of the United States' house?" his voice rose in pitch.

"Yes…"

"President Carter's place?"

"Yes, now listen…"

"No wonder you didn't want to talk to Dad." He chuckled. "So go ahead."

"Well, President Carter has boycotted the Summer Olympics in Moscow…"

"The shithead!"

"No, no, no, it's all good. It's because of the invasion of Afghanistan. Anyway, I'm calling because Dr. Don's offering me a scholarship to dive with him at Mission Viejo," I said.

"That's cool. Train for what, didn't you just say the Olympics are canceled?"

"Not canceled, boycotted. It means the US is making a political stand, or something. I really don't understand everything. But I'll be training for the 1984 Olympics in Los Angeles."

"What about school?" Caine asked.

"Dr. Don wants me to remain in California to finish up and then go to college there." My words were beginning to rush together because of my excitement.

"That's going to be expensive."

"That's where the scholarships come in."

"Scholarship? What does that mean?"

"It means that it's all paid for," I explained.

"Who's paying for it?" he asked.

"Donors and sponsors, I think. I'm not really sure."

"It sounds incredible. Is it something you want to do?" Caine asked.

"I do, I really do."

"Then you do it," he said.

"You're right. Thanks,"

"Don't thank me, you did it all yourself."

"I couldn't have done it without you."

"Aw, shucks," Caine said. "Wait a minute. Would you be able to come home for the wedding?"

"What wedding?"

"I'm doing it. Christi and I are getting hitched." Pride filled his voice.

"Christi who?"

"Christi Cummings," he replied.

"The Christi Cummings in my class?"

"The one and only."

"But she's preg…" Then it dawned on me; that's why she wouldn't go to the dance with me because she was seeing Caine. That's why she told him that I got jumped. "Seriously? When?" I asked.

"July. The date isn't confirmed, but we have to do it before the baby comes. Can you make it?"

"You bet, I wouldn't miss it," I said.

"You can't, because you're the best man," he said.

Mark whispered in my ear, "We have to go."

I nodded. "Listen, Caine, I have to go. I'm so happy for you and Christi and the baby. Tell Mom and Dad that I'm going to stay with Dr. Don, okay?"

"You got it. You did real good, Davy. I'm proud of you." Silence filled the phone. "Okay, bye."

"Talk soon," I said.

The phone's connection ended.

I placed the receiver in its cradle and nodded my head to Mark, "LA Olympics, here we come!"

Mark quickly hung me, and we jumped in a circle. He pulled me at arm's length and gazed into my eyes.

The gaze lingered. Flecks of gold and green swam in the blue ocean of his pupils.

"Let's go tell the others," I nervously pulled away.

Mark stopped me, "David, I need to talk to you."

I couldn't look into his eyes.

"Now that the Olympics have been boycotted and things are going to seem slow for a while, I have been doing some thinking."

He stopped suddenly and looked around. He noticed a more private area on the other side of the coat check and pulled me there.

"Look at me," he lifted my chin. His blue eyes burned with an urgency to speak, and yet he was forcing himself to remain calm. "I'm not sure how to speak about this. I have rehearsed it a million and one times, but I never thought it would be this awkward."

"Just blurt it out," I encouraged.

"You're right." He took a deep breath and joked, "This is scarier than doing a front three-and-a-half from the ten-meter with your eyes glued shut." He took another deep breath. "I realize that I'm a bit older than you."

"Only four years," I added.

Mark nodded, "I'm four years older than you, and I have to go back to Ohio State University to finish this year while you go out to California. I wanted to address the friendship that we have, and I keep thinking of the time in Tønsberg and how much I enjoyed being there with you."

"Mark, what are you talking about?" My palms started sweating.

"You know, like the night you passed out next to my bed…"

I cut him off. "I didn't mean it. I was being so stupid. I don't know what I was thinking…" I pulled away.

He restrained me. "I hope you meant it, and it wasn't stupid."

"What?"

His eyes were filled with longing and care. "Don't."

He reached for my hand. I pulled my hand out of his reach.

"Please, don't make fun of me."

"I'm not intentionally trying to," Mark replied. "It's just that it's been on my mind, and we've never talked about it."

"What's there to talk about?" I crossed my arms against my chest.

"It's just…" He paused and ran his hands through his hair, accenting the cowlick. "After the Worlds, you went back to Aulden and I went to Columbus. I thought we could meet up one weekend, I'd drive down to see you, but you went to dive with Dr. Don. I hoped you would come to this dinner, and when Dr. Don told me you were, I knew I had to talk to you. It's been on my mind, and I think we need to straighten some things out. But every time I've tried to bring it up, other things always seemed to get in the way. Duh, the boycott," he tried to joke.

"I said I was sorry. It didn't mean anything. I was being stupid." I looked past his shoulder to watch more athletes and coaches leave.

"You wanted to see me naked, didn't you?" Mark directly asked.

I wanted to run as hard and as fast as I could. My forehead started sweating, and I could hear my heart beat.

"That's why I went to bed naked," Mark admitted.

"What?"

"I noticed you looking at me when you came to OSU to practice platform," he explained.

"Please stop."

"I thought I was making it up. When you made the World Games team, I was so excited. I noticed you looking over to me then as well."

"You're freakin' Mark Bradley, world and national champion. I was in awe of you," I built my defense.

"That was all, just because I won some medals?" He looked hurt and defeated. "I was mad jealous when you hung out with Giovanni Pizzini."

"He's straight." I dropped my head in shame, realizing that I admitted for the first time that I was gay.

Mark lifted my chin with his fingers and looked deep into my eyes. "I don't care if you're orange, blue, or purple."

I felt my eyes well, and I started backing away. He held tight to my elbows and placed his lips on mine.

I didn't know what to do. His lips were soft and gentle. He didn't force or manipulate the situation. He kissed me. It felt loving and different. It reminded me of Zachary's kiss, but there was something more to it. There was passion and longing.

I gently pulled away and studied his face. It glowed. His eyes sparkled; his cheeks were rosy; and he had a hopeful smile on his lips.

"I had no idea." I took another step back and touched my lips.

"I knew the first time I saw you in Columbus. You were wearing that ugly green Mike Peppe suit. I really knew when you went and changed into Trevor's Speedo. But I was too chicken, and I thought I'd never see you again, being that you are still in high school. Then you made the World team and won the gold medal, it took everything for me not to plant one on you during the medal ceremonies."

"I wish you had." I stepped forward and kissed him the way I have wanted to kiss a man, confident and with passion.

"Wow." He pulled away. "So you like me a little?"

"A smidge," I retorted.

His eyes widened. "If that is any indication of liking me a 'smidge,' I wonder what it would be like if you really 'liked' me."

"I guess you're going to have to wait and find out." He started to in lean in again. "Wait a minute. You're a senior at Ohio State, and I'm going to be a high school senior this fall in California."

"Yes. But you forget that we will both be on the same Mission Viejo team and be going to the same meets."

"What are we going to do in the meantime? Write letters?"

"Shut up and come over here." He pulled me into his chest and kissed me.

Dr. Althea Warner's Office—Dayton, Ohio, July 2015

Althea handed me a gift. "I got this for you for the excellent work you've done."

"You shouldn't have," I said. "Wait a minute, is it chocolate?"

"Open it."

I unwrapped a leather-bound journal. "It's beautiful."

"I want you to continue your journey. We have just scratched the surface of the impact your childhood has had on you. We need to now explore how it affected your acting, relationships, and teaching careers. Are you interested in continuing?"

I nodded, "Yes, I am."

"Let's get it set up." She walked to her desk. "How does next week at three?"

"Sounds great."

Speech taken from

Oettinger, C. (2012). "March 21, 1980: Jimmy Carter announces 1980 Summer Olympics Boycott to the Athletes." Retrieved from http://www.commandposts.com/2012/03/jimmy-carter-announces-1980-summer-olympic-boycott-to-athletes/.

ACKNOWLEDGMENTS

I would like to dedicate this work of art to my soul mate and life partner, Nathan.

I need to also acknowledge the following people for their encouragement and support: my team from Page Publishing—especially my literary development agent, Paula Breheny, and publication coordinator, Danny Yarnell. Editor, Deb McLeod and The Writing Ranch. The people who have read many drafts: Nathan Webber, April Audia, Stacy Emoff, Skip Lang, David Moyer, Illa and MT Taylor, Alisa Nelligan Thomas, Patti Lewis Hickey, Racheal Murdock, Jeanne Weaver, Dr. Joseph S. Leithold and Woodcroft Family Practice and Mike and Judy Webber.

Thanks to Robin Reardon, Leanna Renee Hiebert, Katrina Kittle, and Rick Flynn.

A special thanks to Bella, Barkley, Bailey, and Bryn for their support.

DARKNESS TO LIGHT
END CHILD SEXUAL ABUSE

http://www.d2l.org/site/c.4dICIJOkGcISE/b.6035035/k.8258/
Prevent_Child_Sexual_Abuse.htm#.WDTBkfkrLIU

Mission:

Empower People to Prevent Child Sexual Abuse
Our programs raise awareness of the prevalence and consequences
of child sexual abuse by educating adults about the steps they can
take to prevent, recognize and react responsibly to the reality of child
sexual abuse.

ABOUT THE AUTHOR

John-Michael Lander has relied on his experiences as a competitive diver and traveling the world to write *Surface Tension*. He has had a diverse life that includes competitive diving, coaching, acting (theater, film, and television), teaching, drawing, and writing. He was accepted in the Institute of Children Literature and Long Ridge Writers Group. His master's dissertation was "How Sexual Orientation Affects Male High School Students" and is currently pursuing a PhD in Education in Curriculum, Instruction, and Assessment. He has been artist instructor of *Autism in Shakespeare* for the Human Race Theatre Company in Dayton after teaching for seven years at Stivers High School for the Arts. *Spandau Ballet* and *Saving Balleria* are in the editing process.

CPSIA information can be obtained
at www.ICGtesting.com
Printed in the USA
BVHW071148240619
551796BV00003B/244/P